PRAISE FOR T. M. DORAN'S
Toward the Gleam

NEW OXFORD REVIEW: "[*Toward the Gleam* is] a grand saga in the heroic tradition . . . a complex tale bursting with spirited side-shows and memorable characters . . . [A] sequel to T. M. Doran's extraordinarily stirring new novel is most assuredly in order."

John Granger, TIME MAGAZINE'S Dean of Harry Potter Scholars: "[A] story re-telling how *The Lord of the Rings* was written, with a host of historical figures from Agatha Christie to Winston Churchill [. . .] I confess I wondered how it was possible to pull it off credibly or as engrossing fiction [but] *Toward the Gleam* hit on all cylinders."

David J. Theroux, Founder, C. S. Lewis Society of California: "This is a book richly imaginative, intriguing and metaphysical, exploring many vexing questions of the modern era and enduring truths to be discovered in the process."

THE INKLINGS blog: "Just occasionally, a book comes along that grasps the reader from the first page . . . Indeed, Doran's expert and gradual unveiling of the plot builds the tension to a point that the book is impossible to put down. When the end comes, the tension is broken in the final pages by one of the most satisfying and unanticipated twists of narrative."

GALVESTON DAILY NEWS: "What makes [*Toward the Gleam*] fascinating is, Doran never has the characters doing anything their historical analogues did not do, yet he believably manages to wrap an adventure tale into their lives . . . a delightful book that is as thought provoking as it is entertaining."

Joseph Pearce, Author, TOLKIEN, MAN AND MYTH: "Although [*Toward the Gleam*] basks in the reflected glory of *The Lord of the Rings* and conveys inklings of *That Hideous Strength*, it does not merely reflect the light that Tolkien and Lewis have shown; it refracts it in exciting new directions... *Toward the Gleam* rises above the level of parody or pastiche to reach the heights that few writers have achieved."

THE NEWS-HERALD (Detroit): "[Y]ou don't have to recognize any of the characters for their historical counterparts or the mysterious book at the center of the plot... to enjoy the mystery, the adventure, and the tension that builds throughout *Toward the Gleam*."

Mississippi Valley Archaeology Center: "[T. M. Doran] has created an imaginary world peopled by very historic characters, and this conceit will only add to the delight in this novel, and perhaps will add new delight in re-reading a celebrated trilogy..."

The American Chesterton Society's GILBERT MAGAZINE: "*Toward the Gleam* is a rousing salute to the culture of fandom, celebrating some of the major figures of twentieth-century literature and inserting them into an adventure revolving around a priceless historical manuscript, ruthless super villains, and the hunt for a lost civilization, possibly Atlantis... Doran's melding of minds and adventure is also a place that I would like to explore."

David Mullen, Singer/Songwriter: "This book is so good because it feels so old... What if you put *National Treasure*, C. S. Lewis, Michael Card, and P. D. James in a blender? Think *Da Vinci Code* excitement, without the slovenly intellectual drivel..."

THE LUCIFER EGO

Also By T. M. DORAN

Toward the Gleam

Iota

Terrapin

Circling the Turtle

THE LUCIFER EGO

The sequel to TOWARD THE GLEAM

T. M. DORAN

TMDoranBooks

2018

The Lucifer Ego, by T. M. Doran

Published by TMDoranBooks (tmdoran.com)

Printed by CreateSpace

© 2018 T. M. Doran

The quotation from *The Aeneid* is adapted from the translation by John Dryden.

ISBN: 978-1-7324726-0-0 (print edition)
        978-1-7324726-1-7 (Kindle ebook edition)

Cover and title page illustrations © 2018 by Daniel Johnson (Artisticknack.com)

Editing and book design by Lisa Nicholas of Mitey Editing (miteyediting.com)

"Trust not their presents, nor admit the horse."

Virgil, THE AENEID

THE LUCIFER EGO

PART I

Decisions

AUGUST 5, 2016

Paris

S HE WAS SMILING at the ghost with her most seductive smile.

The stage had been set with great care, all three acts: intimate dinner, diversion, liberation. She'd had help, but it was her production.

Lines rehearsed, props at the ready, necessaries stowed off stage.

"You didn't cook this feast, did you?" the man asked.

"Of course not," the woman answered. "I'm no chef, but the person who prepared this meal is."

"Everything looks and smells delicious, Lina. And may I say you've never looked lovelier."

The woman's blue dress artfully displayed her elegant arms and legs. The combination of the dress, her golden hair, the candlelight, and the makeup she rarely wore produced a spectacular effect.

"A friend recommended this Bordeaux."

Glass uplifted, the man said, "To us."

A one-room apartment: bed; large cabinet with doors; freestanding wardrobe; table and two chairs in the center of the room; water closet in a boxed-out area near the door; sink, oven, and refrigerator on the wall. No carpet or rugs. A lamp on the cabinet, and globe lights over the table and sink.

She viewed this room as a stage, nothing but scenery and props. Her real life was in another place, where she hoped to live with that remarkable man who allowed her to share his life.

Glancing at the hat he'd placed on top of the cabinet, she said, "The jacket and hat become you, Nelly."

They had agreed they wouldn't associate publicly until the transaction was complete, so he had taken the train to Paris and a cab from the train station.

"The chef said *coq au vin* and root vegetables would travel well. More wine . . . yes?" She filled his glass, saying, "I'd like to hear more about the artifact."

"The artifact I hope to be rid of soon."

With the wine, the man's voice ascended the register. "I've been thinking about our family holidays in Brighton. Do you remember our long walks on the beach?"

"*Certainement.*"

"Those were idyllic days," he said.

"Our parents arguing political theories and drinking into the night. Your father a Tory and my mother a Marxist."

"Every year for five years, until my father died."

"You see my apartment. I don't earn a large salary, and neither do you, so we can't afford holidays like those."

The man set down his knife and fork, took a hearty drink of wine, and said, "If it's authentic, the artifact is worth millions. We could live in Saint-Germain. We wouldn't have to work. We could holiday wherever we desired."

"What are you suggesting?"

He was looking at his plate when he said, "Marriage."

"You haven't forgotten we're cousins."

"Neither of us wants children."

"I don't know what to say. I'm not a young girl anymore."

The man pushed back his chair, stood up, and marched to the window that overlooked the street. Even those few steps revealed his limp. At a distance, lit boats, like toys, on the Seine.

Facing the street, he said, "I feel like Quasimodo in that bell tower. Wracked by regret . . . greedy for my Esmeralda."

He turned back to her. "Might you change your mind about us?"

"Please sit. Finish your dinner. Of course, I'm fond of you. If the artifact is as valuable as you suggest, you must have it in a safe place."

"The safest place I could devise."

"Close to you, in your room?"

"In the room, yes . . . This isn't an infatuation, Lina. You have been on my mind since we were children, though I'd given it up until you came to Folkestone. Ever since that day, I've been thinking about you. You can't say you haven't noticed."

"Perhaps you have fallen in love with a memory. I'm not that Brighton girl anymore."

"Why do you think I made off with it, if not for you . . . for us? Don't you remember our conversation in this very room? Why do you think I moved to Germany? I know that money is important to you."

"Yes, I admit it. I've never made it a secret. Your appetite is spoiled, isn't it?"

"Tell me plainly. If I sold the artifact for three, five million, would it change things?"

"Of course, it would. You've always been dear to me. If we had a chance for a new life . . ."

Hammering the table with his fist, the man said, "I have to think, make sure there are no loose ends. Mustn't be arrested . . . or swindled. They'll look for me once it's discovered."

"You said you have until November."

"Yes, if the old fool adheres to his custom."

"Everything will be complete by then."

"We'll have to hide the money or they'll have me, certain," he said.

"Leave that to me. I have a plan. There's no need to hurry."

"There's every reason to hurry, but I won't be reckless. This is our chance, Lina."

She placed her hands over his, leaned across the table, and kissed him.

His face flushed, the man said, "You told me to come straight from the train station. May I stay the night?"

"*All* night," she said.

"I won't fail you," said the man, trying to stand, but falling back into his chair.

"Are you ill?"

"I don't know . . . what's wrong?"

"Are you ill?" she said again, but this time there was no answer.

His head was resting on the table between his two hands. She wasn't in a hurry. There was plenty of time to do what she had to do. Now that she was sure where he kept it, she could rid herself of this troublesome man.

The woman retrieved her phone and sent a text: *Pearl inside shell.*

After she had cleared the supper table, she checked his pulse. Based on the amount of wine he'd drunk, he would be in a deep sleep for at least six hours. Every detail had been planned. They'd never find the body, and even if they did, they'd never connect it with her.

The woman closed the drapes, then walked to the cabinet and opened the doors, revealing a six-foot by three-foot space with no dividers. From inside, she removed a foldable trolley, two plastic body bags, and a small wooden box.

The box contained a syringe, which she removed, then injected the man with the contents. He went limp and would have fallen out of the chair if she hadn't propped him up. After several minutes had passed, she checked his pulse to confirm he was dead.

She lowered the man from the chair to the floor and proceeded to remove his outer clothing. His wallet, keys, and return train ticket would require careful disposal. Though they were the same height, he was forty pounds heavier, so she donned several layers of padded clothing from her wardrobe before dressing herself in his clothes. In the wardrobe was a pair of shoes like his, but her size.

It took almost an hour, but she got the dead man inside one body bag, and then the second, made sure both were secure, dragged him to the cabinet, and manhandled him inside.

She was weary from the hard work, but she was no weakling, and when the doors were closed, she padlocked them tight and attached multiple winching straps to the cabinet.

Those walks on the beach he had so joyfully recalled had been torture for her. If her mother hadn't commanded her, she would never have been seen with him in public.

As they had agreed, he had taken a train and a cab to her apartment, and had paid the fares with cash. He hadn't registered at a hotel. Only the lobby attendant could connect him with this visit to her apartment, and only by sight, not by name, as he had given the man a false name (but even this tenuous connection she intended to rectify).

All of this, and what was to come, was necessary, so that he would vanish without a trace—and not just to protect her, but to make sure any investigation of the artifact came to a dead end.

She practiced his limp, walking back and forth in the room. On the last circuit, she happened to look up and see the shadow on the wall above the door, where the crucifix had been. The previous resident had left it, but after a month she discovered that the sight of it disturbed her, and she'd thrown it in the trash, though the shadow remained. When this business was over, she would repaint the wall, or better yet, move closer to her lover.

Putting on the man's jacket and hat, she left the apartment, took the elevator down to the second floor, then the back stairs to the first floor, and walked to the trash room at the end of the hall. While the door to the hallway was unlocked for the residents' convenience, the trash exit door to the rear alley was latched after nine. She unlatched this door, and went to the dimly-lit first floor lobby, limping past the attendant without looking at him, and saying, "*Bonsoir, monsieur.*"

"*Bonsoir, monsieur,*" was the man's reply as she went into the street.

She walked ten blocks before she put the bag with the hat and jacket in a trash receptacle, then back to her apartment. As she re-entered by the alley door she had unlatched, she locked it again before returning to her apartment.

The dead body a few feet from her bed didn't bother her in the least. She was impatient, but she had been preparing all of this for months and wouldn't do anything to compromise the plan. They would soon have the artifact her lover had been seeking for decades, and he had her to thank for it—a thought that made her glow.

She slept well, as she usually did, and when she awoke she made a simple breakfast and prepared for the day's work.

The movers came midafternoon, placed the cabinet on the trolley, and transported it to the street, where her hired truck was stationed. Up the ramp and into the back of the truck it went.

She wasn't about to leave the truck unattended on the street, not these days, so she immediately embarked on the long drive across the city. Once outside the twentieth *arrondissement*, she continued east for another two hours. By then, it was twilight, and starting to rain. Her navigation device was programmed to take her to the dirt side road that snaked almost a kilometer into the woods before it opened up to several acres that had once been farmland, but were now covered with brush, tall grass, and a few trees.

Long ago, she had come here with Maurice, when they were both students. Even then, the farm that had belonged to his grandparents was long abandoned, the house having been leveled by a wartime bomb that had killed his grandmother. Maurice had been thinking of putting a trailer here and living off the land, far from the urban madness and, in those days, he had been trying to convince her to accompany him.

As for Maurice, they hadn't corresponded in twenty years. He was now General Secretary of the French Communist Party, and living in a luxury apartment amidst that urban madness. Her research had revealed that Maurice still owned the property, and that the land was still unimproved. As he wasn't a farmer, what could he do with such a remote and isolated parcel?

A month earlier, she had made a reconnaissance of the site. She hadn't driven her own car and, once off the road, she had covered the plate on the rental in case someone observed the car and became suspicious. She had to ensure there were no squatters, or anything else that would preclude disposing of the body here.

What made the site ideal was the underground bunker behind the ruins of the farmhouse. She parked the truck adjacent to the bunker, put on the miner's hat, and exited the truck. So far from the road, it was pitch dark except for the truck and helmet lamps. Misty and warm, no wind. The woman walked to the bunker and pulled away the rotting plywood cover someone had used to replace the hinged metal door. She opened the rear of the truck and put the ramp down. After making sure the winches were tight, she rolled the cabinet to the ground. Painstakingly, she pushed the cabinet toward the bunker hatch. Fortunately, the ground was relatively dry, or she might have been stymied at the end of the final act.

When the trolley reached the edge of the bunker, she didn't hesitate, pushing even harder until the assembly went over and down with a loud crash.

From the rear of the truck, she removed plastic panels she had picked up on the way and placed them over the bunker opening before she replaced the plywood, as this would extend the life of the cover.

Her production, though her lover had introduced ideas in the course of conversations: the double poisoning, body bag, disguise accents, unconventional caskets.

Of course, there were things she couldn't control: the truck might have broken down on the way, her victim might have informed someone he was coming to Paris, he might have forgotten to wear the jacket and hat, someone might have latched the alley door, someone might discover the cabinet—but she wasn't worried. She knew there were no perfect crimes. She also knew the police were far from perfect.

Up went the ramp. No need to delay. The apartment had to be wiped down and scrubbed clean, and the rest of his clothes and personal articles deposited where no one would ever find them. She had liberated *dear Nelly* from the artifact, from police pursuit, and from his obsession with her.

DECEMBER 6, 2016

☻-☻-☻

St. Hugh's Charterhouse, Sussex

L IBERA NOS A MALO.

Lyle Stuart read those words on a placard above the door as Porter escorted him into the Abbot's office, a room with an all-purpose table, wooden chairs, a bookshelf, a crucifix on the wall, and a small window with crosshatched metal rods, the only concession to the times being a computer on the corner of the table.

"How are you, my dear Frodo?" the Abbot said to Lyle, after Porter had closed the door. "Take a chair."

"I'm well enough, and curious about this summons. Your invitation reeked of mystery, Uncle."

"I had to make sure the lure was powerful enough to get you here."

"I won't be able to join the Order. I already have a job."

"Of course, you do, though you're on sabbatical, aren't you? Care for a glass of our world-famous ale?"

"You could talk me into it," Lyle answered.

The Abbot exited the room, returning with two water glasses filled to the brim with honey-colored ale. Touching Lyle's glass with his, the Abbot said, "To truth."

"I thought you set all that aside when you cast your lot with this lot." Lyle didn't see his Uncle Henry very often anymore, but when he did, both were inclined to engage in friendly mischief.

"That's a narrow view for a man of science. Are you in a hurry?"

"That depends on what your mysterious summons is all about."

In his sixties, Abbot Henry was a handsome man with a long narrow face, a patrician nose, and eyes that danced when he smiled. He was wearing the traditional garments of his Order, with nothing to distinguish him from Porter or any of the other monks. Though not a small man, he was light on his feet, and could pass for fifty. Before he'd joined the Order, Lyle's uncle had been a theoretical physicist, and was the person who first kindled his love of science.

"Your ale's reputation is well deserved. As for your invitation, my mother would have been distressed if I'd ignored her favorite brother," Lyle said.

"Your dear mother. How I miss her. When she was a girl, she loved to write stories about animals, like Beatrix Potter. She'd read out loud at the dinner table about this mouse or that goose, and she was so animated it felt like a performance rather than a recitation."

"Why did she stop writing?" said Lyle, recalling his mother's vibrancy when she read to him and his brother.

"I'm not sure she did. Perhaps it became a private enterprise."

"She read to Sam and me, even after she became ill."

"I know all about that, a particular pleasure of hers."

The banter and reminiscences didn't amend Lyle's impression that his uncle was nervous and reticent, something he'd never witnessed in this man.

"What do you want to tell me?" Lyle said.

"The truth is, something's been stolen from this monastery."

What could a theft at the monastery have to do with him? "A job for the police, Uncle."

"They've come and gone, without success, and with little encouragement."

"Are you confusing me with Sam? He's the one you want if the police aren't up to finding your old bone—or patch of skin."

"An artifact, not a relic."

"Give the police time, and if you can't wait, call Sam."

"I need someone with special skills. *Your* skills, Frodo."

Since his mother's passing, Lyle's Uncle Henry was the only person who called Frodo Lyle Stuart by that name. Hardly anyone even knew his first name was Frodo, and those who asked about the F were told it stood for Frederick. His brother Samwise had had an easier time of it, having shortened his name to Sam. As for their mother, she had been too good to him to hold it against her.

Lyle said, "I'll have another ale if you'll join me."

"You'll get me into trouble if I'm not careful."

When the Abbot had returned with the ale and seated himself again, he tapped Lyle's glass with his, and said, "Last month, a valuable artifact was stolen from this monastery. I should say, I discovered the theft last month. It could have been stolen as long as a year ago.

"Where to start? At the beginning, I suppose. In 1972, an old man calling himself John Hill came into this room with an ordinary looking crate that contained an artifact he insisted had come from a high civilization that existed thirty to forty thousand years ago."

"Then this thing was a fraud," said Lyle. "There were no high civilizations prior to six millennia ago—the Sumerians, the Nile and Indus valley cultures, and those societies are only considered high in relation to their contemporaries."

"Let me finish my story. The old man wanted us to keep and protect the artifact, and my predecessor agreed to his request."

"You've seen this thing?"

"I visit the repository where the artifact is kept once a year, on the anniversary of John Hill's donation. To the best of my knowledge, the artifact has never been removed from this keeping place since it was installed there by the abbot who received it from Hill."

"What else can you tell me about it?" Lyle asked.

"Inside the crate Hill brought here— placed on this very table—was another box, if one can use so pedestrian a word, and inside that smaller container was a bound manuscript that chronicled events Hill believed had occurred tens of thousands of years ago, along with the long-lost cities and civilizations that existed in those times."

"Hill duped your abbot, or perhaps he'd been duped himself."

Abbot raised a cautioning hand. "The manuscript was composed in an unknown language, with unknown glyphs, or so Hill called them. He was a master linguist, and he told our abbot he'd spent decades translating the manuscript."

"A professional duping."

"The books the man who called himself Hill produced from the manuscript became famous, as did he."

Lyle's eyes widened. "You aren't saying . . ."

"I am saying it. I understand there was a dramatic story attached to the manuscript while it was in Hill's possession, but if he related that story to my predecessor, I haven't heard it."

Lyle lifted his glass and drank, his eyes never leaving the Abbot's face. "Uncle Henry, as you well know, my line of research is prehistoric archaeology, and I can unequivocally say that a high civilization thirty to forty thousand years ago is impossible."

"You're certain you know what happened that long ago, before several ice ages and their glaciers swept over Europe? Are there no anomalies concerning that era that resist explanation?"

"At Oxford, we operate on evidence, data, artifacts we can see, hold, test. There's absolutely zero evidence for such a civilization, and your climatological reference hardly proves that such a civilization might have existed, much less that it did exist."

"Hill was an Oxford professor, too, and he claimed to have discovered such an artifact."

"My mother read us those stories when we were young. You

can't expect me to believe all that really happened. It was a clever story, but just a story."

"That's not what Hill represented. If nothing else, he was a man of integrity and character."

"People with integrity can be mistaken—or deceived."

Abbot Henry wagged his head. "Whenever I'm tempted to think that man has answered every question, I remind myself that our wise men once believed the stars and planets revolved around a flat Earth, and in Newton's day our wise men believed in a mechanical universe. Every age has its blind spots, with its wise men proclaiming that blind spots have been eradicated on their watch."

The Abbot leaned in and over Lyle, saying, "Listen, Frodo, I'm not fully convinced of the authenticity of this artifact, either but, whatever it is, it's special. I'm its caretaker now, and in that I've failed."

"Don't be so hard on yourself, and chances are it's not nearly as valuable as you think it is."

Staring out the cramped window, the Abbot said, "My experience tells me, if something has worldly value, it will be appropriated—or stolen—no matter how well guarded, as such things are in the nature of man. But I wish it hadn't happened on my watch. Come with me."

"I haven't agreed to get involved," Lyle protested.

"I understand, but come anyway. I want to show you something."

Abbot Henry led him out of the room and around a corner. After passing the empty refectory, they started down a long windowless corridor with stone floor and walls, and a vaulted ceiling, giving Lyle the same feeling he had when he was underground at an archaeological site. Though lights had been attached to the wall, he recognized the inserts where oil lamps had once been lodged.

"I had these electric lamps installed," remarked Abbot Henry. "No sense tripping and knocking our heads when we don't have to. As it is, this place is a rabbit warren of halls and rooms."

At the end of the passageway, unlit branches turned to the right and left, with the right-hand passage leading into darkness, and the left extending a short distance to a blank wall. Lyle expected his uncle to turn right, but the Abbot switched on the electric lantern he was carrying and led his nephew to the wall at the end of the short passageway.

Lyle heard a grinding sound, and a portion of the wall opened like a door, until there was a large enough space for them to pass.

The Abbot said, "Mind that lintel . . . Those who came before us may not have had a sliver of our technology, but many were every bit as intelligent as our wise men and women."

Was his uncle referring to Lyle? He could never be sure with this unpredictable man.

The room they entered was cramped and musty. The Abbot said, "I close the door when I come here, but we'll make an exception this time, since the brothers are in chapel."

"Was the thing that was stolen kept here?"

"The artifact resided here. In part, it resides here still."

"How can it have been stolen and still be here?"

The Abbot pointed to an almost invisible niche in the wall opposite the door, and handing Lyle the lantern, said, "Hold it up, Frodo."

When Lyle elevated the lantern, he could see the niche more clearly, along with something tucked inside.

The Abbot reached into the crevice and came away with a wooden box that Lyle judged to be old, but hardly an antiquity. The older man placed it on a narrow shelf attached to a sidewall and asked Lyle to set the lantern next to it, bathing that corner of the repository in light.

"An improvement on oil lamps when it comes to this sort of thing," the Abbot observed, unlatching the box at each end, opening it up, and extracting a second container that immediately commanded Lyle's full attention.

The metal surface, or whatever the material was, had the appearance of water on a still pond beneath a full moon—as if liquid, or molten. The visible surface was etched with runes and embellished with geometric designs. The container seemed to magnify light, so that it appeared even brighter than the lantern.

"Here . . . hold it," the Abbot said to Lyle, who had set the wooden box on the floor.

The container was heavier than it looked, suggesting that something was inside, though Lyle could distinguish nothing like a latch, or even a seam where the object might open.

The Abbot placed his thumbs on each side of the container, and it slowly opened, revealing a silk lining and a blood-red book cover.

"I thought you said the artifact had been stolen."

"Open the book . . . go ahead, open it," said the Abbot, taking hold of the container.

Doing as his uncle had instructed, Lyle saw that the original pages had been removed—each page having been cut loose, as with a razor—and replaced with blank sheets of paper.

Abbot Henry said, "If you had seen those pages as they were— the fabric, pictures, calligraphy, embellishments—you'd realize the extent of defacement that's taken place, worse than if the Mona Lisa had been ripped from its frame."

"You exaggerate, but I take your meaning."

"I don't exaggerate. You haven't seen those pages, as I have, and, even if they aren't forty thousand years old, they are ancient, and the most spectacular art I've seen. I tell you, Frodo, I can't stand to look at what the thief has done."

He closed the book and again put his thumbs to the sides of the container, which slowly and silently closed.

"I dare you to find a seam," the Abbot said.

Lyle examined the container, but he saw not so much as a hair of a line where the two parts had come together.

"With a brighter light, a magnifier . . ." he said.

The Abbot shook his head vigorously.

Lyle said, "However that mechanism works, it's far too sophisticated to have been produced in antiquity."

"How do you know that?"

"Because I've never seen or heard of an antiquarian mechanism that approaches this one in complexity."

"Does that give you pause to reconsider your view?"

"On the contrary, it confirms my view that the container and book are modern inventions, and believing this ought to disqualify me from helping you retrieve it."

"*On the contrary*," said Abbot Henry, his eyes twinkling, "that confirms *my* view that you're ideal for the job. I want a skeptic, so he'll focus on the facts and not lose himself in the mystery and drama."

"Uncle Henry, I'm on sabbatical, not retired. I have plans to visit a site in Bosnia-Herzegovina, and to finish a paper on the weaponry of an ancient tribe."

"If you recover the manuscript in a month, you'll have eleven months for your project."

"Apart from my affection for you, what makes you think I'd consider such a bizarre idea? I may be an archaeologist, but my name is Lyle Stuart, not Indiana Jones."

"I know you better than you think," his uncle said. "You decided to read archaeology because you love the challenge of answering millennia old mysteries. And despite what you say, you're intrigued by this artifact . . . unconvinced it's a modern invention. The most important thing is, you can see around corners—you've always been able to. All those questions about the universe I used to pepper you with. You didn't have every answer, but you were never intimidated or dismayed. Now, come back to the office with me. You need not make a decision, but know I'm convinced you're the man for the job."

Lyle wasn't sure about seeing around corners, though his most acclaimed work had demonstrated that art, fetishes, fertility figures that were thought to have been associated with Cro-Magnon in southeastern Europe had actually been produced by culturally advanced Neanderthals, and he had done this by linking the artifacts to objects and art at obscure Neanderthal sites, a painstaking investigation that resembled modern police forensics. Knowing his uncle had always taken an interest in his career, Lyle wouldn't have been surprised to learn this man was well aware of his Nis Neanderthal notoriety.

"Even if such a thing were possible, where would this civilization have originated?" Lyle asked.

"Hill suggested that high civilization originated on an island in the ocean—was, in fact, the mythical Atlantis."

"That's what Hill believed? You're saying Atlantis was in the manuscript he acquired."

"Or something much like it. The authentic Atlantis, you could say."

"How convenient. He explains the high civilization in his stories by invoking a prior high civilization. This is a lot to absorb, Uncle, an eons-old civilization, predated by an Atlantis that really existed. Makes for a marvelous story, but it can't have happened."

"I'm telling you what *he* believed, or so I judge by what I've learned. As for recovering the manuscript, I'm sure Sam will assist you if you ask him."

"I don't think his organization condones *extempore* assignments," countered Lyle.

On the verge of placing the container back inside the crate, the Abbot paused and said, "Hill wasn't a scientist, so this container, as spectacular as it is, wouldn't have impressed him as it does us and, as he was a linguist, the manuscript would have impressed him more than it would either of us."

"Why do you store it in that old crate?"

"A question Brother Gregory asked my predecessor when he brought us here. The story my predecessor heard was that John Hill made this crate himself and, when he grew concerned about a secure place for the artifact, he settled on putting the crate in plain view on a shelf in his office, reasoning that no one would suspect that something so valuable would be left unprotected, and so easily accessible. The Poe principle, you might say."

The container was halfway back into its crate, when Lyle said, "Wait a moment," extending his hands and accepting it from his uncle.

Had his eyes deceived him? Had the magnificence of this thing dazzled him into seeing something that wasn't there?

As it happened, Lyle had been trained by archeology and experience to observe things differently than the vast majority of observers, to look deeper and longer. The container wasn't square. The lines didn't meet at right angles. The divergence was minute, but without cognitive recognition he had immediately sensed it. Now, holding the object in his hands, turning it this way and that, he was certain of it.

He was certain of something else: the person or people who had made this thing were too talented to have done this by mistake. Then why?

It wasn't in Lyle's nature to put aside puzzles without speculating. He looked at the thing from every angle to confirm his eyes weren't playing tricks on him. Less than a few degrees off square, but there it was.

If intentional—and Lyle was convinced it was—was this an expression of the maker's sense of form—beauty? A test, or a jest? Or perhaps a bow to the natural world, where seemingly straight lines and right angles weren't perfectly geometrical.

With the box and the container restored to the niche, and the repository door closed, the Abbot led the way back to his office, where Lyle asked, "Who knew the artifact resided here?"

"Besides myself, Brother Gregory, Brother Claude, and Brother Thomas, our Novice Master . . . and the bishop."

"Who knew how to get into the repository?"

"Brother Gregory and Brother Claude."

"Not the bishop?"

"He's never viewed the artifact. Too busy, and a skeptic, or so I've heard. The previous bishop was our porter on the day Hill delivered the manuscript."

"Who's actually seen the artifact?"

"Just Brother Gregory, to the best of my knowledge. You realize a professional could get into this monastery easily enough, and into that room, too, I imagine."

"Why was Brother Gregory allowed to view it?"

"Both of us were considered for abbot when my predecessor died, and he thought it wise to let us see the artifact when he received word he had a terminal illness and not long to live."

Lyle said, "I'd like to speak to Brother Gregory, Brother Claude, and Brother Thomas."

"Brother Gregory left the Order five years ago. We kept in touch for a while, but I lost track of him when he was at the Sorbonne in Paris."

"Are the police looking for him?"

"Perhaps."

"How much did you tell the police?"

"What they needed to know to restore the artifact. I decided there was no need to bring . . . John Hill into it, or the age Hill represented the artifact to be."

A wise decision if his uncle wanted the police to take the matter seriously. "What have they told you?"

"That they're investigating the matter, though I don't think it has a high priority. When it comes to the value of the artifact, I suspect the police and the bishop are of like minds."

"Have they located Brother Gregory, where's he's living now?"

"Not as of a few days ago."

"You said Hill translated the manuscript."

"I was told he translated much of it, not all, and that was after decades of work by one of the top linguists in the world."

"His story is the story contained in the manuscript . . . is that what you're saying?"

"That's what I was told by my predecessor, who was told that by the abbot who met Hill. I was also informed there were parts of the manuscript Hill had succeeded in translating, but had decided never to reveal."

"For what reason?"

"The subject matter was said to be perilous."

"How could something that was perilous forty thousand years ago be dangerous today?"

"A question I can't answer. I'm telling you what I was told."

"Could Brother Gregory . . ."

"He goes by his secular name now, Noel Dekeyser."

"Could Dekeyser be behind this?"

"I certainly hope not."

"But you don't rule it out."

"Noel is a psychologist. After leaving the Order, he worked at a clinic in Folkestone, and then moved to the Sorbonne."

"And then disappeared."

"I didn't say that. I lost touch with him, and I haven't been searching for him."

"You said the police haven't found him."

"Presuming they are actually seeking him. It's my impression the police think a professional learned about the artifact and went after it. Whatever Brother . . . Noel was, he wasn't a thief."

"That's just an opinion, Uncle."

"An informed opinion. He was my brother in this Order for over ten years."

"Why did he leave?"

Lyle noticed his uncle's hesitation. "He wasn't satisfied with the direction we were taking."

"An exemplary monk?"

"Determined . . . conscientious."

"I know determined and conscientious men I wouldn't call exemplary."

"That's the best I can do, Frodo. Before you go, I'd like you to see another manuscript, something your mother composed. I hadn't thought about it for years, but talking about her stories reminded me. I'll fetch it from our library."

Lyle was going to be late for the faculty meeting, not that missing one of Dawson's gabfests mattered to him. Still, he'd better text him, or the man might wait for him.

The Abbot returned with a bound manuscript and, handing it to Lyle, said, "A book she composed over thirty years ago. By all means, keep it."

"What's it about?"

"A turtle, of all things."

Lyle couldn't resist opening the manuscript and reading a few paragraphs:

> Beakie didn't think he'd been injured in the fall, and though he'd escaped from the box he was still inside the house. He crawled to the nearest wall and found there were no holes large enough for a skipper, much less a shell. He had done a lot of work and had only escaped a small box to be trapped in a larger one.
>
> Shells in deep water
> Where is the sun
> Cold water and danger
> Need to find light
> Too bold is too reckless
> Come to the surface
>
> That was how Beakie felt, as if he had been in deep water for too long. But how was he supposed to get to the surface, to get out of this house?

A knock on the door and, before the Abbot could say a word, an old man with sunken eyes and a foot-long beard walked in.

"May I speak with him, Father Abbot?" the old monk asked.

Apparently accustomed to this man's direct manner, the Abbot said, "You may, Brother Claude. I'll walk him to your cell shortly."

The monk cast a critical eye at Lyle and said, "I'll be there another hour."

"He's the eldest brother at St. Hugh's," said the Abbot, after Brother Claude had left. "He was here when Hill visited."

"How much has he been told?"

"Most of it, and he's probably deduced the rest. Brother Claude doesn't say much, and he doesn't miss much."

Walking to the window, Lyle said, "What does recovering this artifact have to do with being abbot? Why is bringing it back so important?"

"I'm human, and I take my human responsibilities seriously. I feel a powerful need to restore this thing to the monastery . . . for John Hill, my brothers, my brother abbots who once cared for the artifact, and to remove suspicion from Noel."

"He may be the thief. He could have snuck into the monastery and repository."

"I hope not . . . to truth," said Abbot Henry, clanking his empty glass against Lyle's.

Led by the Abbot to Brother Claude's cell, Lyle knocked on the door and was instructed to enter. He hadn't expected much in the way of size or appointments, but this space was more severe than he ever imagined: a mat on the floor, tiny desk and chair, and a crucifix and an icon of the Virgin and Child on the wall. Standing next to the mat, the monk said, "Be seated."

"Where will you sit?"

Brother Claude pointed at the only chair, and Lyle sat.

"Did you meet John Hill?" Lyle asked him.

The old monk shook his head. "Not me, though I remember that night, and the stir it caused. I don't think you, or anyone else, will find it."

"Why not?"

"Because Noel will have sold it for a handsome price to someone who can lock it up as tight as a drum."

"A black market collector . . . tomb raiders. I have experience with that sort. Why are you convinced it's Dekeyser?"

None of the reticence Lyle had detected in his uncle when Brother Claude said, "He wanted to be abbot, and when he lost out, he walked away."

"You knew him well?"

"Gregory the Great, obsequious to superiors and dismissive of everyone else."

"What else can you tell me?"

"It would be hard for someone, even a professional thief, to get into and out of this monastery without being seen, and they'd have to know about the door and how to open it."

"You don't think anyone's in physical danger, do you?"

"Why wouldn't they be, if this thing is worth as much as Henry believes? Greed does bad things to a person, and that includes harming people who get in the way."

Thinking of the container, Lyle said, "Surely Dekeyser wouldn't harm one of the monks."

"I don't think he would, either, but he's not in this alone, you can count on it."

"Why did you ask to speak to me?"

"It would do your uncle a great service if you can help him, even if you can't restore this . . . thing. He's beside himself. Thinks he's a failure. I've never seen Henry like this, and I don't like it. To hell with the artifact, I want our abbot back."

DECEMBER 13, 2016

☻-☻-☻

Oxford

LYLE FREQUENTED THIS small Oxford pub because it wasn't popular with tourists, wasn't famous or notorious, and the food and beer were better than average. It wasn't pretentious, either, a twelve-table, ale-and-sandwich pub that knew what it was.

A lovely day for mid-December, with bright sun and light jacket temperatures. He'd arrived before lunch so he could hold down a corner table for Sam and Beatrice, who walked in together. Sam was average-looking, someone who'd go unnoticed on the street, with more hair than the balding Lyle; Beatrice bronze-skinned and curvy, with cropped hair and chocolate eyes, sturdy and steady. Though Sam had only been with Beatrice on two other occasions, they got on so well that Lyle sometimes felt the odd man out.

As his brother approached the booth, Lyle noticed that Sam was a little thicker around the middle than he remembered. Ten years younger than Sam, the boy Lyle had revered his older brother and, behind their adult banter, he retained a deeply rooted respect for Sam Stuart. As for Beatrice Adams, his feelings for her ranged from an attraction he'd never felt for anyone else to head-shaking confusion. So different were they from one another, he sometimes wondered why either bothered with the relationship. As someone who liked to put things—and people, too, for that matter—in neat little boxes, he found this frustrating.

Since the theft of the manuscript was a criminal matter, it was easy to understand why he had sought out his brother, but he still wasn't sure why he'd invited Beatrice.

"I know you haven't called me here to announce you're getting married, because I asked her on the street," said Sam, causing Lyle to flush, before he realized that Beatrice was in on it, too.

"Lyle's smitten with his Neanderthal girl," Beatrice said, referring to the skeleton of a young woman in the Archaeology lab.

"I was worried you were too busy tailing Russians to bother with me," Lyle said to Sam.

"The other way around, I'm afraid. Polonium in your martini, if you're not careful."

"Don't you mean plutonium?" Lyle said.

"Polonium-210, a radioactive isotope, millions of times more lethal than cyanide, or so I've been told—what the Russians used on Litvinenko in that Mayfair bar. They're neck-and-neck with Mossad when it comes to who's the most deadly."

"Yes, we'll have beer and sandwiches," Lyle said to the waitress. After the young woman had left with their orders, he said to Sam and Beatrice, "I need your advice. I saw Uncle Henry a few days ago ..."

Giving Beatrice a peck on the cheek, Sam said, "With a ravishing woman like this, you're thinking about taking the cowl?"

"Uncle Henry asked me to help him."

Their beer arrived, and Sam took a big swallow. "I take it this wasn't a routine request. Let's hear what's on Henry's mind."

Lyle told them everything he could remember, including his conversation with Brother Claude. When he'd finished, Sam said, "Is the old boy getting woolly?"

"Except for that bizarre story, his wits seemed intact to me."

"Hmm . . . whether this manuscript's worth anything or not, it obviously means a lot to Henry."

"Are you certain the artifact isn't authentic?" asked Beatrice.

"I'm certain," Lyle responded. "Though the container and manuscript are real enough, the story attached to them is . . . well, chimerical."

"If you're positive about things that happened—or didn't happen—forty thousand years ago, you're smarter than I thought you were."

Beatrice's witticisms often had a sharp edge, and Lyle wasn't shielded from cuts when she had a point to make. He said, "Four hundred years ago, the Dutch established an outpost on Manhattan Island. Where New York City is today, there were hills and waterfalls, forests and streams. Forty thousand years ago represents one hundred years for every year from the present to Dutch Manhattan. That length of time is inconceivable to us, and a high civilization so long ago is even more inconceivable. It's alright for my uncle to take things on faith, but I'm a scientist . . . May I have a pickle?" he asked their passing waitress.

Lyle knew Beatrice couldn't let that comment go unchallenged, and she didn't disappoint him. "Faith means openness to truth, even when an anchoring heuristic is challenged—when something contradicts what we're predisposed to believe."

"I'm not predisposed to believe anything," Lyle answered her, "and psych jargon won't convince me either."

Beatrice was a lecturer in the psychology department at the university, also a polymath, fluent in English, French, and German, along with three or four Ugandan dialects. She hadn't known anyone when she came to Oxford from Uganda and, for a reason Lyle had never understood, she had gravitated to him, and he to her, first as friends, and then more than friends.

Sam said, "Henry believes this old man . . ."

"John Hill, that's what he was told by his predecessor, who heard it from the abbot who received Hill."

"Henry believes this old man bequeathed them the manuscript on which his stories were based."

"That's right. One night, Hill came with the artifact and left without it."

"Why do you keep calling him Hill when you know his real name?" asked Beatrice.

"Do I? I know the name of the man who wrote the stories our mother read us. This is an altogether different man, and until I can reconcile the two, he shall be John Hill."

Beatrice said, "It's all a piece with Lyle's general skepticism."

"Sam . . . Sam . . . are you listening?" Lyle said.

"Sorry, I thought I saw Li Hwang walking past the pub. Probably mistaken . . . haven't seen him for years."

"Who is he?" Beatrice asked Sam.

"A right vicious bastard, and he doesn't belong in Oxford. He's the Chinese security chief. At the center of the web these days, not in the field anymore."

"How do you know him?" Lyle said.

Sam made a move to stand up, but checked himself. "He *turned* a friend of mine. A look-alike, that's all . . . You're considering Henry's request, aren't you?"

"Certainly not."

"Then why are we here?"

Sam still seemed distracted to Lyle, who said, "I thought I could give our uncle some advice."

"He didn't ask for advice," Beatrice said. "He asked for *you.*"

Sam said, "Relying on what you told us, what do we know? First, give me a few minutes to work on this sandwich, and I'll have another beer, if it's on little brother's tab."

Beatrice said to Lyle, "Speaking of look-alikes, I saw a man today that looked so much like Paul I followed him for two blocks."

"Who's Paul?" said Sam.

"My brother. I never saw his body, but I'm sure he's dead."

"Her brother was ... killed by Ugandan rebels," Lyle said to Sam.

"When?" asked Sam.

"In 2002. Of course, the man I followed looked like Paul did then. He'd look different now. I knew that, but I wanted to believe it was him."

"You were close to your brother?" said Sam.

"I love him. I looked up to him. I thought he could do anything ... he could, almost."

"How did you get an English name?" Sam inquired.

"An *American* name. An ancestor of ours was an American slave, and when he escaped north, President Adams'swife, Abigail, helped him get to Africa. He honored her by taking the name, and the family carried it forward."

After they'd finished eating, Lyle said, "We know the pages were stolen by someone who knew about the artifact, and how to get into the monastery and repository without being detected."

Sam said, "A professional, or someone familiar with the ins and outs of the place."

"And schedules ... where the monks are, and when," said Beatrice. "The thief could have taken the container if he'd wanted to. Why didn't he? Because he's cautious and calculating. He knew your uncle periodically viewed the artifact, and knew there was plenty of money to be made from the manuscript, so he left the container and manuscript cover behind to give the impression the artifact was intact."

"I agree," Sam said. "This thief was after money, and he figured he could delay pursuit by leaving the container behind. Now, if Henry knows what he's talking about, Dekeyser, Brother Claude, and Brother Thomas are the primary suspects. Brother Claude and Brother Thomas aren't supposed to have seen it, but they were close enough to the secret. If Henry's wrong about who knew, there may be others in the Order and the bishop's office we can add to our list. That would complicate things, though it's still a small circle."

"If one of them recruited a professional . . ."

"We still concentrate on the smaller circle, and identify the recruiter. Drill him good and hard until we know everything he does."

"Is that legal?" inquired Beatrice.

Sam's nose was in his beer glass, and he didn't bother to answer.

Lyle said to Sam, "Where would you start?"

"If it were me," said Sam, "I'd talk to Brother Thomas, the bishop, and the police, and if I didn't learn anything new, I'd zero in on Dekeyser like a fox on a rabbit."

"Could you find him?" Lyle asked his brother.

"If I couldn't, he isn't findable."

"What's wrong with you helping your uncle for a month or two?" Beatrice asked Lyle, to which he replied, "Everything imaginable."

Sam said, "Give Henry everything we gave you and wash your hands of it—like Caesar."

Beatrice shot a glance at Lyle, who had no idea if his brother was serious, or pulling his leg, as Sam could be as smart or as dull as he wanted to be.

"Anything I've missed?" Lyle asked them.

Sam said, "When an artifact is stolen, it often goes unrecovered for years or decades. Once the recipient takes delivery, he stores it in a safe place and only reveals it to a select few. One thing you should consider is that dead people can't do anything about an archaeologist barging into their tombs and houses, but live people who find out you're searching for them *can* do something about it."

Sam's observation reminded Lyle of what Brother Claude had said about the level of danger.

"Lyle will have to make sure all his food and drink are sealed tight, so no polonium gets in," Beatrice said.

Sam said, "Sealed tight is a relative term. We have a tool that can get into and out of glass and metal containers and leave something behind without anyone being the wiser."

"Surely no one would go so far as to violate a beer bottle," said Lyle, with affected outrage. "Smacks of boys with toys."

"Except ours are rather dangerous toys."

"How does your tool work?"

"I can't tell you that, though it's neat and quick. What I mean to say is people who pursue thieves need to be on guard."

"How would someone begin such a project?" Lyle said.

"If I didn't learn anything new, I'd follow Dekeyser's path from the monastery, starting in Folkestone."

"Even though we know he's moved on?" asked Lyle.

"Just because Dekeyser's moved on doesn't mean the manuscript went with him, if he intended to sell it. After Folkestone, I'd go to the Sorbonne and try to pick up his trail. If Dekeyser's the thief, I doubt he still has the manuscript, but he'd be the most likely person to know who does. That's where *I'd* start, brother, but where it'd take me, who can say? So, when do *you* start?" said Sam.

Lyle put the beer glass to his lips, and when he lowered it, he said, "I'll give Uncle Henry this information and go on with a clear conscience."

"You won't have a clear conscience, and you know it," said Beatrice, "and you haven't asked how I'd start. In Uganda, we have a saying, 'Look at a man's eyes, not his hands and feet'—what's going on inside rather than what he's doing. In my business, we're taught how to look into people's eyes."

"How do you look into the thief's eyes, when we don't know who he or she is, or where they are?" Lyle asked her.

"By learning as much as we can about him. We've already surmised that he's cautious, and more interested in money than in possessing the artifact. Otherwise, he wouldn't have defaced it.

Brother Claude gave us a better look into Dekeyser's eyes than your uncle did—haughty, egotistical."

"There you are, Lyle," said Sam, finishing his second beer. "A roadmap and a psych profile in an hour."

"Information for the professional investigator Uncle Henry hires," Lyle remarked.

Beatrice and Sam gave each other knowing looks. She said, "You've made the decision to help your uncle. You just don't know it yet."

"Lyle's no James Bond. When he was a boy, he was run over by a poodle. Split his chin and sent him to hospital."

"A sixty-pound standard poodle—came at me like a boar."

"Brother Thomas, the bishop, then Folkestone," said Sam.

Lyle was as satisfied and content as he'd ever been, a respected archaeologist at a prestigious university, living in a town he liked. Unlike many of his colleagues, he enjoyed teaching and working in the field, despite the often-harsh conditions. The decision he was on the verge of making would have been unimaginable a week ago, and there was the risk that it would irreparably damage the reputation he'd worked so hard to achieve.

After settling the bill, he said, "Sam, you'll need to talk to the police."

OCTOBER 21, 2002

Albania & Uganda

THE HOUSES ON BOTH sides of the narrow Gjirokaster lane were honeycombed with apartments. Even though the day was cool and gray, men were on porches, on the street, or in the claustrophobic and shadowy alleys between houses, drinking from ceramic cups or smoking water pipes.

For almost a month, he'd been keeping an eye on a man the Chinese were using to make trouble for the incipient democracy.

Pakistanis and Afghanis, he told himself. The two men at the corner would be in his path if he kept on. Pakistani . . . no, something was amiss. Too alert, too observant, too indolent-seeming. He knew what that meant and they were two, while he was one.

He'd never make the safe house, not from here. As nonchalantly as he could, he trotted up the stairs to his left. They'd read him too, in spite of the air of unconcern he tried to project. Two teenagers in jeans and hoodies made room for him. Now, he was in the foyer, and he knew the pair would be on him soon unless he acted with vigor and boldness. Up the dirty, uneven stairs he went at a gallop, every tread bowing and moaning as he ascended. At the first landing, the window resisted until he shocked the casement with his heel. Clambering outside, he pushed the window closed, and shinnied up a drainpipe that overlooked the empty alley. So much for his freshly laundered shirt and pants.

The drain wasn't difficult to negotiate, not for him. Second floor, third floor, the roof. They weren't going to get the drop on him as they had on Nestor Stuart. He stood up on the pitched tile, looked and listened. In view, stark mountain ridges and the eighteenth-century minaret.

He'd been right. They were following him. Could he go from roof to roof? The tile was slick, but after two steps he'd adjusted to it. Laughter from below. A shout, then a few words in a language he didn't recognize. He trotted toward the chimney and crawled behind it.

The chimney bowl was sooty, and now so was he.

Could one of the two be Patrick? He might have been mistaken, but he didn't think so. Best friends once. How many beers together? Like brothers.

I'm in danger if it's Patrick. And a second man, maybe more dangerous than Patrick, though he doubted it. He wasn't a runner, but he didn't relish the thought of mortal combat with Patrick.

He's hunting you, and he'll be here any second.

Getting darker now, even on the roof. They might have night vision. Better assume so. He needed to strike fast. Take risks they wouldn't expect him to take.

Here they come. The first pursuer hoisted himself onto the roof. Not Patrick; not yet.

Sam removed his pistol from its holster. As he always did, he checked the clip.

Empty.

He'd checked it just before Nicholetta had arrived to spend the night with him at the Babameto House, in the shadow of the Romanesque citadel.

Empty, with the pair bearing down on him.

He had the dart, just one, for enemies that were close enough—or for himself, if the situation was hopeless. All he had to do was pierce flesh, and the pea-sized pump would push the deadly poison in the shaft into the victim's nervous system. A few seconds was all it took to kill.

Sam broke the needle seal and stepped out from behind the chimney. A risk they wouldn't expect him to take. Knowing he'd have checked his clip as soon as he realized they were after him, they'd expect him to run. It was getting dark, but the pursuer saw him, lifted his pistol.

Never got off a shot. The dart lodged in the man's neck and down he went.

"This isn't your patch, Sam."

In the few seconds from the time the first attacker died and Patrick made the roof, Sam had retrieved the dead man's gun. Maybe Patrick knew it, and maybe he didn't. His former comrade had the dexterity of an orangutan, the eyes of a hawk, but he thought so much of himself he sometimes overlooked things. Such as this gun? And Patrick had been better than Sam at almost everything. That would make him even more confident.

His adversary had the advantage of superior skills, but Sam's advantage came from knowing he wasn't the smartest, fastest, most talented operative. If this hadn't made him Patrick's equal in combat, it had made him a kind of Samwise Gamgee who knew that being resourceful was the most important thing and, though Patrick and the rest scorned the SOE "amateurs," Sam had sought out the last of them, old Brooks, and learned everything he could from a man who had wreaked havoc in Nazi-occupied France with nothing but guile and guts.

Another roof behind him. If Patrick didn't move to his right or left, he wouldn't see or hear Sam until he landed on top of the next building. What Sam needed to do was harder—let Patrick see him moving, but not long enough to be picked off.

"Sam . . . parley . . . a beer, like old times. Miss the old house, and your mum."

He wouldn't let himself remember. Calculating the arc of flight, Sam made for the next roof. Patrick had seen him exposed for an instant. Hadn't taken a shot. That was like Patrick. Not until he was sure, and in one more second he would have been sure.

Almost too dark to see now. On his hands and knees, Sam crept back to the chimney and huddled tight against the bricks, almost indistinguishable from the stack.

By all rights, Patrick should have waited for him to gain the next roof before he picked him off, but Sam suspected his old comrade would come on hard. As Patrick passed the chimney, he deduced what was really happening, but an instant later Sam had dropped him with two bullets to the head and one to the heart.

No need to touch him. Better not to.

Nicholetta would have cleared out of the house by the time he returned. If Sam were killed, she wouldn't want to face the police, nor Sam if he managed to survive.

Three minutes later, he was on the street again. More lights now, and more people out and about.

No one bothered him.

BEATRICE, HER FAMILY, and two of Paul's friends were on a wilderness trail that would bring them to Kampala in three or four days, if they weren't waylaid along the way. All the men had guns, including her father, though she had little hope they could hold their own in a firefight with the Salafi rebels.

They'd barely escaped as their village was being raided, as the men were being killed and the women and children taken prisoner. Only Paul's and his friends' knowledge of obscure woodland paths had saved them.

As for her, she had given up hope of escape. Her mind had gone numb, as if she'd been given an anesthetic drug. It wasn't the punch in the face that did it, or the hands on her neck—whatever had caused the numbness had come from inside her.

One of the hundreds of bullets that were fired in the village had pierced the flimsy wall and had struck the rebel commander in the side of the neck. Paralyzed with terror, she hadn't noticed until the warm blood soaked her shirtsleeve. How she had escaped the chaotic village and caught up to her family, she never knew, nor did they ask her.

They had been on the run for two days now with only the food and drink they'd been able to forage along their route, almost all of it given to the girls and her parents. Guns were the only things they'd managed to bring, apart from the clothes on their backs.

Those nights in the open she had reclined between Cornelia and Maria, as close as they could huddle, with one of her arms over each of the girls. Paul had sought camps as dry and sheltered as possible, and one of the young men was always on guard. Even so, getting more than a few hours' sleep had been impossible.

"I'm thirsty," Cornelia said, in their Buya dialect.

"Soon, dear," her mother said to her. "Your brother will find us water and food."

Soon enough to keep them from perishing from thirst and hunger? Beatrice wondered. Paul had said the river was up ahead, but how far?

The river reminded her of their snake pond. One of her earliest memories was of her brother taking her to the pond, identifying every creature that patrolled those waters, from insects to amphibians, reptiles, birds, and mammals. He had told her stories, too—some from the Bible, as she later learned, many from African lore. He was her hero.

She had sprained an ankle and was covered with insect bites, but her mother, who suffered and went on without complaint, kept her going.

The relatively open ground they'd been traversing all night was giving way to a forest, crowned with the rising sun.

"We're not far," Paul's friend, Jonathan, said, as Paul lifted little Maria and put her monkey-wise on his back.

"A forest can mean safety or danger," Beatrice's father said. "Be watchful. Be prayerful."

The strap that secured the knife to her belt had loosened, and securing it reminded her that she had brought it as a last resort in case the rebels took her. If such a thing happened again, how would she use the knife?

Normally fastidious about her appearance and cleanliness, she was filthy now. The forest they were entering was quiet, too quiet for her liking. When Cornelia complained of being too tired to go on, Paul reminded her that until they reached the river there was no water.

"And how is my little Beatrice?" he said to his sister, after having quieted Cornelia. Now twenty, she would always be her brother's "little Beatrice."

"She can go as far and as fast as you can," she said, trying to sound more confident than she felt.

"When we reach the river, we will rest."

"How will we cross? We'll be trapped by the water."

"Jonathan and I have a plan. First, rest and drink, and fish if we're lucky."

Paul and Jonathan reminded her of goatherds, in the way they kept the company moving and in order, and though she knew her brother to be as resourceful as they came, trekking cross country with women and children—with the rebels tracking them—was more than even he could handle. Adding to her apprehensions, there was no doubt they were being followed, as Isaac, the fleetest of the young men, had informed them after a reconnaissance.

Beatrice said to her brother, "Instead of catching fish, I'd rather you turn us into fish, like the old magician in the story, so we can swim across."

A gunshot, and Isaac cried out. He'd been hit, though he kept moving. From the corner of her eye, Beatrice saw a band of men—how many, impossible to tell—emerging from the woods, rifles at the ready.

The strong hand on her shoulder was Paul's, who said, "To the right. Keep them moving . . . go!"

She grabbed one of Maria's hands and one of her mother's and pulled them along, and when she realized her father was torn between staying with the young men and coming with them, she called out, "Father, bring Cornelia. Quickly."

Her words resolved his indecision, and the five of them loped toward the woods, and away from the rebels.

There were too many gunshots for her to count. She didn't have time to cry, though she knew the best her brother and his friends could do before they were slaughtered was slow down the rebels.

The forest was soon quiet again. The rebels would expect their prey to flee in the opposite direction, so she would circle back to the area where the fighters had come out of the forest, using the dense brush as cover. Whether this stratagem would work hardly mattered now, as in a few hours they would be caught, or too hungry to go on.

"Where are we going?" a terrified Cornelia asked her.

"We're going to Kampala, to a new house."

"Will there be food?"

"Plenty of food. Mother, keep up."

Half an hour later, they might have been where Beatrice intended them to be, they might have been anywhere. She thought the river was to their right, though that was nothing more than a guess, so she led them in that direction, hoping they didn't cross the killing field where her brother had died, subjecting her parents to that horror.

She smelled the river before she saw it, and that kept her going when she was on the verge of giving up. A hundred-yard patch of tall grass between them and the river. All was quiet, a bad sign, but one she didn't have the luxury to heed.

The company was within thirty yards of the river when a man with a gun—surely one of the fighters, as he was dressed like them—showed himself and called out, "Come here, now. Drop that gun," he said to Beatrice's father, "or I will shoot the women."

As the rebel's rifle was pointed at them, there was nothing to do but obey. Perhaps he would shoot them all, Beatrice thought. End this misery.

The rebel led them to a narrow, heavily shingled riverbank. The young man, just a boy with his orders, had a motorboat moored at the water's edge.

"Sit here," the boy-man commanded them, and when they were all on the ground, he hit Beatrice's father hard on the side of the head with the butt of his gun, causing the older man to topple over and her mother to cry out.

Not giving the stunned man a second thought, the rebel retrieved a walkie-talkie from his coat pocket and put it against his ear.

Beatrice's mother had crawled over to her husband, and the two girls were huddled together and whimpering. Beatrice took in the scene, knowing the rebel was alerting their pursuers to having captured them. The blood on her sleeve that had dried to a crusty black reminded her of the direness of their position. Not just her, but all of them, even the girls. She began crawling in her father's direction. The rebel glanced at her, but he was preoccupied with his conversation. When she was within a few feet of her father, she leapt to her feet, lunged ahead, and drove the knife into the rebel's neck. She was young and strong, and the one arm he'd used to fend her off hadn't hindered her.

She had scored a direct hit. Blood gushed out of the wound like a geyser. The walkie-talkie slipped from the man's hand. He stood in place for several seconds, as if he'd been stung by a bee, then dropped like a felled tree.

Beatrice's heart was hammering in her chest. Glancing at the bleeding and twitching youth on the ground, she could feel the bile surge in her throat, had to swallow three times to staunch it. Now wasn't the time to show weakness. She wiped the blade on the grass until every speck of blood was gone. The girls and her mother were looking at her as if she were a stranger. Her father was sitting up, but too dazed to understand what had happened.

As panicked as she was, she forced herself to act. She picked up the walkie-talkie and threw it into the river, returned her father's gun, and took the rebel's gun for herself.

"Get in the boat . . . everyone. Father, we need you in the boat, to take us up the river. Come, girls. We're going for a boat ride."

DECEMBER 19, 2016

Oxford

FOR A MAN WHOSE BREAD and butter were the ancient and antiquarian, it was ironic that Lyle hadn't been aware of the Consolidated Archives.

The reception area might have been attached to a library or reading room, except that it was walled off from the rest of the structure. A timid-looking man at the desk, small in stature, thin-haired, and wearing a red and gray pullover, verified Lyle's identity and, a few minutes later, a bulbous uniformed man entered from the room's only interior door.

"Bin 421," said the clerk to the guard, who opened the door and motioned Lyle through.

Sam had informed Lyle that because a portion of the material archived here had been restricted by British Intelligence after World War II, the entire building had been removed from the public information grid, and was now thought to be a warehouse. Discovering a John Hill archive here, a diligent Sam had secured permission for his brother to examine the contents, telling Lyle it was his policy to learn as much as possible about the principals before embarking on a mission. For his part, Lyle viewed this as a pro forma exercise, with no expectation he'd learn anything that would help him locate the manuscript.

Upon entering the archival area, Lyle had been searched and fitted with an electronic wristband to alert the guard if he strayed. Formerly an eighteenth-century Recitation Hall, of stone, brick, and timber construction, the building now combined old and new, with all of the interior architecture having been removed to make way for row upon row of fenced and gated areas. The stone walls and high ceiling remained; not the stone floor, which had been paved over to facilitate trolley traffic. A modern air conditioning system made the structure suitable for archival activities, and, to adequately illuminate this cavernous space, motion-activated pendant lamps extended from a latticework of aluminum framing.

Though there was nothing ostentatious about this archive, Lyle suspected that many of the items retained here would fetch fortunes on the open market, considering their age or who had once composed, drawn, built, or owned them.

Stopping abruptly, the guard used a card key to open a gate. "The beeper'll tell me when you're finished," he said, as the gate clanged shut behind Lyle.

The fenced area was twelve by twelve feet, with boxes stacked to a height of ten feet on steel shelving that backed up to the fencing. Next to the gate were a movable wooden chair and a five-tread stepladder. Silent as a tomb, the air cool and still, the building reminded Lyle of an enormous cave, dark everywhere except for the immediate vicinity of Bin 421.

Lyle's uncle had facilitated interviews with Brother Thomas and the bishop. Though not as frank as Brother Claude, Brother Thomas had expressed no sadness over Dekeyser's departure. He was aware that Dekeyser had gone to work in Folkestone, though not that the former monk had later moved to the Sorbonne. Brother Thomas had thought he'd seen Dekeyser on the grounds earlier that year, but hadn't been sure, and the man had walked off when hailed.

How sure had he been that it was Dekeyser? Not at all sure, though the man had the same halting gait as Brother Gregory. So, why hadn't Lyle's uncle mentioned this to him?

As for the bishop, before he had said a dozen words, Lyle had calibrated his expectations, receiving the impression this man was preoccupied with far weightier matters.

Had a valuable artifact been kept at the monastery? Something sensational had been stored there, but whether it was an artifact, as commonly understood, who could say? How concerned was the bishop with having it restored? Anything that was important to the Order was important to the bishop. Had he spoken to the police? Certainly, though he had turned the matter over to Abbot Henry.

There must have been a hundred boxes in Bin 421, all labeled, so where was Lyle supposed to start? The box labels suggested that most of the material was connected to the man's linguistic and literary research, with everything related to those famous stories kept elsewhere. One by one, Lyle read the labels and brief summaries of the contents, an activity that took some time, considering the number of boxes. He was on the verge of signaling the guard when he found a box labeled *Odds & Ends*.

Lyle knew that Beatrice would ask him about the archive. Nothing she did was done superficially, and she was keen on Lyle being as well prepared for this mission as possible. If he examined the contents of one box, he could tell her he'd made an earnest search, and she was nothing if not earnest.

Odds & Ends proved to be an apt description of the contents of that box: a diary, old envelopes with nothing inside them, a grade school primer, a worn Roman Missal, a shaving brush, prayer cards, heavy cardboard postcards. Holding up a card, Lyle was struck by the realization that these things had once belonged to a man who was as legendary as his stories.

In short order, Lyle realized that the diary hadn't belonged to the man whose materials were archived here, but to someone else.

When he opened the small book, he hadn't expected to give it much attention, but as he turned pages, he grew more intrigued by the person who'd inscribed her name on the first page: Agnes CurLio.

Commencing in 1916 and ending in 1932, the diary showed gaps of weeks and months without anything being recorded. An early entry identified Agnes as a schoolgirl in 1916, so only in her thirties in 1932. Had she died then? Lost the diary? How had it come to the man whose work was enshrined in this archive?

Lyle read more carefully when he came to an entry that was especially enlightening or intriguing.

> *1916—My proudest and most frightening moment on the same night. Portraying Peter Pan in the school play. Shaking as I delivered my first lines but calm after a few minutes. Grandfather Arthur can't go anywhere without his wheeled chair, but he was there in the first row with mother and father. I could see how proud they were and probably more anxious than me. How shall I ever sleep tonight?*

> *1919—I've tried to resist. Tomorrow, I'll join him. Mother and father will never understand. Shall I tell them or waft away like Peter Pan? I only know my planet must orbit Adler's star.*

> *1921—They took him away before I could so much as see him. A. told me it was for the best, that he had died an hour later. I whispered to A. the name I wanted him to have. How terrible life can be.*

> *1924—We eliminated three of A's adversaries today, two in Argentina, and one in Brazil. As usual, he left nothing to chance. The Brazil assassination was so delicate he dispatched Christopher to oversee the operation. How enthusiastic A. is when he's stalking and hunting.*

> *1925—A. gave me the privilege of joining him in his secret puzzle room tonight. Pitch dark. A thousand-piece puzzle on an invisible table. What I think is he wants me to know I'm a piece of his puzzle and no matter where in the world I go, he will find me and put me in my proper place.*

1926—It was living inside a Mammillaria Matude, in Oaxaca. Not an impressive cactaceae, or an impressive scolopendra. But how doggedly deadly.

1927—I lack for nothing, or so it seems. Outwardly, I behave as any good lieutenant would behave. All the captains take my orders as if they came from A. As for Christopher, who can say what that one is thinking? Only A. knows, and he never tells. All this instead of children. That's the choice I've made, or the choice that made me.

1928—A. gave me a diamond-studded broach to wear to the President's Ball tonight. Every woman's eyes were on it, and most of the men's. I overheard the American ambassador telling someone it's worth a million dollars, and that A. is a fool to let me wear it in public. I was tempted to tell him that whatever A. is, he isn't a fool. I expected him to ask for it when we returned to the compound, for safekeeping if nothing else, but he never said a word. Perhaps he's distracted by his eagerness to return to Europe.

1928—An enemy was executed here in Buenos Aires, or so A. informed me. Columbian golden frog venom. Our poison of choice. A single one-inch specimen with enough poison to kill a dozen men. I hope the poor soul deserved it, and I told A. so. Perhaps I can save a few along the way. That's what I keep telling myself.

1929— "You considered that one hair fluttering at my neck; you gazed at it upon my neck, and it captivated you." I shall never be the same after finding the book. I've been made fallow by what I've seen and experienced in the last five years. The book will force me to decide, and soon. Henceforth, I must protect this diary with my life.

1930—I left him today, unimaginable a few years ago. Left the broach in my jewelry box. Left him and didn't look back. He shall look back though, and send them for me.

Lyle looked up, took a deep breath. Still wondering why he was spending half a day here, though he had to admit this woman's experiences were fascinating.

1931 — Urchins stole my bag today on an Algiers street, my arm wrenched, but the pain is subsiding. My cache of toxins stolen. The book stolen. Not the creature I left in a matchbox in my room, the last arrow in my quiver.

1931 — Thomas came with information about G's whereabouts, a sanitarium in Port d'Ivry. As if I don't have enough problems, he told me a woman named Rosman is trying to find me, a person who seems to be after what A. is after. How good it was to see Thomas again before he went off on the Brough.

1931 — G. is here with me. Not in this room but nearby. I woke at three and couldn't get back to sleep. Can you blame me after what I've been through? Even here, in this place of peace, there's no peace for me. Tomorrow we move again.

1932 — The channel boat tonight. Almost sure the big man I saw on deck is following me. Why should that surprise me? I've upped the ante with G. and Christopher, haven't I?

1932 — I'm seeing the Oxford teacher today, and I'm leaving this diary behind. Even if A's people take me, something of me will remain in this little book.

Lyle tried to imagine this articulate, intelligent, sensitive woman, with a strong will that had succumbed to a stronger will, but had eventually broken free. Not the first time he had indulged his imagination when he'd encountered a human-produced artifact.

Turning brittle pages that had received scant protection from the ravages of an oxygen-laden atmosphere, and knowing what he knew about the man who had called himself John Hill, Lyle expected that care would have been taken every time the manuscript was removed from the container, its pages exposed only as long as necessary for transcribing the contents. But what of the manuscript since it was stolen? How well protected was it now, and how would it fare in an exposed state?

He reminded himself why he had embarked on this mission: to assist his uncle, to accept the intellectual challenge, and to impress Beatrice, if he were honest with himself. Though Beatrice hadn't sent him on this mission, he knew that how he conducted himself, how diligent he was, mattered a great deal to her.

He put the diary back in the box with the other odds and ends and re-shelved it. He'd give his uncle one month. He hadn't talked to his Department Head about this, or any of his colleagues, and he didn't intend to, as his absence would be put down to working on the logistics of his upcoming expedition.

The guard escorted Lyle to the reception area and searched him without a trace of self-consciousness. Fortunately, Lyle had left his umbrella at the entrance, as a steady rain was falling from a lead-gray sky.

The absurdity of taking on this assignment engulfed him like the rain that pounded against his umbrella. Though his uncle believed Lyle could see around corners, he knew he'd need daily assistance from Sam, and colossal good fortune, to accomplish what he was setting out to do.

Good fortune? Water was running down the side of Lyle's face and into his collar. His umbrella was leaking.

MAY 3, 1932

☻-☻-☻

Soho, London

WHEN SHE OPENED HER EYES, he was standing over her. Had he said or done something to wake her, or had she sensed his presence in her sleep?

Hardly a physically intimidating man, he was the most dangerous person in the world.

She wasn't frightened, merely weary of pretending and running.

"May I turn on the lamp?" he asked her.

"As you wish."

"That's better." He took in the room, and said, "You've come down in the world."

"Have I? I rather think I'm ascending."

"And what have you done to yourself? You are hardly the grand dame who went to balls and fêtes on my arm."

There was only one chair in the room, and that chipped and unbalanced. The man dragged the chair from the wall, turned it toward the woman on the bed, and sat.

"That's not much of a throne."

"I've missed your wit," said the man.

"Should I be flattered you came yourself?"

"I wouldn't have had it any other way. You ought to know that."

She had raised herself to a sitting position, with her back against the headboard and her legs and feet beneath the stained counterpane.

"If this is what you call ascending, I'd hate to see what descending looks like. I want to know why."

"You wouldn't understand."

"Probably not, but I still need to know."

"I was on a path to destruction, and I decided to take a different path."

"You were never in danger, not while you were with me."

"I couldn't go on with the murders, the destruction of lives, the superficiality."

"The superficiality, if I understand you correctly, is the only thing that matters in life."

"I know that's what you believe."

"You believed it once, Agnes."

"Not as you do. I couldn't stay, and I couldn't tell you I was leaving, so I ran."

"And two years later, here you are, in this pathetic little room, sleeping with lice."

"That's one way to look at it."

"That is the only way to look at it."

She said, "You won't convince me, and I won't convince you."

"A stalemate, you mean."

"Hardly. You're never stalemated."

"You've learned a few things from our time together."

"I've been trying to forget as much as I can."

"Oh, how cutting you are, my dear. If only you hadn't meddled in my business."

"You're talking about your brother, your only living relative."

He extended both hands. "My brother, my business, not yours. Then you compounded it with Christopher. You know how I relied on him. That was inexcusable."

"Christopher left me no other choice, Adler, and I'd do it again to free Gregory."

She saw the pique in his eyes. No one else would have recognized it, but she did.

The man said, "I will find Gregory, and have him back, and as for the fool pretending to be John Hill, he's at the end of his rope . . . rather, *my* rope. You know him, I think."

"You eliminate both of us and take what you want."

"I couldn't have said it better myself. Then, I'll settle that fat meddler's hash."

"Another poor soul in your sights? You weren't always so bitter."

"You did it. Betrayal did it."

Even when they were allies, and much more than allies, she had never been able to look him in the eye, but now, as imperiled as anyone ever could be, she met his eyes, and held them.

"I changed. You could change too. You can do anything you set your mind to do."

"Follow your path? I prefer blazing my own."

Their eyes were still locked when she said, "I'll come back, if you leave the teacher and his family alone."

"That impostor and liar? And what makes you think I want you back? That's not a bargain I'd ever make . . . never in a hundred years. My, what an inflated opinion you have of yourself."

"I do now." Her eyes fell to the bedspread. If she had been watching the man, she might have detected a hint of doubt.

"Will you give me the diary, or must we search?"

"You'll have to search. It's private, John. That's your given name. Your grandfather destroyed you."

"I made my own choices. You ought to know that by now . . . The child is alive."

She snapped to attention. During their time together, both had learned to extract meaning from just a few of the other's words.

"You're saying that to hurt me."

"I've never lied to you."

"Were you lying when you told me he was dead, or now, when you say he's alive? Everyone else takes your word as law, so you've forgotten what truth is."

"As this is the end, I wanted you to know he's alive."

"To bless me, or curse me?"

The man rose from the chair, walked to the bedside, and kissed her cheek. At that moment, she felt a prick in the shoulder where he'd placed his hand to steady himself.

"How long?" she said.

"Thirty minutes. I promise it won't be painful. You are the only person in the world I cannot bear to see suffer, even after you defied and betrayed me. After you're gone, we will have to make a show with your remains, to demonstrate the price of betrayal."

"Do what you have to do. I don't mind. I forgive you. Everything."

It was as if she'd slapped his face. The man backed to the door. "All I ever wanted was your loyalty. Was that so much to ask, after everything I've given you?"

"I left the broach in the jewelry box."

"You are cruel."

"Is he being cared for?"

"His needs are being met. I've seen to that. They are trying to fix him."

"Is he broken?"

"Of course, he is."

"Do you see him? Talk to him?"

"He's far from here, and my business consumes me. You ought to know that."

"I'm getting sleepy. Perhaps you ought to go."

"Is there anything I can do for you afterwards?"

"I told you I forgive you. I want you to remember that . . . afterwards. I mean it with all my heart . . . I forgive everything."

Though her eyes were shut, she heard the door open and close. She was fortunate, she told herself. How many knew the exact moment they would die, and could prepare themselves for it. She would use these few minutes to remember the beauty, and to put herself in the hands of the one she trusted.

"A boy . . ." she whispered.

DECEMBER 19, 2016

◉-◉-◉

Oxford

RETURNING TO HIS APARTMENT from the Consolidated Archives, Lyle had been fortunate to find a parking space on the street, but when he exited the car the first thing he heard was, "Haven't seen you about."

Though it had stopped raining, Lyle was still wet, and the last thing he needed was William Horrigan. If he'd been paying attention, hadn't been thinking about Agnes CurLio and all the work he had to do before he left town, he might have avoided the man by going to the back-street car park.

William resided in the Waterloo Creek Apartments across the street from Lyle's flat. Except for the ambulances, and the movers that came a few days later, Lyle didn't often think about the old people across the street. With all new buildings and features, Lyle's side of the street catered to University teachers and administrators, while the Waterloo side featured drab nineteen-fifties apartments.

Lyle sometimes waited for William to walk out of sight before he left his flat, knowing the man would barrage him with a flurry of topics and questions.

Wearing his trademark blue sweatshirt and accompanied by his brown standard poodle, William said, "Just got back from radiation."

Decorum forcing him to reply, Lyle said, "What's wrong?"

"Prostate cancer. Treatments wear me down. Anxious, too. Always been a good sleeper . . . till now. Stay, Lucia. Don't bother the Professor."

"How many treatments?" said Lyle, backing away from the dog, and the memories that accompanied the animal.

"Three months, twice a week. Going to any jungles or deserts?" William thought jungles and deserts were the only places that interested archaeologists. Once, he'd asked Lyle if he'd bring him back a souvenir.

Though William was talking to Lyle, he was watching an old man with a cane, bent over almost ninety degrees, creeping toward the front door of the Waterloo Apartments. Lyle had seen this man often enough, had even spoken a few words to him, but couldn't remember his name.

"Harold doesn't give up. Makes me ashamed to complain about the radiation. I talked to your lady friend when she visited. Whip-smart."

"She teaches at the University."

"What's her subject?"

Why had he volunteered information, when it only led to more questions and conversation?

"Psychology."

"They help people with anxiety, don't they? . . . Lucia likes you."

The poodle was nudging Lyle's hand with its nose.

"I have work to do, William."

"Maybe your lady friend could help me with my nerves."

"I'll mention it." In fact, he didn't plan to do anything that got Beatrice involved with William. Just another excuse for the man to seek him out. "Take care of yourself," he said, distractedly.

"Oh, I will . . . no worries, mate," William said to Lyle, who was already halfway to the door of his flat.

JANUARY 3, 2017

☯-☯-☯

Oxford

B EATRICE GREETED HIM wearing jeans and a sweater.
"No exotic aromas tonight," he said as he removed his coat and scarf.

"That's because we're having an English meal, roast beef, gravy, carrots, pudding."

"Is there such a thing as an English meal anymore?"

The Miles Davis album he had given her for her birthday was playing on the turntable. Her tidy apartment was an eclectic mixture of African and Western furniture and decorative objects. He had learned that Beatrice could reach into any culture for inspiration.

The only photograph displayed was a picture of her family, with a backdrop of a grotto and a statue of the Virgin. All were smiling, even her brother, standing as ramrod straight as a soldier. Her parents were in the center, with Beatrice herself off to one side, her younger sisters each holding one of her hands. This Beatrice, more slender in body and face, had an expression of unconstrained gaiety that Lyle hadn't witnessed in the woman he had come to know.

"I thought you'd enjoy a home-cooked meal before you take to the road. Are you resigned to helping your uncle?"

"Resigned is the right word. I'm packed, and reservations are made."

"Look on it as an adventure."

"I prefer adventuring at seven-thousand-year-old sites."

"If your uncle is right, the artifact is much older than that."

"A few weeks, then back to things that matter."

"Psychologists take words seriously, and yours tell me you don't consider your uncle's concern to be serious."

"I don't, and I'd be dishonest if I pretended otherwise."

She handed him a glass of wine and perched beside him on the sofa. "Aren't you curious about the manuscript? Wouldn't you like to see it for yourself?"

"I'd love to see the thing Uncle Henry described, the thing he believes it to be, but no, I'd rather not waste my time with a modern invention, or a fraud."

"Your uncle's a scientist, and a wise man. Don't you think he'd recognize a modern invention, or a fraud?"

"Probably, unless his religious beliefs got in the way."

"You think of faith as putting on blinders, don't you?" Beatrice said, playing a game they'd played before.

"If he wanted to see things a certain way, it might color his judgment, that's all."

"Are you telling me you've never met scientists who wanted to see things a certain way?"

"Of course, I have." He looked down at the purple liquid in his glass, swirled it gently, and said, "This wine is delicious."

"Thank you. Let's eat."

At the table, he poured each of them another glass of wine, then waited while she lowered her head, something he'd gotten used to.

They were an unlikely couple. Soon after Beatrice had arrived at Oxford, she'd attended a holiday party at Lyle's School, she pressed into coming by Angela Hurst, and he by Donald Cooper, the two most sociable instructors in a department of idiosyncratic men and women. Since neither Lyle nor Beatrice was a mixer, they had come together at a corner table and introduced themselves, and what had struck Lyle from the beginning was her genuineness.

They didn't see each other again for several months, when they happened to meet at a town concert and managed to sit together. Afterwards, plans for dinner at a restaurant they both liked.

He looked forward to being with her. More than that, self-reliant Lyle understood that life would be less without her. Her spontaneity was refreshing, and his witticisms, which he had learned weren't for everyone—for very few, if he were honest with himself—she took in stride. What was next for them—if there was a next for them—was a question he wasn't ready to tackle.

"I received a letter from my sister today," she said, as she handed him a tray of carrots.

Beatrice's family in Uganda was a topic fraught with anxiety—all of them had been hunted by terrorists. Her mother and father were now dead, her older brother murdered, her younger sisters safe and sound at the moment, though things could and did change rapidly.

"They're fine," she said. "Maria is having a baby in May." Maria, twenty-five, was Beatrice's baby sister. "How's the meat?"

"Exquisite. And Cornelia?"

"Grayson found a better job, so they finally have a few shillings to spare."

On more than one occasion, Lyle had been on the verge of asking if he could help her family, but he wasn't sure how Beatrice would receive such an offer. Whereas Sam would have come right out and asked her, let her say yes or no, Lyle's public image of self-assurance masked the real man, who always calculated the risk of rejection.

"You're leaving tomorrow?" she asked.

"Bright and early. Sooner off, sooner . . ." But the look in her eyes kept him from finishing the thought.

"Tell me what Sam learned."

"Without Sam, I might as well tie a blindfold over my eyes. He's supplied the itinerary: Folkestone, the Sorbonne, the Johannes Gutenberg University of Mainz—Dekeyser's most recent job. The CID told him they haven't located Dekeyser or made any progress, and that the matter isn't a high priority—no one hurt, nothing damaged, the item not insured and of unknown value, the bishop not interested. Sam told me he's also consulted the German *firm* and several other friendly firms, along with the Mainz police, and they had nothing on Dekeyser. Maybe more telling, Sam said there's been nothing with Dekeyser's digital fingerprint—credit cards, phone, computer accounts—for months, as if the man's fallen off the face of the Earth."

"Or was helped off," said Beatrice, collecting their plates.

He saw her glance at the photograph on the wall as she made her way to the kitchen.

"May I help?"

"Not tonight. This is your *bon voyage* celebration."

"Sam gave me Dekeyser's physical dossier. All I can say is, I wouldn't want my life reduced to something like that."

"What will you say when you meet him?"

"Dekeyser? You mean *if,* don't you, and an unlikely if, in my opinion. I'm not sure. Like an excavation, depends on what I find when I get there."

"Before you go to a site, I'm sure you plan and prepare, so what's your plan for Dekeyser?"

"To engage him for as long as I can. As to the manuscript, bide my time."

Beatrice had resumed her perch on the corner of the sofa. "Excellent, psychologically speaking. Did Sam say anything else?"

"To check in with him every day."

"Did he sound worried?"

"He sounded like an older brother."

"You'd better listen to him. Investigations are his business."

"I'm not sure I'd call what he does investigating, and I don't plan to talk to any nefarious characters, just Dekeyser's former employers."

Her hand on his shoulder, Beatrice said, "Wouldn't it be wonderful if you recovered your uncle's manuscript?"

"That possibility hasn't crossed my mind."

Off went the hand. "There you go again. You could stand to have a pin stuck in you once in a while. What if it turns out to be the most valuable artifact in the world?"

"That's not something I've considered, even though I'm embarking on a wild goose chase to find it."

"Just make sure your *apochen* isn't cooked. That's a Ugandan goose, for your information."

Lyle poured her half a glass, and himself too. He might have detected a cautionary look from Beatrice but, if he had, it vanished quickly. It could have been his oversensitivity to what had happened on that earlier night, a night he'd been trying hard to forget.

As they drank their wine, they discussed the classes they were teaching, what was going on in their departments, and finally, when the wine had run out, she said, "Have you heard from your uncle?"

"He sent me an article describing how Gödel proved that no theory of physics based on mathematical formulations can be proven with certainty. Without coming out and saying it, he's telling me science doesn't have all the answers."

"But you know that already," Beatrice said. "By the way, I wouldn't mind hearing from you either."

"Every day?"

"If you'd like."

"Thanks for dinner, wine, music . . . everything."

"If you're leaving early in the morning, I'd better get you home."

"Sam told me to leave the Spider in the garage and rent something practical."

"Don't tell me you're going to drive that thing just to be contrary."

"First of all, it isn't a *thing*, it's a roadster, and it'll suit me just fine."

"Until there's an inch of snow. If Sam can't talk you out of taking it, I don't stand a chance."

The Spider Lusso had been an impulsive purchase, and even after owning the car for five years, he still felt out of place behind the wheel. What Sam had actually said when Lyle told him he intended to take the Spider to Europe was, "Toad must have his motorcar . . . poop-poop."

Lyle was already in the hall when he turned back, put his arms around her, and kissed her.

"Don't let any poodles run you over," she said.

JANUARY 3, 2017

☻-☻-☻

Oxford Archaeology Laboratory

THOUGH HE INTENDED to leave town early the next morning, Lyle had too much anxious energy to return to his apartment, so he made for the Archaeology lab and library instead.

BBA—before Beatrice Adams—he had spent most of his evenings here, planning, researching, reading. Even now, this rambling old lab, stuffed to the gills with the remnants and artifacts of past instructors, was the most congenial place in the world to Dr. Stuart.

More than congenial, a *safe* place. After his mother's long illness and painful death, while Sam had doubled down on his work, Lyle had succumbed to bitterness and despondency. When he finally emerged from this state, he had committed himself to science, what could be seen, heard, touched, and measured, things that would never let him down or require faith in any sense of the word.

Twenty years later, Lyle imagined that he had conquered his boyhood sense of alienation, despite not having any close friendships until Beatrice.

The lab was drafty and dusty, the benches, cabinets, and floor scarred, and the air rich with earthy scents, the residue of countless expeditions to the Middle East, Africa, China, everywhere, with these scents differing from bench to bench and from corner to corner as spices in a kitchen cabinet differ from one another.

Making for the opposite end, where the library was located, Lyle passed Andrea Fitzgerald's lit office. She was on the phone and didn't bother to acknowledge him, though she was looking right at him as he passed. The urge to enter his own office and do some Lido-related work was powerful, but he resisted and continued on to the stacks.

A few minutes in front of a computer informed him that the gold standard for what he was seeking was a book published in 1923 by a University of Heidelberg paleo-geologist, Pepin Hermann, entitled *Geology, Geography, and Climatology of Upper Paleolithic Europe.*

Except for Andrea, he was the only one in the lab; an uncommon experience. After locating the book, Lyle sat at his favorite worktable next to the skeleton of a Neanderthal girl, with the area light illuminating the two of them as if they were both figures in a diorama.

The girl's skeleton and era had been the inspiration for several pages of speculative notes concerning her likely physical appearance, her clan, the cause of her death, and even her personality— what might have made her happy or frightened her. Except for the facts that she had been five-foot-one, twelve to sixteen years old, and had lived on the European continent seventy to ninety thousand years ago, it was impossible to say how close he had come to the truth.

Before opening Hermann's text, Lyle returned to the stacks and retrieved that epic fantasy story, his mother's handwritten name on the front leaf, still where he'd placed it years ago, in an obscure location where no one was likely to encounter it.

He couldn't look at this book without admitting that it had once evoked and nurtured his interest in archaeology, even if by the time he'd begun to read the subject he had learned to keep this a secret, had been embarrassed to admit it to others. Eventually, he was embarrassed to admit his childhood motivation even to himself, something that made him keep the story he'd once loved at arm's length, in the stacks rather than in his office library.

Two books: one a serious scientific treatise, the other a fairy tale, but, if Lyle's uncle were to be believed, they intersected in history, in a specific time and place.

Lyle jumped halfway out of his chair when he felt something press against his shoulder.

"Sorry, just me," said the familiar voice.

He took a breath and turned around. Agnese Leone, a colleague in the Archaeology Department.

Lyle closed the novel and folded his hands over it. "The least you could do is wear shoes that make a little noise . . . or hail at a distance. That happened to me once at a site in Greece when a snake dropped on me from a tree limb."

Originally from northern Spain, Agnese was in her late fifties, short and round, with frizzy hair that wasn't often brushed, or didn't pay attention when it was. To hear student testimonials, she was one of the best teachers in the Department, and the most entertaining.

"I was wearing these house shoes when I had the inspiration to come here, and I forgot to change them."

That wasn't all Agnese had forgotten, as she had put her coat over pajamas and a red and purple bathrobe.

"You didn't walk, did you?"

"You know I live just a block from here."

"Aren't your feet cold?"

"When you get older you don't notice."

"They'll pick you up for a vagrant if you're not careful."

"Lido research?" she said, ignoring the admonition.

Lyle nodded, though he couldn't make himself confirm it verbally. His folded hands made a poor shield. Fortunately, Agnese was too preoccupied to examine the books.

"I hear you're off to the Continent."

"Tomorrow."

"*Bon voyage,* then," she said, padding away.

An hour later, the side-by-side books were opened to pages displaying maps, and the similarities couldn't be denied: a grand north to south mountain range with an east-west leg at the southern end, a vast ocean on the western edge of the continent, a land bridge between the continent and a place that resembled Britain, with Ireland attached to Wales.

Lyle knew that ancient maps were often tools of persuasion, visual rhetoric, rather than precise delineations of geographical distances and features, especially geographical features that were outside the realms and borders of the mapmaker's patron, and were thus depicted as less expansive to denote lesser importance. Contrivances such as these went hand in hand with extending the boundaries of the patron's realm based on metaphysical considerations rather than legal or other *bona fide* rights. He wouldn't have expected perfect congruency, even if these maps represented the same territory and time period.

The most glaring discrepancy was the absence of the Mediterranean Sea to the south. If the maps in the manuscript were historical, how could such a prominent geographical feature be missing, as the Sea had been formed by a sudden onrushing of the Atlantic Ocean through the Straits of Gibraltar over five million years ago? Conversely, why wouldn't a modern fraud, or something produced in recent centuries, have included the Sea? What was gained by leaving out so prominent a geographical feature in a document that purported to depict a prehistoric civilization?

Hermann described temperate periods in Europe from sixty to thirty thousand years ago, aligning with what Lyle already knew: that trees, rivers, lakes, and an environment generally congenial to human life had prevailed over multi-millennia stretches.

There were discrepancies between Hermann's maps and the

story's maps, but the alignment was striking. None of which demonstrated the existence of a high civilization, nor did Hermann so much as hint at anything of the sort. Mightn't the author of the story have visited these stacks, referenced this book, and constructed his fictional lands accordingly? Wasn't that the most likely explanation for the similarities?

Lyle's uncle had asked for his help in locating the manuscript. Beatrice had encouraged him to accede to his uncle's request. What's more, she had given him some valuable insights into his quarry's motivation and character. And Sam had agreed to assist Lyle by applying the firm's considerable investigatory resources. Nevertheless, Lyle knew this assignment to be whimsy, and what he was doing here and now was appropriate preparation for the whimsy on which he would soon embark.

Still, to hold, examine, study such an artifact (if it were genuine) would be to stand atop the tallest mountain in the archaeological world, and to breathe air no archaeologist had ever breathed—a thought that excited him, even as his mind ridiculed the idea.

At the monastery, when his uncle asked him about anomalies from this period, Lyle had recalled, but hadn't mentioned, the fierce debate that had raged the year he was preparing to test for his doctorate.

Old, and notoriously eccentric, Lefebvre had insisted that stone at a Normandy excavation was road flagging, and the archaeological world had risen up in scorn, as Lefebvre's excavation had been dated at thirty-eight thousand years BCE, when there were only unimproved and temporary tribal trails. The obvious answer was that Lefebvre had excavated into a deposit of granite that fortuitously mimicked cut stone.

Fortuitous mimicry rather than an anomaly, the end of Lefebvre's career as a serious archaeologist, and a cautionary tale for Lyle, if he were to be too closely associated with his uncle's manuscript.

The nearby water dispenser appeared to be empty, but Lyle shook a small cup of water loose and drank it down. A glance at his Neanderthal girl made him realize that he was already assembling mental notes about Noel Dekeyser based on the skimpy evidence at hand, as he had done more deliberately with this prehistoric girl.

He slapped both books closed and returned them to the stacks. By this time next year, he hoped to have identified a much earlier date for Bronze Age activity in Europe, but this would require hard work, work that would now be delayed by weeks.

Andrea's office was dark as he made his way to the exit. Agnese Leone was nowhere to be seen, but her name reminded him of the woman whose diary he'd discovered. He had an intuition, something he believed proceeds from unrecognized evidence, that the Agnes CurLio of the diary was connected to the manuscript and its strange path to his uncle's monastery—but what could that unrecognized evidence possibly be? As he closed and locked the door, he couldn't help wondering what he'd know about the manuscript and Dekeyser, if anything at all, when he next crossed this threshold.

JUNE 12 & 28, 1942

☻-☻-☻

Albany, New York

"WHAT'S YOUR NAME, KID?" said the Ringmaster.
"Alembert."

"Alembert what?"

"Just Alembert."

"Okay, but to the rubes you're *The Flying Freak of Nature.* If they ask, that's who you are."

"That suits me fine."

The two men were under the Big Top, the patchy grass strewn with a layer of straw and sawdust. Above them, riggers and rousta-bouts were assembling platforms and trapeze cables. Not much activity at the moment: men steadying a quarter pole, and, in a far corner of the big top, a woman working out two liberty horses.

"Anyone ever tell you you're the spittin' image of Errol Flynn?" said the Ringmaster. "Too bad the rest of you ain't. Where'd you learn to be a flyer?"

"When you rely on your arms, the trapeze comes naturally."

"You from England?"

"How did you guess?"

"We got enough clowns, pal." Pointing at the trapeze platform, the Ringmaster said, "No brodies from up there. You fall, the rubes get more'n they paid for, and the boss don't care."

"I won't fall."

"What're you doing over here anyway?"

"Training."

"For what?"

"Making people do what I want them to do."

"That's funny. A freak oughta be worried about feeding hisself."

"I've never missed a meal. When do I go up?"

"The boss says no net for the likes of you, so pay attention when you're up there. This ain't no training, not with bright lights in your eyes and so much noise you can't hear yourself think. Easy to fall . . . seen it often enough."

"What's your name?" said Alembert.

"*My* name? Why you want to know that?"

"Because I may want you to work for me."

"In that case," said the immaculately dressed, theatrically erect man, "it's Edgar Bogart, with a E and a B."

"This is your lucky day, Eddie."

"The artists call me Mr. Bogart. That's the way it works around here. So, what do you want done?" said the amused man.

"That depends. I'm searching for something."

"Money, I suppose."

"You suppose wrong. I have plenty of money."

"Then what?"

"I'm not certain."

"People generally know what they're searchin' for."

"Ordinary people do. What can you tell me about Santini?"

"Highest paid artist in the Show."

"So I understand. Why is that?"

"You ain't seen his act yet. He works wherever they pay best, so only the big shows can afford him. He brings 'em in, and they come back, two, three times. Ever seen a man who can change hisself from a emperor to a witch to a coolie to a whorehouse madam in the wink of a eye, without no masks . . . just drapes and hats?"

"How does he do it?"

"Have to see for yourself. He makes 'em believe. Convinces 'em he's what he pretends to be. Ain't called The Great Santini for nothin', not this guy. It's inside him, that's what I say."

"How did he get his start?"

"One of the old zanies says Vaudeville. Magician at first, then the theater, till he learned he could get a piece of the gate at the shows."

"Have you talked to him about how he does it?"

"Santini don't tell his secrets to no one."

"He'll talk to me."

"If he won't talk to me, why'd he talk to a freak?"

An animal roar from outside the tent caught their attention.

"The bear," said Bogart. "He's new . . . touchy."

"I'll need a Ringmaster for what I'm planning. You're an orphan, aren't you?"

"How'd you guess?"

"I never guess. Where were you raised?"

"Milwaukee. Used to take the trolley when the matrons weren't payin' attention and patrol the beach. Watched people swim and play, lifted what I could. Never had any food with me. *I* missed plenty of meals when I was a kid. Took the last trolley back and got whipped."

"Resourceful . . . and no illusions. Ever killed a man, Eddie?"

"Might of, when I had to," with the Ringmaster surprised he'd volunteered this to a virtual stranger.

"Did it bother you?"

"Not excessive. You better be thinkin' about that fly bar."

"Where I grew up, they had a gymnasium. As it happened, I was the only one who lived there, and I used the equipment to make my arms and hands strong. Day in and day out, year after year. Want to arm wrestle, Eddie?"

THE LARGEST TRAILER in the Show, a palace in comparison to his tiny berth in the flyers' trailer.

"Will you have a lemon ice while you wait?" asked the woman. Handing him the glass, she said, "I'm amazed Billy's seeing you so often. He isn't the type to mingle, you know."

"We have much in common," the young man said, leaving unsaid that he'd been arriving early to see and talk to her.

From the moment he had met her, he could scarcely believe how she affected him. Though not especially intelligent, talented, or physically attractive, she was different than every other woman he'd met, a virtual magnet for his thoughts ever since he'd first spoken to her. In fact, he had paid her the greatest compliment in that he would never seek to manipulate her, or her kindness and interest in him would be contaminated, a thought he couldn't bear to contemplate.

"I wish you would tell me your first name," she said.

"How do you know it isn't Alembert, and why use two names when one suffices?"

"Men with one name have big dreams. What are your dreams?" she asked him.

"I'm afraid you'd find them rather shabby. Speaking of dreams, why are you with Billy?"

"The truth is, I don't know. He swept me up, you could say. I'm not a . . . you know what, and it would pain me terribly for you to think so."

"I would never think such a thing. Not in a million years, Madeline."

Her smile warmed him. "I have a feeling that if we put our dreams together they'd add up to something fine."

He had never considered that dreams might be additive, or fine, except in the sense of obtaining what he desired.

"May I ask where you got that name?"

"My father's name."

"He must have been an impressive man to have a son like you."

"He was a man with dreams, big dreams, like Billy."

"I see, but yours can be different than his and Billy's. You told me you were studying psychology. Why did you give it up?"

"I haven't. This Show is a field exercise. Putting theories to the test, you could say."

"You'll be a wonderful psychologist. You see inside people. I can tell. You can help them, heal them, make their dreams finer."

She had been prescient in saying that he had a rare talent for seeing inside people. In the eyes of even the kindly disposed, he had always detected revulsion, or, at best, pity, with a few better than the rest at disguising these sentiments, but never had he observed this in Madeline, only warmth and admiration.

Everything that made him who he was—talent, foresight, a mind that was different than other minds—told him if he didn't act soon, maybe this minute, the old equilibrium would be reestablished, and his dreams would revert to those shabby ends.

"You are always early, Alembert," said the man who had stepped into the vestibule. Though it wasn't a cold day, this tall, lean man wore a cape and a fedora adorned with a delicate scarlet feather.

"If you will excuse us, Madeline dear, Alembert and I have things to discuss. And take your pocketbook with you."

The peremptory dismissal infuriated Alembert, who suspected the man's words had been chosen for this purpose.

After Madeline left the trailer, Billy poured them glasses of bourbon, and said, "The most successful sharks in the ocean are acutely aware of the movement of the water, the movement of other creatures and especially their prey, even the moon that influences the water and what lives and moves in it."

"You refer to more than physical movement," Alembert remarked.

"Of course. Moving minds is a far more interesting occupation. You see it too, and the more subtly this occurs, the more effective it is. Anything you can employ to burrow deeper—emotions, religious beliefs, pathologies—is fair game. Affections are especially ripe with opportunity. What the shark does in its physical environment. A trifle when it comes to the rabble, harder and more satisfying when it involves adept minds."

"Your act," said Alembert. "Where did you learn this art?" but the man waved him off, saying, "Don't confuse art with higher things."

Alembert glanced at the clock on the wall, and said, "We're practicing a new triple hang in a few minutes. Can we talk again tomorrow?"

The Great Santini said, "That won't be possible. I'm leaving the Show, an opportunity to tour South America, not a moment to lose. I'm sorry to say that Madeline is coming with me. We will both miss you."

"This is sudden," said Alembert.

"In the works for a while. Never tip your hand, m'boy. She wouldn't be good for you. Impedimenta in the grand scheme of things."

"She's everything to you, isn't she?"

"She is nothing to me, but you shan't have her. No one takes so much as a penny from me."

Affections are especially ripe with opportunity. Billy had won this contest of wits and wills. "Where is she?"

"At this moment, Loki is escorting her to our car, so there will be no opportunities for fond farewells."

Loki, a man with a hard, bony face, who prowled the circus with an elephant hook, and who had the look of someone who liked to use it.

"You have taught me a great deal," Alembert said.

"Yet, when we met, you didn't think there was much to learn, a trick or two perhaps."

"I won't make that mistake again."

"I don't think you will either, m'boy."

AUGUST 3, 1953

⊙-⊙-⊙

Barcelona

"YOUR NOTE SAID YOU HAVE something vital to tell me. Be quick about it."

"Some hotel," the visitor said.

"The Colon is the best hotel in Barcelona. My contract stipulates lodging at the city's finest hotel."

"Better'n a trailer."

Both men were tall and thin, though the visitor's attire was noticeably humbler. He opened a box he'd been carrying under one arm and set a bottle of Courvoisier on the table.

"How did you acquire a Josephine bottle, Bogart?"

"I know you appreciate good cognac, Billy."

Immediately, the other man raised a hand and said, "I'll thank you not to call me by that name. I am Señor Santini."

"Whatever you say. If you'll fetch the glasses, we'll share a drink."

Looking hard at the cognac, Santini said, "Ten minutes is all I can spare."

Bogart removed the cork from the bottle and stashed it in his pocket, and when Santini returned with the glasses, he let his visitor fill them.

81

"Your health," said Bogart.

"What do you want to tell me?"

Bogart lowered the glass he had put to his lips. "You're performin' at the Goya?"

"To full houses, night after night."

"How long'll you be in Barcelona?"

"A month. Lovely women. Passionate. What are you doing with yourself? Have you fallen on hard times?"

"I'm workin' for Alembert. You remember him?"

"The freak that pined for Madeline. I haven't thought of him in years. Where is he now?"

"Vienna, at the University."

"Enough about that little monster. Tell me your vital news, Bogart. I'm expecting company, and I won't be keeping her waiting."

Bogart's eyes were trained on his glass of cognac when he said, "Alembert learned that Madeline died in Brazil."

"Poor thing. She took ill not long after we arrived."

Bogart lifted his glass, but before he could take a drink, he said, "A long sickness, right?"

"What does that have to do with you, or me?"

"You left her there to die. That's what we was told."

"What if I did? It's no business of yours. Now, get out," Santini erupted, refilling his empty glass, and wiping his damp brow with a handkerchief.

"Alembert was beside hisself when he found out."

"I imagine he was. I'll see you to the door." Santini started to rise, sank back into his chair, and said, "I'm not feeling well."

"When you left Albany, you told the boss I was preyin' on local girls. He ran me off, and the word went from show to show."

"That's a lie. Why would I care what happened to you? Crawl back to your monster boss on the rat line that brought you here. I'm sick, Bogart. Get out . . . now!"

"Admit it, damn you."

Santini's eyelids descended, and he slumped to the floor.

Bogart's glass was still full. Without hesitation, he removed a knife from inside his coat and stabbed the unconscious Santini in the heart, once, twice. Then, he walked briskly to the sink, cleaned the knife, emptied the cognac down the drain, and rinsed the bottle. From a small flask, he added a little cognac to the bottle, dried everything, put the bottle in the cabinet and the knife in the drawer.

Bogart lifted the note he'd sent to Santini and stuffed it in his pocket. "Not so great anymore, are ya'?"

PART II

Destinations

JANUARY 5, 2017

Folkestone

Dear Frodo,

Though I am exceedingly grateful for your help in recovering the manuscript, need I remind you that no THING is as precious to me as my dear nephew? Keep your eyes wide open. Clear out immediately if you sense peril.

Your Uncle,

Henry

A TINY ROOM AT THE nineteenth century Red Cow Inn, with the Dover cliffs a few blocks away, rather than Lyle's familiar apartment, his battered plexiglass suitcase against the wall, with compartments for clothes, notebooks, electronic devices, and his field kit.

At the last minute, he had packed his mother's story about the turtle. Now, looking for something to read, Lyle removed the manuscript from the case, then stowed it again and retrieved a journal instead.

In spite of getting to sleep late, waking up late, and encountering a construction detour, he had managed to arrive at the

Folkestone Regional Psychiatric Clinic on time.

The attendant in the lobby removed a tube of lipstick from her purse, attentively applied it to her lips, and without looking at him, said, "Dr. Remington will see you now."

Lyle followed the woman into the business side of the building. He had secured this interview with Peter Remington, the director of the clinic, only because someone Sam knew had spoken to someone Remington knew.

"Here we are," she said, as if he were a patient she was eager to hand off.

Remington's office featured displays of fine art, and first class carpeting and paneling.

"Dr. Stuart," said Remington, without rising from his chair. "I was informed you have questions about Noel Dekeyser. I'm afraid I don't have much to tell you, as he worked here for less than a year."

An economical welcome and dismissal. Lyle noted the man had a cup of tea or coffee on his desk, yet neither the director nor the attendant had offered him anything.

In his early fifties, wearing a dark suit and tie, Peter Remington was a big, energy-exuding man and, though Remington's eyes were trained on his visitor, Lyle wasn't convinced the director was thinking about him or the subject of their meeting.

"You know I'm trying to track him down," Lyle said.

"He's done something wrong?"

"Not that we know. Questions, that's all."

"An Oxford archaeologist going to a lot of trouble to find a man who hasn't done anything wrong. It's been years since he worked here. Why are you seeing me now?"

"To learn if something Dekeyser said or did while he was at the clinic can help me locate him. Was he a good employee?"

"I'm instructed not to answer questions of that sort. But for you . . ." Remington showed bright white teeth. "There were no problems of note, other than a quick temper. That's the way it is with these churchmen. They're not who they pretend to be. Full of repressed wrath. Dekeyser was a workmanlike psychologist, but not particularly gifted."

"Why did he leave the clinic?"

"He was vague about it. A woman from the Sorbonne visited him while he was here. I know that because I ran into her in Dekeyser's office, and he introduced us. Just a hunch, but I think they were already acquainted. I wouldn't be surprised to learn she recruited him, though I can't imagine why the Sorbonne would be interested in Dekeyser."

What Lyle had gotten accustomed to in recent years, had come to rely on, was deference, respect. He wasn't used to the role of supplicant, and he didn't like it. For a moment, he imagined himself back in Katrivesis's lab, feeling as he had when he was that imperious man's doctoral student. "Do you remember the woman's name?"

"Desrosier. I had a schoolmate with that name. We went boating one day and had too much to drink. He fell into the river and never came up . . . Guy Desrosier."

Lyle could tell the memory was still affecting Remington, who said, "What else do you want to know?"

"Did Dekeyser have friends at the clinic?"

Remington shook his head. "Not that I know."

"Lovers?"

A raised eyebrow.

"Did he ever talk to you about artifacts?" said Lyle, trying to make the question sound routine.

Remington was paying attention now. "Artifacts? Did he steal something from that monastery?"

"Not that we know," Lyle repeated himself.

"But what you suspect is an altogether different matter, isn't it? You don't have to answer. If there was a theft, why aren't the police speaking to me?"

"Because the police don't have any reason to suspect him."

"That could mean several things. Dekeyser never spoke to me about artifacts. We had conversations about the art I display in this office. He asked about the figure on the corner of my work table," said Remington, pointing over his shoulder.

Lyle trained his eyes on the one-foot-tall, bone-white statue of an angel enfurled in bat-like wings.

"A miniature of the white marble statue that's displayed in the Cathedral of Liège. Dekeyser thought it was an angel."

"What is it?" asked Lyle.

Remington gave him a look of strange significance. "Lucifer . . . the liberator. I keep it here as a reminder that man needs to be liberated from inhibitions, from slavery to superstition."

It seemed to Lyle that Remington was waiting for affirmation from him, or perhaps the man had decided to treat the interruption as an entertainment. Lyle said, "What did Dekeyser say when you told him that?"

"He was troubled. I'm trained to notice things like that, and all the tells were there. Let's strip the world of all this divinity nonsense, the inhibitions these gods impose, and replace it with the autonomy of art in the broad creative sense. Goethe's view of art: *My* art will be my god."

"Did Dekeyser ever ask you about art dealers?"

"As a matter of fact, he did ask, but I didn't take him seriously because Dekeyser didn't impress me as someone who knew anything about art. By the way, what does your brother do for the government?"

"He's a paper pusher, or so he says."

"A paper pusher with influence."

"Did anyone else ever contact you about Dekeyser?"

"Let's see," Remington said, checking his wristwatch. "I recall a reference check from someone in Mainz. They were considering

Dekeyser for a teaching position a few years ago. Now, if you will excuse me."

As Lyle rose from his chair, the miniature Lucifer drew his eye, reminding him of Remington's outing with his friend on the lake. It was one thing to shed your inhibitions when you're immortal and indestructible, and quite another thing when it came to mere mortals on a boat.

Lyle was back in his car when he called the paper pusher. He had to leave a message, and it wasn't until he was in his room that his brother returned the call.

"How's the sea air?"

"I'm not sunbathing," Lyle said. "Can you track down a woman named Desrosier at the Sorbonne?"

"What's her connection to Dekeyser?"

"She visited him in Folkestone. The clinic director thinks she might have recruited him to the Sorbonne."

"Learn anything else?"

"Dekeyser was looking for art brokers. He asked the director for a recommendation."

"We know the manuscript has been missing for less than fourteen months because Henry viewed it in November of 2016, so Dekeyser didn't possess the artifact when he worked in Folkestone, or at the Sorbonne, but that doesn't mean he wasn't making plans . . . scheming."

"What was Dekeyser doing in Mainz?" Lyle asked Sam.

"Working at the School for Cognitive Studies as a . . . let me check my notes . . . a *Lehrbeauftragter*, an adjunct."

"How long ago did he leave?"

"Five months, but he didn't leave—resign or get sacked, that is—he disappeared. We haven't discovered anything about him after that. I'll let you know about the woman."

After dinner that night at a local restaurant, as he was preparing to return to his room, Lyle received a school-wide message from

Julius Marks, who announced a joint expedition with Andrea Fitzgerald to a site near Jericho. Lyle could read Marks's excitement
between the lines, and why not, with the prospect of a months-long
partnership with Andrea? While Lyle was in Folkestone, with several more weeks of wasted hours and days ahead of him, instead of
actively planning his own project.

He couldn't help feeling envious of Marks. Andrea had come on
the scene like a supernova, rather, like an asteroid that roasts the
landscape when it crashes, upsetting relationships, making enemies of friends, and collaborators of former adversaries. She
happened to be a diligent scientist, along with being as telegenic as
any film star. She had kept Lyle at arm's length for three years,
until she realized that he was dating Beatrice, and then she let him
know she was interested in him. Lyle guessed Andrea wouldn't
throw him out of her flat for having a little too much to drink, as
Beatrice had.

He was here now, he reminded himself, not preparing to embark with Marks and Andrea, not making plans to visit Popa and
the Lido site. Here, in Folkestone, and on his way to Paris. Was it
significant that Dekeyser was interested in art brokers, or had the
assignment Lyle had accepted given the information greater
weight than it warranted? Figuratively speaking, had Dekeyser
fallen, or been pushed, off a boat? Was Lyle following a flesh and
blood man, or a ghost?

As he had a few days before his meeting in Paris, Lyle had arranged to visit a retired colleague in a nearby town rather than
returning to Oxford or spending the weekend alone in Paris, but
whether it was his uncle's mission or his friend, he couldn't shake
the feeling that he was wasting time.

Folkestone, a waystation for Dekeyser, and for Lyle.

In a few days, the channel tunnel and Paris.

SEPTEMBER 22, 1958

Oxford & Mainz

A KNOCK ON THE DOOR, and a voice said, "Exterminators Unlimited. We heard you have an arachnid problem."

The man working at his desk said, "Come in, scoundrel."

The visitor resembled the occupant, though he was younger and, unlike the older man at the desk, his hair was neatly combed and his shoes were shined.

"What a delightful surprise," the older man exclaimed, as he rose from his chair and extended a bony hand. "You'll stay for dinner?"

"Sorry, Father. Have to be off in an hour."

"Your mother will be disappointed."

"Perhaps you shouldn't tell her I was here . . . forget I said that. Mother seems to know everything."

"She always has."

"I'll never forget that night, though, when we were in your old Pembroke College office," the visitor said.

His father sat back and packed a pipe, then pointed to his bookshelves and shook his head, saying, "Your courage was all the more commendable considering your boyhood fear of spiders."

"Those weren't your sentiments that night. Today, they call it shock therapy."

"I was proud of you. I still am."

"Thank you, Father."

"How are the children?"

"Growing, giving me the shakes."

"Bring them for a visit soon. Your mother would like that . . . so would I."

"I listened to your conversation with the woman earlier that day, but you know that, and I know you possessed something that put you in grave danger, something a man named Alembert was desperate to acquire."

The older man's pipe was smoking and his eyes were bright. "Between us spider stalkers, I possess it still."

"The danger is past?"

"*That* danger is long past, but the human inclination . . . the *temptation* that motivated the danger is alive and well in the world."

"Is the thing safe?"

"Who can say? I'm worried someone knows I have it."

"Why do you say so?"

"Someone has searched this office, and the house."

"You know this?"

"As to the office, yes. As to the house, your mother has so advised me, and I can tell you she was up in arms about it."

"No threats since the danger you experienced when I was a boy until these new . . . invasions?"

"I wouldn't go quite so far. About ten years ago, a woman visited me here and pressed me about this *thing*. Not naming it, or quite threatening me, but suggesting she had knowledge about it that surpassed what I knew, and she would share this information if I let her examine it."

"You turned her down, of course."

"If she was angry with me, she disguised it, and if she searched my possessions for this thing . . . an invasion, she did it so expertly that your mother and I never noticed."

"Did she tell you her name?"

"Rosman—an entomologist, or so she said. I conducted a search in the literature and was unsuccessful at identifying a Rosman in that field of study."

"How did she strike you, Father?"

"Intelligent, determined, a person who might be charming or deceitful, and quite attractive in the fashion of Jack's White Witch. Believe it or not, she had me considering her proposal, until I shook off the cobwebs."

"You never heard from her again?"

"Never, and if she's behind this new mischief, why has she waited so long? I tell you, I sometimes desire to be relieved of this thing, though I always end with 'Not yet.' Does that sound familiar, Michael?"

"Here's an idea for the time when 'Not yet' becomes 'Not a day longer.' John told me about a monastery where he'd gone on retreat. He was impressed by the abbot and monks. You might give them this thing for safekeeping."

The older man took several pulls on his pipe before saying, "I'm grateful for the suggestion. You know that all things in this life come to an end. I shall only occupy this office one more year. Your mother and I aren't as spry as we once were, and long hours at this desk wear on me, so it behooves me to make sure this thing is as secure as can be when it passes from my care."

"Whatever happened to the woman who came to our home that day?"

"She perished a few days after she came to me. I'm sure Alembert was behind it, a man profligate and stingy with the wrong things. I often wonder if she would have lived if she hadn't come to warn me. A lamb with the heart of a lion . . . Agnes CurLio, that was her name."

"I TOLD YOU never to come here," said the man behind the desk. "What do you want, Eddie?"

"I need money," said the tall man, silently closing the door.

"No, do not sit. You won't be here long. You need money, do you? I sent you to England to find something, and you came back empty-handed."

"Not for lack o' tryin'. I got into the places you told me to, and it wasn't there, or I'd a found it."

"That's what you *told* me."

"I done what you said, like always."

"You were instructed to find it and bring it to me, and all you did was burgle."

"I been with you a long time. Done a lot for you, dangerous business, too."

"That's right, Eddie, but it's time to part company."

"Not without fair payment."

"You've been more than fairly paid."

"That's a matter o' opinion, boss. Burgling people's houses is pair-luss work. Never know when a cop might shine his lamp in your eyes. And Billy"—the man couldn't help turning his head toward the hanging bones in a corner of the office—"was more pair-luss yet. Worth somethin' to keep all that to ourselves."

"You did that for your own reasons—Billy's lies."

"As I figured then. Now, I ain't so sure. I seen and heard a lot workin' for you."

The man behind the desk said, "How long have you known me, Eddie?"

"Let's see. Fifteen years, I guess."

"Sixteen to be precise. Have you ever known me to be careless?" said the man, with a forensic gaze he might have bestowed on a troublesome insect.

The visitor shifted from one foot to another. "Not as I can remember."

"There's not a shred of evidence you work for me. When that professor's house and office were invaded, I was here in Mainz, while you were in England. That's what your passport says. When Billy was murdered in Barcelona—a bloody business—I was in Vienna, and you were in Spain. Your passport attests to it. Communicating these coincidences to the police might shine a lamp on *you*."

"I'd tell 'em everything."

"And I'd tell 'em I've been treating you for various manias. That should satisfy them when there's no evidence we are otherwise associated."

The tall man wrung his hands. "I guess you got me there. You always think ahead, boss."

"You ought to know that by now, Eddie."

"Can you spare a few marks to see me through?"

"You've always been careless with money. Haven't I told you so?"

"You have, boss."

"I'd prefer you leave the Continent."

"I'm too old for the shows, and Helga's here."

The little man opened a desk drawer, removed a key from his vest, and opened a box. "Take this . . . and leave."

Eddie put the money away and extended a hand, but the man in the chair ignored it.

After the visitor had left the office, the man lifted his telephone and dialed a number. "Helga," he said, shifting from English to German with the ease of an otter going from land to water. "I thought you'd like to know Eddie's leaving town . . . a woman? Yes, I'm sure of it . . . he'll be at his apartment tonight . . . yes, do come and see me . . . now? For you, Helga, I will make time . . . I'm sorry. You have been so faithful, and look at how he treats you."

The man hung up the telephone. He knew she had a pistol, and he thought she knew how to use it, but he'd make sure.

JULY 4, 1963

☯-☯-☯

Glasgow

THE WINDOWS BEHIND Jacob Basile's desk looked out on an industrial landscape populated by sprawling buildings, smokestacks, and a horde of vehicles as busy as ants.

Basile didn't offer to shake the visitor's hand, nor did he offer the man a seat. "My secretary said your name is Albert."

"Al-um-bear, Lord Paisley, and you would not have seen me unless that name meant something to you."

"What do you want Mr. . . . Al-um-bear?"

Leaning on ebony canes, the visitor said, "Information. Would it help to inform you I've already spoken to Anton and Jones, and that Cherukuri would have been on the list if he were still alive?"

Basile reclined in his desk chair and said, "My secretary can bring a suitable chair if you'd like."

"By all means. How long have you owned these steel works?"

Basile picked up his desk phone, said a few words, and replaced the receiver. "Twenty years. I took over during the war, when production was badly lagging."

"And made a grand success, I understand."

The stout bald man behind the desk inclined his head.

"You are wealthy. A lordship came from your service during the war."

"That's public knowledge."

"Where did you acquire the nest egg to purchase the company?"

"Hard work and good fortune," Basile replied. "How did *you acquire* that name, or did you appropriate it?"

"The name belongs to me."

"I doubt that."

"What you believe or doubt means nothing to me."

A knock on the door preceded a striking young woman and a man in work clothes, carrying a small chair.

"Anywhere is fine," the visitor told them, looking from the woman to Basile.

After the pair had left the office, the now-seated man said, "I'm writing a book about Adler Alembert. I've been researching this project for years, and I am well aware of your involvement in that man's criminal empire."

"What is he to you?"

"We are connected by blood . . . and interests."

"When was I supposed to have known this man?"

"You were employed by Alembert from 1925 to 1932, when he disappeared, and his empire unraveled."

Basile produced a decanter and glass from one of his desk drawers, poured himself a drink, and consumed it.

"Is this blackmail masquerading as journalism? If it is, say so directly and let's get on with it."

"I want to interview you about Alembert and, if I decide you are being honest and forthcoming, I will give you an affidavit with my legal commitment to keep your name out of the book."

"That's all you want?"

"Nothing else, and you need never see me again. Here's the affidavit. All it lacks is my signature."

The visitor pushed the paper across the desk to Basile, who read it and set it aside.

"That's your real name?"

"My legal name, yes."

"Then, ask your questions."

Though the chair was small, the visitor's feet didn't touch the floor. "When was the last time you saw Alembert?"

"Aren't you going to take notes?"

"Have no doubt about that, but I don't need pen and paper."

Basile's eyes narrowed. "He had that talent too. England was my turf. In May, 1932, Alembert came over to confront a man using the alias John Hill . . ."

"I know all about that imposture."

" . . . and to personally eliminate an enemy."

"What was this enemy's name?"

"I don't recall."

"Honest and forthcoming, or no affidavit."

Basile twirled a pen between his fingers like a baton. "Agnes CurLio. She'd been his mistress and confidante, but she left him and . . . made trouble."

"What kind of trouble?"

"There was a rumor in the organization that she killed Alembert's right-hand man."

"Whose name was?"

Basile looked longingly at the empty glass. "Christopher Niiri."

"Good. That corroborates what Anton told me."

Basile closed his eyes. "What is he doing these days?"

"Bathhouses, when he has the money. He's old and down on his luck, so I gave him a few shillings for his trouble. The last time you saw Alembert?"

"Anton, Jones, and I, and some foot soldiers, accompanied him to the impostor's office at Pembroke College. We were to guard the building and alert Alembert if we observed anything suspicious or threatening."

"You were competent to do this?"

"Alembert saw to that."

"And how did he ensure such competence?"

"In the first place, Alembert was a keen judge of talent, and he adopted the Roman dictum that the best soldiers fear their own officers more than the enemy. Before Alembert arrived in Oxford, he put us in charge of battering the impostor's psyche."

"You touch on a subject that's dear to me."

"We were instructed to introduce certain . . . unnerving creatures to the man's office, not to cause grave harm, to disarm him emotionally."

"What happened the night Alembert visited this man?"

"He never came out of the building. We confronted the impostor the next morning. He told us Alembert had been alarmed by someone he'd seen, had exited through a tunnel beneath the building."

"You believed him?"

"Cherukuri had joined us by then, and we were shown the tunnel. We walked the entire length, but found no trace of Alembert."

"Did that man tell you what Alembert wanted?"

"He said the matter involved an ancient urn. Antiquities were Alembert's passion—the older, the better. We were on the lookout for anything that was said to be both ancient and exceptional, especially objects with writing on them . . . runes, glyphs."

"No one ever heard from Alembert after that night?"

"Not to my knowledge. I can't imagine him being alive and letting his organization erode as it did."

"What do you think happened to him?"

"I suspect someone tracked him in the tunnel, killed him there, or at the other end of the tunnel, and disposed of the body. A very capable assassin, or several. Not that impostor. He was no match for Alembert."

"My theory is this man had something Alembert wanted, but this *thing* was well hidden, and your commander needed to keep the man alive until he located it. You were there. You were inside the organization. Does that ring true to you?"

"Your theory fits what I knew at the time."

"The man Alembert met that night was a linguist. Today, he's a famous author. Was it ever suggested that this man possessed an ancient manuscript?"

Basile was already shaking his head. "We pressed the man hard the next morning. That's when he told us about the urn, and the tunnel. Are you suggesting this ancient manuscript is connected to that man's books?"

"I'm asking whether it was more likely for that man to have possessed an ancient manuscript than an urn."

Basile clasped his hands and said, "I haven't heard Alembert's name for thirty years. Why do you need this information?"

"Read my book when it's published—it's all there. I'll send you a signed copy."

"Don't bother. I wouldn't be talking to you if I had a choice. For the record, I never knew Alembert was doing anything illegal."

"Oh, spare me, Lord Paisley. All right, I'll go along, as you have been *honest and forthcoming.*"

The visitor retrieved the affidavit and signed it, saying, "I trust this satisfies you."

Pointing at the glass-encased butterfly on a table behind Basile's desk, the visitor said, "Where did you acquire that?"

"None of your business."

"It is, if it belonged to Alembert."

"You can't prove it."

When Basile frowned, his fleshy face encroached on his eyes, so they were almost invisible. "If you darken my doorstep again, I'll see to it that every bone in your body is broken."

Loki's elephant hook had been primitive and crude in comparison with how the visitor made his subjects feel, think, and do what he desired. "To be clear, Lord Paisley, my promise not to include you in the book doesn't mean my private files won't contain a record of this conversation, including that threat and the affair you're conducting with your secretary, which may be of interest to the current Lady Paisley. I hear she's rather temperamental. If something happens to me, this record will be made public. The twin hammers of public and private obloquy, milord. Do we understand each other?"

"Perfectly," Basile said, refilling his glass.

JANUARY 9, 2017

Paris

BENEATH THE STRAITS of Dover in the Eurotunnel, Lyle recalled the first time his mother had read to him about the company passing through the tunnel and caves under the mountain. His route through the Eurotunnel was thirty miles and took thirty minutes, while the company in the story had traversed their thirty rugged miles in three days, they had lost their leader, and the rest had barely escaped with their lives.

The Spider Lusso was impractical for lengthy trips and unsuitable for winter driving. Even so, he loved the invigorating feeling he had when he was behind the wheel, the roof down, cruising at night on two-lane country roads. Of course, the roof wasn't down on his trip from the coast to Paris, though he'd sought out smaller, valley roads where he could experience a bit of the *joie de vivre.*

The last time Lyle had been in Paris, he'd spent a weekend here with an art teacher, under the pretense of visiting art and archaeology museums, though both had known they would share a bed. The problem was, Lyle had considered it a recreational trip, while the woman had seen it as a bonding event. While there had been no recriminations on the return trip, there had been little conversation either, and Lyle had never seen the woman again. Every time he thought about that weekend, he felt guilty, and here he was in Paris, where he couldn't help remembering Colleen and what she had said to him the first time they made love.

He couldn't imagine Beatrice sharing a room, much less a bed, with him before their relationship was formalized, nor could he imagine her misreading him so egregiously. Before Lyle had met Beatrice, everything had been transactional. Not relentless bunkering, but always through a *quid pro quo* lens. Though he wouldn't go so far as to say she had made him a new man, he wasn't the same man who had brought Colleen to Paris.

Driving through the city, Lyle detoured to view the *Museé du Louvre*, circling the museum three times, impressed as he always was with the size and majesty of the structure. Was it imaginable that he was searching for something more valuable, more important, than anything in this museum?

"I MISS YOU. I've grown accustomed to your face."

Beatrice called him just as he was preparing to enter a building where he'd be interviewing Richard Lourdes, the Adler Alembert Chair of Paleoarchaeology at the Sorbonne. Sam had confirmed that Caroline Desrosier was still employed at the Sorbonne, and that she worked for Lourdes, so Lyle hoped to interview her, too.

One of Lourdes's duties was to manage the Alembert archives, where Noel Dekeyser had assisted when he was in Paris. That begged the question of why a psychologist had been working in the archives of a long-dead paleohistorian.

An even more mysterious question had been lodged in Lyle's mind ever since he learned that Dekeyser had worked at the Alembert archive. Could the "Adler," the A. in Agnes's diary, be Adler Alembert? The time period matched, and Adler wasn't a common name.

"Want to join me?" Lyle said into his phone.

"I have work to do here."

"So do I—there, I mean—rather than wasting time in Folkestone and Paris, places Dekeyser left years ago."

"Remember that Sam said the manuscript may be in a different place than Dekeyser, if he's already sold it. Maybe someone he met in Folkestone or Paris has it, or knows who does. Do you know where Dekeyser is now?"

"You know I don't."

"Then why not proceed step by step, the way you would at a site? You're still accumulating evidence . . . meta-analysis, rather than cognitive closure."

"I'm trying, but it's frustrating."

"And if you indulge the frustration, it will disrupt what you're trying to accomplish."

"How much do I owe you for the therapy session, doc?"

"A big hug the next time you see me. Don't rush what you're doing in Paris. Dekeyser was after something there and, whether he found it or not, you're accumulating evidence that may lead you to him and the artifact. Anything new from Sam or your uncle?"

"Sam hasn't been able to locate Dekeyser, and neither have the police."

"If no one else has said this, I'm telling you to be careful. Meddling in the affairs of people who vanish is dangerous business, something I learned the hard way in Uganda. You can do your uncle a service without putting yourself in danger."

"Maybe I should come home and give you that hug."

"Maybe you should. Call me when you get back to the hotel."

"Don't worry about me. I've been on digs in some wild places."

"That's what they all say before . . . you know what."

On his way to Lourdes's office, Lyle was thinking about the dream from which he'd anxiously awakened that morning. A faceless man in a robe and cowl, carrying a candle, had come into his room and had revealed page after page of text that had been typed on a manual typewriter.

"They tell me it's worth a fortune. Everyone says so."

"But it's typed," Lyle had protested.

"That's what makes it valuable."

RICHARD LOURDES stood and gripped Lyle's hand firmly, saying, "Good to make your acquaintance, Dr. Stuart. I know your work."

The Adler Alembert Chair of Paleoarchaeology stood as one taller than his actual height, which might have been five-seven. He wore a suit and tie, and had an oval face with fair skin and artfully combed gray hair. Lyle knew the man was in his seventies, though Lourdes's posture and strong voice suggested a younger man.

In the corner was a low bookcase packed with heavy volumes, and several metal filing cabinets.

"Please sit. You want to see the Alembert archive," said Lourdes, in a way that suggested he was as comfortable speaking English as French.

"If it can be arranged."

"Certainly. What's your interest, if I may ask."

Lyle had thought about how much to reveal to Lourdes. "I'm trying to locate Noel Dekeyser. He was a monk in my uncle's Order. Some loose ends my uncle would like to tie up."

"I see," said Lourdes, in a way that suggested Lyle's answer was less than satisfying. "Where is Noel these days?"

"That's just it. We can't find him."

"What makes you think something in the archive will lead you to him?"

"I admit I'm excavating a site I don't know much about. Perhaps something you or Caroline Desrosier tell me will help me find him." Lyle hadn't answered Lourdes's question, though he hoped he'd said enough to keep the man at bay.

A luscious indigo, burgundy, and avocado cloisonné bowl on the side of the desk seemed out of place in the midst of Lourdes's academic paraphernalia, and when the man saw Lyle gazing at it, he said, "A gift from a dear friend. What do you know about Professor Alembert?"

"Not a thing, except he has an archive here."

"Since you'll be examining his archive, here's some background on the man. Professor Alembert inherited a small fortune from his grandfather and turned it into a large fortune in South America. He taught at this university, and disappeared in 1932 in what was thought to be a botched kidnapping. A generous man, another Schweitzer."

Lourdes had given this biographical summary in the practiced way Lyle often did with familiar subjects he was asked to address, though he was hoping the man had more for him than rote recitals. One thing stood out: Adler Alembert had made a fortune in South America, as had Agnes's "Adler."

"Alembert was a paleohistorian. In those days, the field had a broader scope. Now we're all specialists. One of my colleagues insists on being called a paleosudsinoarchaeologist," Lourdes said, in such subtle English and with an accent so muted that Lyle had forgotten the man's native language was French.

"How long has the archive been here?"

"Since 1940. Alembert was a self-effacing man, so few knew of him during his lifetime, and even fewer after he disappeared. If you examine the ledger, you'll see that only a few hundred people have visited the archive in almost eighty years."

"May I look at the list?"

Lourdes's brows furrowed. "I don't see why not." Going to a sidewall shelf, the man removed a thin book and handed it to Lyle. "We've had so few visitors that we're still using the first ledger; something of an artifact itself now."

Caroline Desrosier had visited five times between 2009 and 2014, and there was Noel Dekeyser, who had visited twice in 2013 and once in 2014. What had he been looking for in the archive of a dead paleohistorian, and how could those visits not be connected to the artifact Lyle was seeking?

"Why did Desrosier and Dekeyser bother to sign the ledger?"

"Because I requested they do so. You know how things are when it comes to funding, and the few Euros we receive for the archive are easier to justify if we can point to actual visitors. If we were to go a few years without any visitors, even the small stipend we receive might be eliminated. So, if you would kindly sign the ledger, I'd be grateful."

One more ledger entry caught Lyle's eye: *Russell, Mainz,* because that's where Dekeyser had gone when he'd left the Sorbonne, and because this man or woman had visited three times from 1952 to 1976.

Though reticent to give Lourdes too much information, Lyle said, "Did Dekeyser ask your advice about art or artifact dealers?"

"Ah," Lourdes said, clasping hands that looked older than he did. "I can safely say we never discussed those subjects. Was he a collector?"

How to answer? Like Remington, this man could add two plus two easily enough.

Lourdes freed Lyle from the obligation to respond by hopping to his feet. "I'll take you to the archive, though I'm afraid that's a pretentious word for the room that holds Professor Alembert's material."

Lourdes removed a key from a hook on the wall behind the office door, a far cry from the security Lyle had encountered in the Oxford archives. Walking down the hall, Lyle said, "I'm hoping to speak to Caroline Desrosier too."

"That can be arranged. First things first."

Lourdes opened a door at the end of the hall and led Lyle into a windowless room, flipping a wall switch to illuminate the archive. "Surprised?" the man asked.

Seven mismatched boxes lined up against the wall.

"You are welcome to examine them. I'll be in my office until six."

"Would you ask Mademoiselle Desrosier to meet me here if she's available?"

"I shall. See me when you're finished so I may lock the door, and I'd like to know if you find anything of interest."

"Gladly. You've been a great help, Professor."

The door closed, and Lyle walked to the nearest box. To refer to this room as an archive stretched the meaning of the word past any reasonable interpretation. He had interns with more material than this. Moreover, he told himself, just because the past was at the heart of his own work didn't mean that past events had anything to do with a manuscript stolen in 2016.

Lyle dispensed with six of the boxes in short order, as these contained uninspiring and mostly derivative historical and archaeological material that would have been of negligible interest even in Alembert's day. Very little had been authored by Alembert himself, which made Lyle wonder if the man's business interests had distracted him from his academic work. The seventh box was identified in faded longhand as *Paléomythologie*. On the top, a spectacular butterfly was displayed between glass plates and, though at least eighty years old, the creature retained vibrant colors and looked as if it had been recently mounted. Having an eight or nine-inch wingspan, its wings were a kaleidoscopic blend of scarlet, gold, and violet, unlike any butterfly Lyle had ever seen.

Setting the butterfly display aside, Lyle discovered an extensive collection of material about Atlantis, and related Atlantean legends: books, monograms, Thule Society newsletters, excerpts from longer articles and texts, many of these purporting to be serious works. Though he knew there were intriguing links between ancient societies in different parts of the world, no one had ever discovered anything—not a single artifact—that supported the existence of Atlantis, or any civilization like it. That hadn't kept feverish advocates of the myth, including some renegade archaeologists, from asserting the existence of a high civilization that had informed and formed Mesolithic, Neolithic, and even Bronze Age societies east and west of the Atlantic Ocean.

A 1930 letter to Alembert from a Yale archaeologist caught his eye, because the subject line read *Atlantis reconditus.*

> *Apart from that grand myth, and myth it surely is, the idea of a seafaring civilization exerting hegemony over geographically distant lands and peoples is not as outrageous as many think. Consider the Phoenicians, the Vikings, and Spain in the New World. Especially in territories with daunting terrain, seafaring expertise permits rapid access to, and conquest of, coastal cities and towns along navigable rivers. Think of the Normans and the Seine. Such advantages would be multiplied for technologically advanced societies, meaning seafaring colonizers might supplant or subjugate indigenous populations.*

All fine and good, Lyle reflected, though the gap between historical Vikings and a mythical civilization rendered logic-based comparisons irrelevant.

He came to a one-page letter on *Hotel du Louvre* stationery, where a name on the first line caught his eye: Rosman. He had recently heard or read that name, but where? On the verge of putting the letter back in the box, he suddenly remembered another box, and Agnes's diary entry.

April 17, 1929

Dear Professor Alembert:

My name is Elana Rosman, and I am an entomology researcher at a university in Spain. I am aware that you have an interest in the insect world, and butterflies in particular.

I have a spectacular specimen that has never been catalogued, and that I am certain you have never seen. I would be delighted to let you view this beautiful creature.

I understand you are presently in Paris. You may contact me at the Hotel du Louvre to schedule a viewing. You will not be disappointed.

E. Rosman, D. Entomology

The unsigned letter had been typed. A handwritten note at the bottom read: *Have Basile research this person—who is she?*

The woman who swiftly entered the room spoke with a pronounced French accent. "I am Car-oh-leen Des-rose-ee-ay. Dr. Lourdes asked me to speak with you."

"*Bonjour, Mademoiselle.*"

A woman who might have been twenty-eight or forty-eight, blue eyes like turquoises, her hair short and golden, her cream-colored skin like a china doll's. Not a classically beautiful woman, though someone who'd draw admiring eyes.

"I'm interested in Noel Dekeyser."

"What would you like to know?" she asked, her bright eyes fixed on the open box.

Lyle had noticed the woman's reticence straightaway. "Did you recruit him to the Sorbonne?"

"He applied for a position, and I was sent to interview him."

Working in one wilderness after another, in all kinds of weather, had taught Lyle a laconic directness. "What were his duties?"

"He assisted Dr. Lourdes with department matters, and with the archive."

"Did you know he was a psychologist?"

"*Certainement* . . . of course."

"Did he ever explain what attracted him to this position?"

"It's not uncommon for people to take positions outside their educational training. I've done so myself."

"Were you friends?"

"We were courteous to one another. We didn't socialize. You can decide whether that qualifies as friendship."

"Why did Dekeyser go to Mainz?"

"As I recall, an open adjunct position in the School for Cognitive Studies. I was a librarian at the University of Mainz before I came here, and he asked me questions about the city and university."

"How long were you there?"

Lyle's probing questions were a dog whistle to this woman. "What else would you like to know about *Noel?*"

"Did he ever talk to you about art . . . artifacts?"

"No, never."

"How often did you hear from him after he went to Mainz?"

"What makes you think we kept in touch?"

Lyle was convinced they had, though he guessed she wasn't about to admit it unless she had to.

"The ledger says you've spent time in the archive."

"Me again? I was curious about the man who endowed Dr. Lourdes's Chair, and Dr. Lourdes likes me to come here now and again, for his own reasons."

"Is Noel Dekeyser still at the University of Mainz?"

"I don't know."

"You're familiar with the contents of these boxes?"

"I thought I'd made it clear I wasn't answering any questions about myself. Now, if you will excuse me, I have an urgent appointment."

"I apologize if I've said anything out of turn. Thank you for talking to me."

"You may thank Dr. Lourdes," Desrosier said, halfway out the door.

Lyle had to admit that he was a woefully inadequate interrogator. It was humbling to step out of his area of expertise, his comfort zone, and feel so incompetent. Moreover, he was going through a box of things that had belonged to a man who'd been dead for decades, a man who had no known link to Noel Dekeyser or the manuscript. He'd been to enough unpromising archaeological sites to know when to pack up and move on.

Lyle replaced the items in the *Paléomythologie* box, though he still had half the contents to examine. As for Caroline Desrosier's mulish attitude, there could be any number of reasons for it, including Lyle's interrogatory style that didn't suit everyone.

Lourdes was at his desk, writing on a notepad. "Finished already?"

The question had a jarring effect on Lyle. He had been in that room less than an hour. Had Desrosier's words and attitude distracted him? Hard to believe she had done it intentionally. So what if he didn't believe the manuscript was what it purported to be? There *was* a manuscript. Noel Dekeyser *was* a real person. Lyle's brother *was* actively engaged in this search. Why not think of this as an intellectual puzzle and try to learn as much as he could, even if he never found Dekeyser or the manuscript? As long as he was here why not excavate to the bottom of the box? Even unpromising sites had been known to produce a treasure or two.

Lyle said, "I have a few questions about the archive. Why is there so little material?"

"Professor Alembert was a spare man in many respects, including what he chose to retain. To be truthful . . . *entre nous*, you understand, if he hadn't endowed this Chair, there would be no archive, no remembrance of the man."

Lyle said, "The Atlantis box . . ."

"You examined it? In his day, Alembert enjoyed a reputation as something of a fabulist. Frankly, we retain the material because we have so little else of his."

"Are you aware of any other Alembert collections?"

"Nothing, to the best of my knowledge. The man lived an uneventful life by all accounts, the only spark of genius being the mountain of money he made in South America."

"Why did Dekeyser apply for this position?"

"I've been waiting for you to ask that question. He told me he was interested in a close associate of Alembert's in Buenos Aires, an innovator in some branch of psychology, and was hoping to find something in the Alembert archive. As it turned out, there was nothing, but Noel stayed because the post gave him the time and University resources to pursue his research interests."

Desrosier had said nothing about a research project when Lyle had asked her this question, but then, she seemed to know little about Dekeyser.

"Did he give you any details about this project?"

"Nothing. I don't even recall him mentioning the Argentine's name."

"Your specialty is early Mesoamerican civilizations."

Lourdes beamed, though the man's reaction would have been less enthusiastic had he known Lyle had researched his work as a courtesy rather than knowing Lourdes by reputation.

"If you're familiar with my work, you know I'm trying to correlate the extinction of large South American mammals with the geographic expansion of those early civilizations. You see, I have an interest in South America in common with our benefactor, though I haven't hit any gold veins as of yet. Alembert had it all over me in that respect."

Lyle said, "Did you send Mademoiselle Desrosier to interview Dekeyser in Folkestone?"

"If I did, I have no recollection of it. Did she say so?"

"She suggested as much."

"We're an informal group here. She may have understood some questions I had about Dekeyser to mean she should have a personal conversation with him, and she could have made the trip in a single day."

"One more thing. Can you recommend a restaurant near the Hotel Marat?"

"A little café on the corner. Nothing pleasing to the eye, but the *bouillabaisse* is quite nice . . . they have a Marseille chef. The oysters at the *Pied de Cochon* are lovely, but a bit of a hike . . . well worth it if you have the time. I'd invite you to dinner, but a friend and I are dining tonight at a rather *haute* establishment . . . not for everyone."

Lyle found the place in the *Paléomythologie* box where he'd suspended his search. More articles and essays on Atlantis, with several taking the view that this prehistoric civilization was a proven fact.

A fabulist, Lourdes had said—the simplest explanation. A harmless hobby, like the butterfly.

At the bottom of the box were some brittle photographs, along with what Lyle recognized as Autochrome plates that still retained clarity and color. One of these depicted a man staring wide-eyed into the camera, a Napoleon-like figure leaning in with arms behind his back. Alembert? Another depicted a young woman with this same man, both in evening dress. But the Autochrome that most interested Lyle revealed an ornate cup, or goblet, with runes on the facing, and a faded note on the Plate's side margin: *Hill could read.*

The same hand as the note on the Rosman letter?

Lyle's mind was so scrambled that the plate slipped from his hand and rattled on the floor.

JANUARY 10, 2017

☙☙☙

The Road from Paris to Mainz

BOUILLABAISSE AND A half-bottle of a tasty *Haut Brion* had put Lyle into a sound sleep, and left him with warm memories of the little restaurant and the man who had recommended it—better memories of Paris than his last visit.

Snow slowed him as he drove east, though he wasn't about to mention it to Beatrice or Sam. As he drove, he was reminded of this archaeological site or that, as other motorists note quaint towns or interesting natural features. At one such reminder—Byrne's Macromanni tribe encampment—he was barely attending to deteriorating conditions, when the Spider Lusso skidded off the snowy road and came within inches of sliding into a deep ditch.

Breathing hard, his jaws clamped shut, he could feel his heart pounding. His foot was on the brake—actually pressing on the brake as hard as he could. How could a man who so meticulously prepared for an expedition be driving a sports car in this weather?

If he couldn't admit to Sam and Beatrice that taking the Spider had been a bad idea, he could surely admit it to himself.

He was careful getting the car back on the road, creeping along the shoulder until he found a safe access point. Still shaken from the near disaster, he hadn't gone five miles when he arrived at the town of Sankt Ingbert, not far from the border, and decided to stop for something to eat.

Though it was a cold day, it felt good to get out of the car, breathe the crisp air, view the white hills that surrounded the town, and walk again. Instead of taking a direct route to the Restaurant Delphi, he decided to circle the block to stretch his legs.

Anchored by a red brick Gothic church, the town featured buildings with white walls and red roofs, homes and businesses alike. A sky like ice from end to end, and the town so still the leaves seemed rooted to the ground.

At the restaurant, Lyle was seated in an intimate red and gold room that displayed classically inspired statuettes and faux friezes, with real linen napkins and tablecloths. The wood stove against the wall must have been real, because a black cat was stretched out in front of it.

With coffee and a liverwurst sandwich, he set himself to reconstructing the expeditionary program he'd worked out prior to the mishap on the road. If Beatrice were here, she'd use one of her mnemonic techniques to help him bring everything back. On the other hand, he couldn't see Beatrice driving cross-country in the Spider, especially in the middle of winter. No, it was best he was alone, and chastened enough by the close shave to practice extreme caution for the remainder of the trip.

Of the ten tables in this side dining room, only three were occupied, the other two by couples. The room's antiquarian motif reminded Lyle of the goblet, and the words, *Hill could read.* Every time he thought of the goblet, he felt that excitement of discovery anew, the same sensation he felt at a site when he discovered a game-changing artifact. He'd been too startled to formulate questions at the time, but now he wondered if someone—perhaps Dekeyser—hadn't planted the picture in the box as a red herring.

Though Dekeyser had assisted at the archive, how could he have known that anyone would bother to search the boxes, and where would he have acquired the resources and skill to produce an authentic-looking Autochrome plate?

Lyle was convinced that Desrosier knew more about Dekeyser than she'd admitted, and equally convinced that someone more adept than he would be needed to pry it out of her.

He declined a refill, though he had some sandwich yet to consume. As for Lourdes, Lyle didn't think the Adler Alembert Chair was hiding anything, when it came to Dekeyser at least, though how could he be sure after spending so little time with the man?

Then, there was dead Alembert, the sort of person that made Lyle comfortable—not living, breathing, or modifying the historical record. He preferred his mysteries static rather than kinetic. As to Alembert, everything he'd heard from Lourdes, and everything he'd seen in the archive—until the goblet—had suggested mediocrity, though perhaps this Atlantis fabulist had acquired the already-inscribed Autochrome plate by good fortune and had squirreled it away with his other Atlantean oddments.

As for the elusive Dekeyser, Lyle had placed the physical dossier Sam had given him on the table, with their quarry's anthropometry reduced to layman's terms for Lyle's benefit.

Age: 46
Height: 5 ft., 9 inches
Weight: 170 pounds
Build: heavier lower torso
Hair: wheat, thinning on top
Eyes: blue-gray
Face: prominent features, beak nose
Complexion: fair to pale
Dialect: northern England
Temperament: melancholic
Childhood nickname: Nelly
Other identifying features: congenital limp

Clipped to his notes were photographs Sam had sent him. Lyle was pursuing a man he'd never met, had never spoken to, had not heard of until a few weeks ago, but even though he was on a wild *apochen* chase, he consoled himself by likening this assignment to deciphering a skeleton he'd excavated at a site, the step-by-step process of reassembling a life from the evidence. The problem with Dekeyser was the *kinetic* element, —or was there a kinetic element?

The CurLio diary connected Agnes CurLio, Adler Alembert, and John Hill. She had followed "Adler" to South America and had cooperated in the man's criminal enterprise. In one entry, she had recorded his eagerness to return to Europe. On the run, she had visited an Oxford teacher and had left her diary with that man. In addition, Lyle was now aware of the connection between Alembert and John Hill. With all this evidence, how could those three not have been linked by the manuscript John Hill had discovered? And one more thing: an entomologist named Elana Rosman had shown up in both Agnes's and Alembert's effects, making Lyle wonder if she was also connected to Hill.

After taking care of the bill, Lyle was surprised by a message from his doctoral candidate, Gorsey, informing him in words reeking with humility and contrition that he was joining Marks and Fitzgerald on their expedition to the Jericho region—which meant he wouldn't be able to assist in preparing for Lido.

Lyle could scarcely believe his eyes. How could *his* student make such an announcement so cavalierly?

As it turned out, the answer suggested itself in Andrea Fitzgerald's message below Gorsey's, which the student had neglected to delete before forwarding his *apologia* to Lyle.

> Jericho-A72 will advance your knowledge and prestige far more than packing bottles and bags for Lido.

He could send an irate message to Gorsey. He supposed he could even prevent the young man from going to Jericho, though with Andrea at the helm that was no sure thing.

"What's wrong with you helping your uncle for a month or two?" Beatrice had asked him. "Everything imaginable," he had responded, and here was an example.

Precisely the narrow, calculating thinking Beatrice had tried to get him to question, or at least examine, his strong inclination to think that only what's tangible is real and worthy of consideration. Lyle was thought by many to be a great catch, having earned a reputation that transcended the archaeology community—*Time Magazine's* Nis article had done that—but he suspected he was the lucky one, and wondered if Beatrice would tire of what she perceived as his narrowness.

"All right, Beatrice," he whispered. If Gorsey wanted to go, he could go. If Andrea wanted to punish him, Lyle wasn't going to try to stop her, not this time anyway.

For the time being, he would attend to roads and ditches.

MARCH 8, 1995

☻-☻-☻

University of Cambridge

WITH THE WALLS in need of fresh paint, no awards or honoraria displayed, and busy whiteboards and sheets tacked and taped everywhere, this unpretentious office didn't look as if it housed one of the most acclaimed geneticists in the world,

"How can I help you, Professor?" said a burly man, who looked more like a carpenter than a Nobel laureate.

"I was told by Dr. Berger there's no one better than Nathan Harte to answer my questions."

"Hans is well, I trust?"

"Quite well. He sends his regards."

"Hans suggested your questions were of a speculative nature."

"Just so, Dr. Harte. I'm interested in evolutionary adaptations and their applicability to the human species. For instance, amphibians grow new limbs, as do trees. Some trees have been alive for hundreds or thousands of years. I have heard the Greenland shark can live to five hundred years. My understanding is these organisms evolved and adapted to be long-lived, to regenerate lost limbs, so might the human species do the same, and not by magic, unless one ascribes these adaptations to supernatural forces?"

Harte repressed a smile. "With an organism as complex as *Homo sapiens*, the adaptations you describe would be radical indeed. I can say that we're far from understanding how such things could be accomplished, but I wouldn't say they're impossible, as many of the diagnostic tests and cellular therapies we practice today would have been considered impossible by scientists a hundred, even fifty, years ago."

"I understand you are working with lower forms of life, reptiles and amphibians, to accelerate and enhance such processes."

"Genetic enhancement is painstaking work—mapping the genetic code and then identifying how changes affect the organism."

Eyes trained on the geneticist, the visitor said, "If we could obtain a formula—if such an imprecise word can be used to describe the application of this process to man—from another world, or civilization—could modern science apply it?"

Giving the visitor and his twin canes a searching look, Harte said, "You refer to modifying the human genetic code to promote limb regeneration."

"And longer and more virile lives."

Harte's eyes were twinkling when he said, "As this is a speculative question, involving a speculative world or civilization, I must give you a speculative response: if the formula, as you call it, was intelligible, we might be able to apply it."

"Intelligible in what sense?" the visitor probed.

"I see you are keen on this question."

"A fancy I can't put down without hearing from an expert."

"This formula would have to be rigorously mathematical and rigorously defined with chemical equations, along with specifying the physical conditions under which the work would proceed. Only then would we stand a chance of applying it. To be even more critical, a single gap in the formula would be enough to nullify its application because we don't possess adequate theoretical knowledge."

"You are saying that no matter how graphic, a word description would not suffice."

"Never in life, my dear man. Out of the question."

The visitor sat as still as a sunning snake, and Harte said nothing to hurry him.

"One more question, if I may."

"I see you've given this fancy of yours a great deal of thought."

"Psychologists are drawn to puzzles of the mind, and this one has captured my imagination. What if the formula was rigorous, though composed in a language with norms of expression that differ from our own?"

"I suspect you already know the answer, Professor. Only if this formulaic language could be made intelligible to modern science; that is, if this language could be correlated with our own mathematical and chemical equations. And, as you may know, genetic alterations of this kind would be more efficacious if accomplished in the womb than if attempted later in life."

"If the formula was dynamic enough, might an old man be adaptable?"

"Accepting the speculative premise of the existence of such a formula, then why not accept your even wilder premise? As you cannot be serious about such human adaptations, I surmise you're working on an exercise to reveal things that resist conventional psychological techniques."

"Your Olympian reputation falls short, Dr. Harte. You have guessed my secret. An innovation I hope will trigger repressed memories in the disabled."

"An innovation to disarm them?"

"Psychologists would not use that word. You see, our subjects are more temperamental than your cells and mitochondria. Nonetheless, you have captured the essence of my work."

Harte said, "I've read about conventional techniques the psycho-sciences employ to disarm resistant patients . . . psychotropic drugs, physical stimulation . . ."

"Yes, of course, but such hammering techniques should only be employed when one is driving a nail. Those measures are the least effective means to motivate a person. To use your word, I *disarm* patients in ways that make them believe they are motivated to act by their own will, their own self-interests." What the visitor left unsaid was that this was exactly how he had motivated Berger to arrange this meeting.

"Let me know if I can be of further assistance," said Harte. "Anything to advance science, that's my motto."

"And a fine motto it is. I happen to be seeking a . . . resource, an essential resource, that seems to have vanished into thin air, but I shall find it one day. You can depend on it."

JANUARY 12, 2017

☺-☺-☺

Mainz

"L ET ME TELL YOU where I am," said Lyle.

Sam said, "Don't bother. You're parked in the second row, fourth space from the east end, of a lot across the street from the School for Cognitive Studies. I thought you'd like to know that Caroline Desrosier is Noel Dekeyser's cousin."

"She failed to mention that. Anything else?"

Sam said, "I'm so desperate I checked up on Henry's two monks . . . Claude and Tommie. If one of them is up to no good, he's an expert at keeping to the *legend*."

Lyle said, "I've got something for you. I found an old Autochrome plate of a royal drinking cup in the Alembert archive, with a note: *Hill could read.*"

"I don't like it," said Sam. "This is shaping up to be more than a snatch and run. Beatrice and I had dinner last night . . ."

"I'm gone for a week, and you're stealing my girlfriend?"

"We agreed that Dekeyser's disappearance changes things, that you should come home."

"You might locate Dekeyser," Lyle protested.

"We'd have located him by now, if he were alive. Some people leave trails like slugs on tile. Any fool—or professor—can follow

126

them. Some are like dogs in a field. You can follow them, if you know dogs. Some are like birds. Ever tried to follow a bird? The reason I think Dekeyser's dead is, he was a slug that turned into a bird. How likely is that?"

The strange message Lyle had received from his uncle now made sense. All of them: Sam, Beatrice, and Henry were conspiring with each other but playing it sly, at least until now. No doubt Sam was the ringleader, with his research suggesting more danger than they'd originally anticipated.

Lyle said, "As long as I'm here I might as well scratch around for a while."

"If you knew how many people have said that and been scratched out themselves, you'd think again."

"I'm not taking your advice lightly, Sam."

"What I'd expect a lazy thinker to say, not a certified genius."

"This is the last place we know Dekeyser to have been. The manuscript might be here."

"If he's disappeared, you can bet the manuscript has too. By now, it's in Moscow, Beijing, or Riyadh. Who are you seeing?" Sam asked him.

"Ambar Sangal, in the department where Dekeyser worked."

"Talk to him, get in the car, and drive home," said Sam. "Put the roof down while you're at it . . . poop-poop."

"What do you know that I don't?" Lyle asked his brother.

"Nothing, that's the problem. I ought to know a hell of a lot more, so keep to the beaten path. Hold on, you can add an oval birthmark on the right shoulder to Dekeyser's dossier, in case you meet him on the beach."

"No beaches within a hundred miles of Mainz."

"A sauna, then."

"Based on what you've told me, I'd be more likely to meet Dekeyser in a morgue."

When Sam hung up, Lyle still had a few minutes before his

meeting with Sangal. A few minutes for what? Not beaches or saunas, even if he found himself with a few hours or days on his hands. Lyle was more comfortable in a working camp in some out of the way place than he was in any city, because a solitary life was easier to accept when he was working than when he was on holiday, supposedly enjoying himself. Here he was in Mainz, just having come from Paris, and he hadn't made time for any recreation.

He found Mainz to be a typically spic-and-span German city. Navigating the campus revealed that the Johannes Gutenberg Universität Mainz was smaller than Oxford, with many modern buildings—a strikingly different visual environment than Lyle's college.

The Head of the School for Cognitive Studies, or *Institutsdirektor*, was a portly, dark-skinned, wary-looking man with a seamed forehead. Without looking up, Sangal said, "I'll be just a moment. So, how can I help you?"

Since Lyle had already informed Sangal of his interest in Dekeyser, the man had either forgotten or he wanted to compare what Lyle told him now to what had been previously communicated—not unprecedented for someone whose specialty was psychology.

"I'm trying to contact Noel Dekeyser about some unfinished business in England."

Sangal rubbed his shiny forehead. "I have no idea what happened to him."

"Did he resign?"

"He stopped coming to work. He was teaching a course, and one day he was absent and never returned."

"Were the police notified?"

"I can't say. Perhaps Professor Russell can answer that question. He sponsored Dekeyser for the *Lehrbeauftragter* position. As I recall, Russell endorsed Dekeyser teaching our first-year Principles and Concepts course."

"Did anyone ever question you about him?"

Sangal's slumberous eyes didn't signify a slumbering mind. "Is he dead? Is that it?"

Lyle had met Sangal's kind before, men who became bullish when aroused. "I don't know," he said.

"Russell's your man. He's sagacious, in his way."

What could that mean? "Were you satisfied with Dekeyser's work?"

"Russell would know better. No complaints or endorsements from me."

"Have you ever met Caroline Desrosier?"

"The name isn't familiar. Does she work for the University?"

"She used to be a librarian here. Now, she's at the Sorbonne, and assists with the Adler Alembert archive."

Not a hint from Sangal that he recognized the Alembert name.

"Is there anything else you can tell me, Dr. Sangal?"

"I'm afraid not, and I'm not at all clear on why you're here, Professor Stuart."

A dead end, and a barely civil one, Lyle told himself. "Where can I find Professor Russell?"

Glancing up from his work, Sangal said, "Down the hall, take the tunnel to the building on the other side of the road, second floor, far end. I'll let him know you're coming."

"Cognitive Studies has offices in both buildings?"

Sangal's eyes narrowed. "Just Russell."

An outcast? There were a few such men at Oxford.

"Thanks for nothing," Lyle whispered as he exited the office. Should he bother with Russell, or take Sam's advice and debark for England? Last stop, he told himself, turning into the brightly-lit tunnel.

Accounting for different personalities, the interviews with Remington, Lourdes, Desrosier, and now Sangal had been tediously similar, with the subjects exhibiting reticence, suspicion, and truculence in varying degrees, even his fellow archaeologist, Lourdes, and, apart from being inconvenienced, none of them had been distressed that Dekeyser had moved on.

By the time Lyle reached Russell's office, he couldn't help wondering who or what had conspired to consign this man to the wilderness, so far from all his colleagues at the end of a hall full of adjuncts' and interns' warrens. Perhaps this was the office reserved for the youngest or newest faculty member. The placard on the door reinforced this idea: Arthur Russell, *Professor extraordinarius*, which Lyle knew corresponded to assistant professor, or lecturer, at Oxford.

The door was half open and, when Lyle knocked, a melodious voice immediately answered in English, "Come in."

The first thing Lyle noticed when he entered the room was the state of inundation. Stacks of books, magazines, binders, and unbound paper were everywhere: on the floor and on a table against the window wall, and on the desk itself, not to mention the wall-length bookcase behind the desk and another one adjacent to the doorway, that were stuffed with material. Russell had a computer on his desk and two more side by side on the floor against the wall. In the corner opposite the door was the hanging skeleton of a male *Homo sapiens*, suspended from the ceiling as from a gibbet. A true skeleton, Lyle's eyes told him, and not ancient.

He almost missed the man behind the desk for all the clutter, and he couldn't have been more surprised at what he saw. To say the least, the rich voice he'd heard from the hallway was incongruous with the man seated at a desk that was only half the normal height.

In his child's wheelchair, Arthur Russell couldn't have been four and a half feet tall, and was grotesquely misshapen, his legs like sticks while his upper body was stocky. One shoulder was higher than the other, suggesting kyphosis, but despite the deformities and his advanced age, Russell's thin, mobile face was still handsome: clear blue eyes with perfectly horizontal brows, and thick wavy hair that retained a few corn-colored strands and was swept back from a high forehead in a way that suggested wings. As if a statue Lyle had once seen in Iraq, with a god's head perched on the body of a gruesome beast, had come to life.

Hand extended, Russell made the effort to launch himself out of his chair and between the stacks on the desktop. He had a heavy handshake for so small and so old a man, and when he leaned forward Lyle observed his knife-edged trousers in the old-fashioned style—or maybe ancient themselves, like the man wearing them.

"Glad to know you, Dr. Stuart. Sangal informed me you were coming," said Russell, scratching the bridge of an elegant nose, like a bowsprit enhancing the lines of a ship.

"Yes, sir. Thank you for seeing me," said Lyle, mesmerized by the voice that proceeded from this man.

"As you see, my office is an adventure. For obvious reasons, I ask that you avoid rapid movement. Though this place has the appearance of utter chaos, I assure you I know where every book, manuscript, piece of paper resides—those I care about," said Russell, giving Lyle a smile that put him at ease. "The device you see on the floor is a mechanical extender, a substitute for height and functioning legs, fabricated years ago by a man in the engineering department."

"How long have you been here, Professor Russell?"

"Sixty years. I'm ninety-six, the oldest teacher at this University. This wheelchair came later in life, when I was eighty-seven and could no longer walk on the toothpicks nature gave me for legs. A retirement opportunity, or so I was told, but here I am."

Russell was proud of his tenure at the University and his longevity, and why shouldn't he be, thought Lyle, as the man's conversational dexterity and the work that surrounded him suggested he was still intellectually vigorous.

"I gather you were educated in England," said Lyle.

"A private school that could accommodate my disabilities, until I was old enough for college . . . and some adventures, the amazing young man on the flying trapeze, that sort of thing," Russell said. Both men shared a laugh.

"Do you miss England?"

"At my age, one is grateful for any place to hang a hat, and to have a hat to hang. But you're not interested in a Cretaceous Period teacher. You came to learn about Noel. Five months ago, he abruptly stopped coming to work, and it fell to me to complete the course he'd been teaching."

"Were the police notified?"

"I informed Dr. Sangal. I'm not certain what he did with the information, other than insisting I finish teaching Noel's course. Sangal and I don't converse that often," Russell said, giving Lyle a knowing grin.

"Did Dekeyser ever talk to you about art . . . artifacts?"

"Let me think. We might have had a discussion about artifacts. He told me he was once in a religious order. That might have been how the subject was broached."

"Professor?" a voice intruded.

Lyle looked over his shoulder and saw a bespectacled young man standing in the doorway.

"How can I help you, Grohl?" Russell replied in German, a language with which Lyle had limited command.

The young man's response in German: "May I interrupt you for a moment?"

"Certainly," Lyle said to Russell, and while Russell conversed with the man, Lyle scanned the bookshelves and stacks, high and low—ordered clutter according to Russell—observing John Garstang's *The Land of the Hittites*, Sigmund Freud's *The Ego and the Id*, and Abraham Maslow's *Motivation and Personality*. High on the bookshelf, B.F. Skinner's *The Behavior of Organisms*, a black binder hand-labeled *Sed libera nos a malo*, and Ivan Pavlov's

Conditioned Reflexes. Lower on the shelves, Carl Jung's *Psycholog-ical Types,* Albert Einstein's *On the Generalized Theory of Gravitation,* Kurt Gödel's *On Formally Undecidable Propositions of Principia Mathematica and Related Systems,* which Lyle recognized from his uncle's article as Gödel's Incompleteness Theorem, Sir Leonard Woolley's *The Sumerians,* Sir Arthur Evans *Ancient Il-lyria,* and two large jars filled with what looked like rice and tea leaves.

A man with eclectic interests, a blending of the old and new, psychology, archaeology, history, mathematics, physics.

On the wall next to the window was a slightly askew recogni-tion plaque from the Johannes Gutenberg Universität for "Arthur Russell's 50 Years of Devoted Service." Even as Lyle heard the young man's farewell words, the Alembert archive visitors ledger came back to him: *Russell, Mainz.* Could this be the man who had visited the archive as long ago as the 1950s?

"I was never orderly, but things have gotten worse in recent years. There was a time when I opened that window in favorable weather, and kept all kinds of things on the ledge, till one day my best cane went over and, by the time I reached the window, down the street went a little fellow waving it like a pirate's sword."

"Professor, have you examined the Alembert archive at the Sor-bonne?"

"Repeatedly, though not for many years . . . decades, actually. You may wonder what in that archive would attract a psychologist, and the answer is I have an interest in what prehistoric archaeology can tell us about the cognitive processes of early man. When I learned about the Alembert archive, I thought it worth the short trip to Paris, and several more as it turned out."

"Did you examine the *Paléomythologie* file?"

"Cursorily, and only on one occasion. My interest in myth is as psychological phenomena, how myths represent norms, phobias, taboos, and such."

"A woman who works at the archive recruited Dekeyser. She worked here before she went to Paris."

"What is her name?"

"Caroline Desrosier."

"The librarian," said Russell. "Before I was confined to this wheelchair, I often visited the library, and we would occasionally speak. She was interested in the attraction of psychological types to political theories. A bright girl. I saw you scanning my collection as I was speaking to Grohl. Did it make you wonder?"

"Is that a psychological question?"

"All questions are psychological, in their way."

"There were more historical and archaeological references than I would have expected."

"And how would you answer that riddle?"

"They're connected to your interest in the psychology of early man and early civilizations."

"Just so," said Russell, "but enough about this old man. Tell me about yourself, Dr. Stuart, an archaeologist of note, if I may say so. I looked you up after Sangal told me you were coming. Perhaps we can talk more about the psychology of early man before you leave Mainz. Are you married?"

When Lyle answered no, Russell said, "Well, we make our choices, and my physical condition limited the matrimonial field. There was a woman once, but she is long gone, and a union would have been impractical. You happen to be a young, healthy man with a sterling reputation, not the common man's limitations. Tell me about your research."

To meet someone sympathetic, and volubly so, was a new experience on this mission and, though Lyle was eager to get down to business, he couldn't resist telling Russell about his work—the Neanderthal sites, the Lido encampment, and the early domestication of horses.

Russell gave every indication he was fascinated by the Lido site.

"The horse and man. Ulysses' canny invention, Alexander's Bucephalus, Bonaparte's Marengo."

Lyle said, "The horse held a high place in near Eastern, Aegean, and Adriatic cultures and myths. In later periods, the Greeks produced marvelous pottery: cups, *pelikes*, *pateras*, and column *kraters* that featured the horse and horsemen . . . bigas and quadrigas."

"You have seen such art, I presume."

"More than my share. The tribe I'm studying was too preoccupied with survival to produce such things, but there are pictographic representations of horses at some of their encampments. Not war horses and chariots in those times; smaller, stockier horses—transport for men and supplies. I'm trying to establish an earlier date for Bronze Age weaponry in Europe . . . changing paradigms, fresh ideas." Though Lyle knew this to be true, and privately took pride in his trailblazing work, he'd never said it out loud. But something about Russell—his manner, expressions of interest in the subject—had made him comfortable revealing it to this man.

"I look forward to more on this subject, but I am too old and frail to gallop with the young colts and mares, while you are a renowned scientist on a mission, or so I gather from Sangal's few words. So, back to Noel. We may have spoken about artifacts on one occasion. Have you learned something about his whereabouts?"

"Not yet. I was hoping someone at the University could point me in the right direction."

"To have traveled all this way, the matter must be important."

"My uncle asked me to help him, having to do with Dekeyser's time at the monastery."

"Nothing serious, I hope. Noel was always a pleasant enough fellow."

The first time anyone had used a word like that to describe Dekeyser, but maybe this said more about Russell than the man Lyle was seeking.

"Should I speak to anyone else at the University, or in the city?"

"I don't think he had many friends. To be direct, none to my knowledge. We went to dinner on several occasions, and may I observe that Noel was one of those men who didn't seem to need, or desire, close friends, wasn't distraught about it. The most intimate thing I learned about him was his passion for liver, so I brought him to the Café Marseilles, where that dish is a specialty, and expertly prepared."

"That's my favorite meal—has been since my mother introduced me at an early age," Lyle said, enthusiastically.

"Then, you must visit the Café Marseilles, but I warn you they are always busy, so have the hotel concierge make a reservation for you several days in advance."

"I don't think I'll be here that long."

"Too bad, my friend. It's worth an extra day in Mainz. Speaking of nourishment, I see you eyeing the jars on my shelf. I practically subsist on green tea and brown rice. You see, I believe that's the secret of my longevity. When Noel and I dined at the Café Marseille, I made an exception with their liver creation, and not since that night have I consumed anything that approached the succulence of that dish."

"The temptation is powerful," said Lyle.

"Indulge it, if you're able. You won't regret it. Our River Rhine deserves a viewing, and our cathedral is a thousand years old. Somehow, it survived all those bombs. A miracle, some insist."

"I don't believe in miracles, Professor."

"Neither do I, but I believe there's more to this universe than we can imagine."

Lyle said, "Mainz was the northernmost encampment in Roman Gaul."

"More than an encampment. Portions of the Roman aqueduct and theater remain. You are familiar with the mathematical concept of chaos theory?"

"I'm aware of it, though no deep understanding."

"Do you think chaos theory can be applied to history?"

Though Russell was old and crippled, his imagination was a hummingbird that flitted from flower to flower.

"I'm not sure what you mean," Lyle said.

"That a small, so-called peripheral act can set cataclysmic events in motion."

"I suppose such a thing is possible."

"I believe it's more than possible, Dr. Stuart. I believe such things are common."

"You refer to random acts or events."

"And intentional acts that seem to be insignificant, or unconnected to the cataclysm. I hope to see you again before you return to Oxford, but if I don't, it's been a pleasure talking to you."

Walking to his car, Lyle took stock. He had a viable exit now, a clear path home, endorsed by Sam, Beatrice, and his uncle, buttressed by the Dekeyser dead end. He wasn't getting any more out of Sangal, he suspected Russell had given him everything he had, and Sam's intelligence storehouse was empty. On his own, he had no idea what to do next, and he was fed up with these stultifying interviews.

As for Dekeyser, Lyle had learned little that Sam couldn't have provided without leaving England. If he had a vague sense that something was lurking beneath these still waters, he had no idea how to fish it out. Thinking about his brother's cautionary words, and recalling the thing in Hill's story that was lurking beneath the water in front of the mountain, he admitted some things were better not fished out.

His callused hands reminded him that a reconnaissance of the Lido site before he returned to Oxford made all the sense in the world.

JANUARY 14, 2017

☙☙☙

Bosnia-Herzegovina

THOUGH THE LAST TWO hundred miles of the drive to the Lido site had been on tedious two-lane roads, Lyle felt rejuvenated by doing what he was supposed to be doing. He had spoken to Sam and Beatrice before he embarked, and both had expressed relief that he'd left Mainz.

On the first day out, with the sun shining, he had put the roof down—a finger in Sam's eye—but ten minutes of cold wind cured him of that.

Before he exited the Spider, Lyle looked at his phone and discovered a recent email from Russell, who must have read Lyle's conflicted feelings because he had written:

> You have sacrificed precious time and have done all that duty and obligation demand. You can return to Oxford with a clear conscience. A stab of regret too, at having missed the best preparation of liver this side of Paris. Cordially Yours . . . Russell.

Lyle's destination was a Chalcolithic Age encampment, not far from the better-studied settlement of Pod, where he hoped to advance his knowledge of the weaponry of the tribe that had garrisoned here six millennia ago. A barren, hilly land midway between Bugojno and the Adriatic Sea, and not far from the border with Croatia, with a wind so strong he had to remove his field hat as he made his way to the fenced area where three people were working.

What had attracted him to this proto-Illyrian site was the discovery of tin-enhanced copper spearheads that might fix an earlier onset date for Bronze Age activity in Europe.

The little bandy-legged man who scampered out of the fenced area had a narrow head covered by a broad-brimmed hat with chinstrap. He wore a stained gray coat, ear covers, work gloves, and heavy boots. The stubble on his chin and cheeks suggested distracted shaving rather than an intended effect.

"Dr. Stuart, we weren't expecting you for several weeks, but we're delighted to see you. Welcome to the Lido fortress."

A patch of ground no one but an archaeologist could have mistaken for a fortress. Lyle hadn't met Cornel Popa, an archaeologist at the University of Sarajevo, though the two had corresponded for years.

"I was in Germany. Couldn't pass up the opportunity to see your work."

"You're not staying?"

"Not this trip. I have to return to Oxford to equip myself." And without Gorsey, equipping himself would be a bigger challenge than he'd anticipated.

His eyes fixed on the Spider, Popa said, "How did you fare on the road to the site?"

"I won't be driving that car the next time I come."

"Let me show you our work."

On the way to the fenced area, Popa pointed to the crowning barbed wire. "This won't keep determined thieves out, but it discourages casual collectors. We're staying in a town ten kilometers from here, so we must remove most of the artifacts daily. You can appreciate how hard it is to pack everything up and store it in town, things not available at the site for reference and comparison, but

I'm not complaining. Better than those construction sites with looming bulldozers we so often encounter . . . ah, my assistants, Eva and Josip."

The young people looked up from their ground level work and waved at Lyle. Josip was burly and fair, with long straight hair and an actor's chin, Eva dark haired and almond eyed. Both wore wool caps that covered their ears. Lyle recognized his name when spoken by Josip, and the animation it elicited on Eva's features.

Two field tables had been erected in a corner of the fenced area, one shaded and draped on three sides for computers and other sensitive devices, the other populated with artifacts and bones. Beneath the tables were burlap sheets where dozens of plastic bags were stored and, against the fence, wheelbarrows, sifting screens, and other implements. Not far from these tools were half a dozen spoil piles.

"Spearheads?" asked Lyle.

"Just seven so far," said Popa, "along with a socketed axe head. Once we've mapped the distribution of tin, we're hoping your algorithm can tell us whether the tin is incidental or intentional."

The big question, the answer to which would determine Lyle's level of interest in this site.

"Saddle querns?"

"Certainly, for local grains. We've collected a dozen or so. Fortunate to have so little snow this winter, and warmer than normal, though it's cold enough for us," said Popa, looking skeptically at Lyle's jacket. "When I learned you were coming, I brought in the spearheads. They're on the table. Go ahead and examine them."

An excited Lyle stepped to the table and inspected the side-by-side spearheads. Inadvertent or intentional? That was the question he and Popa needed to answer. In addition to the spearheads were several dozen tools and copper blades, along with horse and other animal bones, with well-preserved palisade posts propped against the table.

"We wrapped the spearheads in acid-free paper, of course. Every precaution has been taken, I assure you."

Lyle lifted his head and scanned the hilly terrain outside the fence, then gazed again at these remedial artifacts. The thought that a high civilization had thrived on this continent tens of thousands of years before this nomadic tribe was nothing short of ludicrous.

Rejoining Popa and his assistants, Lyle said, "What do the timbers tell you?"

"They confirm the climate was cool and dry in those times. Not a Roman Climate Optimum . . . probably accounts for why these people had to move so frequently."

"Human remains?"

They were looking at him oddly, and Lyle realized he was so chilled he'd been hopping from one foot to the other like a dancing bear.

"We haven't located their burial site yet. Nearby, I suspect. We're too busy with the fortress, but we discovered a pit with broken bones, stones, and horsehide remnants."

"Bone grease."

"Meaning this was a more permanent encampment than we first thought."

Lyle said, "My eye test tells me the spearheads were intentional."

"As does mine," said Popa. "How soon do you think you can run the algorithm after we've mapped the metal distribution?"

"A week, including blinds and quality control."

"Excellent. We'll have the data in a month, sooner perhaps. Will you have dinner with us tonight?"

Lyle knew what hospitality entailed in this part of the world, meaning no expense would be spared and every second of the team's evening would be occupied with his entertainment and comfort. Considering they were unprepared for his visit, Lyle said, "When I return, I'll look forward to sharing a meal with you, but I plan to reach the Austrian border tonight. Just a quick trip to see the site and the spearheads, and to meet your team."

A relieved-looking Popa said, "If you insist. When you return, we'll bring food from Sarajevo that would be impossible to find in this little town."

"Any evidence of a connection to the Minoans or Mycenaeans?" asked Lyle.

"Nothing as yet, though contact makes sense considering their proximity and periods of influence."

"You're sure they're not renegade Mycenaeans?"

"Sure? As you know, we must be careful with that word. I'm cautiously confident that our tribe is distinct from the Aegean and Ionian tribes. As to influence, that's another matter. Our people were nomadic, and linked by strong outpost-towns like this one, not builders of cities like Troy or Pylos."

Or as Lyle's mother might have said, Edoras rather than Minas Tirith dwellers.

After Popa had given him a tour of the fortress and surrounding area, Lyle examined the spearheads again, the eye test not often contradicted by analytical data or his algorithm, trying to put himself in the mind of the maker based on what he observed and what he knew of this tribe and the times. Promising, more than promising, he told himself. Data was one thing, but seeing the spearheads and fortress for himself was an altogether different experience.

As he was preparing to embark, Josip sought him out and shook his hand, saying, "It's an honor to meet you, Dr. Stuart."

The same way Lyle had felt when he met Katrivesis, until he began working with the man.

"I've read your work on the Nis Neanderthals."

If he was going to get to the Austrian border before midnight, he didn't have much time for the young researcher. Daunting mountains to negotiate before he exited Bosnia-Herzegovina, and he didn't want to be tired on those narrow switchbacks.

"When I return, we'll have a long talk, but I have to get my car to the road before it's too dark to see the rocks and holes."

No sooner had Lyle separated himself from Josip than Popa and Eva approached, with Popa carrying a bottle and Eva four cups.

"You must please share a drink with us, Dr. Stuart," said Popa.

As there was no declining without hurting the man's feelings, Lyle sat on the cold ground in a cold wind with the three expeditioners as Popa poured purple liquid into their cups.

Lyle was exactly where he wanted to be, in the environment he loved, a *locus amoenus* that most would consider a *locus purgatorius*. He was doubly encouraged after meeting Popa and hearing from the man but, given that he was ill equipped and unprepared, the sooner he returned to Oxford, the sooner he could return to the site. On the other hand, now that his sleuthing was over, a day or two to inspect the Roman ruins in Mainz and taste Russell's heavenly liver sounded better than a mad dash to the coast.

"Hardly suitable vessels for *blatina*, but we shall make do this time. To our colleague and friend, Dr. Stuart," Popa said, raising his cup, with Josip and Eva joining him.

"And to the intrepid Lido expedition," said Lyle, lifting his own cup. Noticing the look Eva was giving him, all the more reason to return to the road as soon as courtesy permitted.

Knowing Lyle had a long drive ahead of him, Popa didn't press him to consume more than the toasts. The expedition's leader had prepared a bag of bread and cheese for the journey, and Lyle was thrilled to get back inside the car, as even the two shirts he was wearing beneath his jacket hadn't kept him from being chilled by the cold wind.

Before leaving the site, he posted several photographs and some observations to the Archaeology Department page.

The Spider seemed to be intact, and when an exhausted Lyle

laid down on his hotel bed several hours later than he'd hoped, he was still preoccupied with weapons of war and the people that had produced them, what he'd seen at Lido, what he hoped Popa's analytical data and his own algorithm would prove, that the spearheads were intentional bronze.

PART III

Devastations

JANUARY 16, 2017

☻-☻-☻

Heidelberg & Mainz

A T THE HOTEL on his way to Lido, Lyle had read a recent issue of *Archaeology Today* that contained an interview with a German woman named Karine Feuer, who was the great-granddaughter of Pepin Hermann, the Heidelberg professor who had authored *Geology, Geography, and Climatology of Upper Paleolithic Europe,* and who was still respected as a groundbreaking paleogeologist. Though an interest piece rather than a substantive article, Feuer stated that her family possessed Hermann's research papers.

Ever since Lyle had examined Hermann's book in the lab, he'd had questions about how much of the cartography was based on evidence versus informed speculation, a distinction not as well documented in Hermann's time. Might this woman share Hermann's papers with Lyle to help answer these questions?

While modern paleogeologists had vastly more investigatory resources at their disposal than had Hermann, most modern researchers had a narrower focus than Hermann's panoramic view of Europe and, as many had built on the foundation Hermann had established, Lyle hoped he could learn something by going back to the source and testing that man's scholarship—information that would aid in his research projects, though in the back of his mind was a fascination with the congruency between the maps he'd examined in the lab.

Feuer had been identified as the owner of a restaurant in Heidelberg, along the route north to Mainz. Lyle had secured a late supper reservation at the *Café Marseille*—and lucky to get it according to the hotel concierge—but he needed something to eat before then. Perhaps he could speak to Feuer or, if she wasn't in, he could leave his card.

As he was getting ready to leave the car in Heidelberg, he received a matter-of-fact message from Andrea Fitzgerald informing him she'd identified two first-year students to do the work Gorsey was supposed to have done. Leave it to Andrea to add insult to injury.

The restaurant's floor, walls, and peaked ceiling, even the elaborate cuckoo clock, were constructed of dark wood, as was everything in the dining room except the fieldstone fireplace.

It was early for lunch, with only a handful of customers. After being seated next to a roaring fire, he removed his jacket and set out several artifacts Popa had sent home with him.

"*Guten tag*," said a young waitress in traditional dress, with cheeks as red as ripe apples.

Looking up, Lyle asked, "Do you speak English?"

"Oh, yes, we all do. It's a requirement. We have many guests from Britain, Canada, and America."

She introduced herself as Marthe, and said, "Do you teach at the University?"

"Oxford. I'm over for a few days. In Mainz, actually."

Looking down at the artifacts, she said, "Are they German?"

"Bosnia-Herzegovina, a site I'm studying."

"Are you an archaeologist?"

"A prehistoric archaeologist. Some call us paleoarchaeologists."

"My mother's great-great-grandfather was a paleogeologist. He taught at the University."

"I often work with paleogeologists. We consult them when we need geological information for the time periods we're studying, and I've heard about Dr. Hermann. Is your grandmother here by any chance?"

"She is. Would you care to speak with her?"

"Tell her I would be grateful if she can spare the time."

Marthe said, "I'm sure you're hungry, and we have the best wiener schnitzel in Heidelberg. My grandmother's recipe. Would you care to start with a Vetter Alt?"

"Is that beer?"

"Delicious beer."

"Perhaps . . . not too large, though. And I'll have a small portion of your wiener schnitzel, if I may."

After Marthe left the table, Lyle looked out the large window at the bridge over the River Neckar, with the University on the opposite side, the snow falling making him glad he and the Spider were almost back to Mainz.

The woman who returned with his beer, trim and in her fifties or early sixties, was dressed in a dark gray frock. She had a candid face, and her yellow-gray hair was tied back in a tight bun.

Taking the seat next to Lyle, she said, "I'm Karine Feuer. My granddaughter said you're a paleoarchaeologist."

"You must be proud of Marthe . . . so friendly and attentive."

"I'm very proud of her. She's studying to be a lawyer."

"Oh-oh."

"As our dear Goethe said, the profession that makes right and wrong similar," observed Karine.

"Marthe told me your great-grandfather was a paleogeologist. In those days, such men were breaking new ground."

"So I've been told."

"The beer is delicious."

"It's popular with our guests. I'm glad you like it."

"I'm Lyle Stuart. I teach at Oxford."

"Are you on holiday?"

"I am now. I just finished an . . . assignment."

"Involving these tools?"

"Not exactly. I don't mean to be cryptic. The assignment wasn't successful, so I decided on a few days recreation."

"I'm glad you chose to visit us, Professor Stuart."

"Lyle will do. I came here because I read your interview in *Archaeology Today.* May I ask some questions about Dr. Hermann?"

"Gladly. May I examine your artifacts? I must have inherited my interest in ancient history from my great-grandfather."

"These are remedial tools, and they would have looked and worked better when they were made. You must be proud of him."

"Of whom?"

"Dr. Hermann."

An odd expression took hold of her handsome face. "I was careful not to say that in the interview."

Lyle said, "I'd like to hear more about Dr. Hermann. To be honest, I'm hoping you'd consider sharing his papers with me."

"Why are you so interested in ninety-year-old research?"

"When I examined Dr. Hermann's book, I wondered where he drew the line between evidence and speculation, as that wasn't clear."

"Is that all?" she asked.

Lyle cast sidelong glances at adjacent tables to make sure no one was listening to their conversation. "That isn't all, though I'd like to keep this between the two of us. I'm intrigued by the congruency . . . similarities between Dr. Hermann's maps of the Europe of forty thousand years ago and a famous fantasy story."

Unexpected vigor shone in Karine's eyes, though she didn't immediately speak, as if she were pondering something. "My grandmother told me a story numerous times because she knew I enjoyed hearing it. Though her father was surly and contentious, when he bothered to speak to his family, he came home from the University one night and told them about an English writer who had interviewed him that day."

She must have noticed Lyle's consternation, because she said, "May I continue? . . . This writer had told him he was doing research, and had inquired about periods one hundred thousand to ten thousand years ago when Europe could have supported human life, even an advanced civilization . . . Have I surprised you?"

"Please go on."

"The Englishman asked about favorable geologic periods, plants and animals, about a land bridge between Europe and Britain, and about a north to south mountain range grander than our Alpine mountains. Great-grandfather made a joke of it and disparaged the man, but grandmother had been amazed at hearing her father talk at such length about anything, and by the idea of such an ancient civilization. She told me she had asked her father if such an idea was possible, and his answer hadn't been kind. I sometimes wonder how a person as generous and gentle as my grandmother could have come from such a brute, and I suppose the answer is he didn't have much to do with raising her. Or perhaps our outlook is more of a choice than psychologists and biologists tell us it is."

"You never knew your great-grandfather?"

The light had gone out of her eyes. "The Nazis didn't tolerate strong and frank opinions, not that his views were any more humane than theirs. Apparently, he had sour words for Hitler's crowd, too. One day in nineteen thirty-six, he didn't return from the University, and the family never learned what happened to him."

Lyle said, "In those days, vicious ideas were on the march."

"And these days, eugenics, euthanasia, population control are accepted, rationalized, psychologized. Children represented as enemies of the environment. Humanism reduced to how man may serve the economy, or the state."

"Are you a philosopher?"

"A student of what's going on, what I see, hear, and read every day. We bury these utopian ideas after thousands ... millions are murdered, but they claw their way out again like ... zombies."

"I haven't experienced what you describe, and I've been all over the world," Lyle said to her.

"Does a fish know it's immersed in water? But you came here for a meal, and you receive a lecture."

"Perhaps I'm due for one, after subjecting my students to so many."

"The ideologies that ravaged the world in my great-grandfather's time are alive and well, Professor Stuart, minus the *Sieg Heils.*

"I doubt I would have remembered my grandmother's story if not for a book I'd read years later, and a map in that book that suggested much the same thing—an advanced civilization, millennia before any known civilizations, in a land much like Europe, with a great north-south mountain range, and connected to a land like Britain. Undoubtedly, the book you read. I was astonished, and ever since I've been curious what an archaeologist would make of it."

Though a month earlier, he'd have been more circumspect, especially with a stranger, it seemed as if everything was conspiring to force this bizarre idea on him, and his natural instinct was to push back. "*This* archaeologist hasn't seen a shred of evidence to support the existence of such a civilization. Do you remember the English writer's name?"

"My grandmother told me, but that was so long ago."

"Hill?"

"Yes, perhaps."

"Even if the English writer who visited your great-grandfather was the author of the story you read, that doesn't prove it's historical."

"Who wouldn't want to believe such a civilization could have existed? Terrible things happened in that world, but there were people of virtue, too, fish that knew they swam in dirty water and were determined to do something about it. You admitted you came here because you were intrigued by the similarities."

Pointing to the Lido artifacts on the table, Lyle said, "These simple tools are more advanced than anything we have from forty thousand years ago."

"Here's your meal. Would you care for another glass of beer?"

"I'd better not. I have a late supper at the Café Marseille in Mainz."

"I've dined there. You're in for a treat."

Karine's story was independent evidence that as early as the nineteen-thirties John Hill had actively sought corroboration of what he'd learned in translating the manuscript, and, in a matter of minutes, she had sensed his conflicted thoughts, whereas it had taken him weeks to recognize it.

Marthe tried to prevent him from paying for his meal, but Lyle insisted on taking care of everything except the beer. Karine met him at the door, where Lyle said, "If I told you I knew everything that happened forty thousand years ago, I'd be a liar, or a fool."

"I hope you're not saying that to make me feel better."

"I had a lovely meal, and I enjoyed our conversation. Archaeologists unpack a fraction of the history they study, and the further they try to go with it, the thinner the limb they're on."

"I would be happy to let you examine my great-grandfather's research . . . Who knows where it might lead?"

As Lyle fired up the Spider under a clearing sky, he went for his sunglasses in the glove compartment and an envelope tumbled out. He'd been in a rush when he had checked out of the hotel in Mainz and had stashed a letter they'd given him in the compartment. Though he was tempted to stow it away again, he tore the envelope open and discovered there were two letters, with the outer envelope containing a communication from Sam and Beatrice, and the one in the inner blue envelope being Noel Dekeyser's resignation from the Order.

Sam had weighed in first.

> *I wanted something in Dekeyser's own words, so I pried this out of Henry. The old bird didn't want me to see it, probably because it doesn't reflect well on his Brother Gregory, but I've pried pearls out of tighter clams than our uncle. Not that it will bring Dekeyser back from the dead, if he's taken that door.*

Below Sam's thoughts were Beatrice's observations, keyed to Dekeyser's statements in his letter to Abbot Henry.

Dear Henry:

[BEATRICE: Not Father Abbot, or Abbot Henry.]

> *I am resigning from the Order and will have departed when you receive this. For some time, I have felt compelled to seek new fields, where fresh perspectives will be received with openness.*

[BEATRICE: The Order is cramped and narrow.]

> *Pardon my directness, though my years with the Order oblige me to speak frankly, with the hope that positive change will come of it.*

[BEATRICE: Reeking condescension.]

> *When I joined the Order, I judged these were fertile grounds for the infusion of modern psychological principles, but I have been discouraged by the resistance to new ideas. Too many rabbits and caretakers. With competent marketing, thousands would come to see the thing you hide in your vault, and the money could be used to modernize the building and beautify the grounds.*

[BEATRICE: "Why was this oil not sold for three hundred days wages and given to the poor?"]

> *If you desire to contact me, I will be working at the Folkestone Regional Psychiatric Clinic.*
>
> *Sincerely,*
>
> *Noel Dekeyser*

[BEATRICE: Could his dramatic departure from the Order and disappearance in Mainz have been grand statements, like the magician vanishing at the end of a performance?]

This was another side of the warm, engaging Beatrice, the cold-eyed analyst pursuing truth based on the evidence. The question remained, had Dekeyser been killed, or had his vanishing been self-orchestrated?

Lyle's analytical and intuitive skills had served him well as an archaeologist, so how could he ignore the mounting evidence in the matter of the manuscript? If he were at an archaeological site, he would retrieve his notebooks and log everything he had learned. Why wouldn't he do the same in this matter?

There were good reasons to leave Mainz, after dinner at the Café Marseilles and an inspection of the Roman ruins. That way, he could stay focused on Lido and what the University expected of him, too.

On the other side of the ledger: Caroline Desrosier was Noel Dekeyser's cousin. Dekeyser had come to the Sorbonne subsequent to a visit from Desrosier. The Alembert archive, where Desrosier worked and Dekeyser once worked, contained an Autochrome plate of a goblet that suggested John Hill could read the runes, and who else could this Hill be, other than that famous linguist? Dekeyser had vanished without a trace in Mainz, vanished so definitively that not even Sam could locate him. Lyle had established a connection—most likely the manuscript—between Agnes CurLio, Adler Alembert, and John Hill. And there was that seamless container that he knew in his heart wasn't a modern invention.

His sober-minded uncle had taken the matter seriously and had given credence to John Hill's story.

Hill himself had traveled to Heidelberg to consult with Hermann, and probably to Paris to meet with Alembert. For all Lyle knew, Hill could have consulted others too. The meeting with Karine had proven that Hill was not just researching a story, but events that man believed had really occurred.

The nagging thought he hadn't been able to dismiss: what if Hill, in his famous story, hadn't revealed everything contained in the manuscript, had held something back, as Lyle's uncle had suggested at the monastery? If someone suspected this, mightn't he want to get his hands on the manuscript and employ the modern diagnostics Hill could never have imagined to translate the entire contents?

There would have been no Nis Neanderthals or Lido for Lyle without his attachment to John Hill's story. He didn't know if anything in the manuscript was true, but from now on he was going to act as if it were, as John Hill had done.

From now on? Hadn't he come to a dead end, such a dead end that not even Sam's prodigious resources could eke out any more information? Sam, Beatrice, and his uncle wanted him back in Oxford. Even Russell had told him he'd done his duty and should return to his work.

More than at any time since he'd embarked on this confusing rota of people and places, Lyle missed Beatrice, her counsel, and especially her reassuring presence. The good news was that he was almost back to Mainz, though what he would do about the manuscript when he arrived was a mystery. First things first, he told himself: a shower, change of clothes, and a good meal.

At the Café Marseille, Lyle was shown to a corner table, a red rose in a vase on the immaculate white tablecloth. Overhead lamps like palm fronds gave the cream-colored ceiling and walls a warm glow. Separated by arched doorways, the elegant dining areas featured red leather booths and chairs, and gold-rimmed green plates with a cursive "CM" in the center.

Several of the men Lyle passed in an adjacent dining area were attired in black tie, causing him to feel underdressed in the gray wool lecture jacket he'd brought with him on the trip.

He was trying to push the decision he had made in Heidelberg out of his mind so he could enjoy this meal to the fullest, but it wasn't easy. Looking up from the wine list and expecting to see his waiter, Lyle observed a young man in a tradesman's blue uniform, carrying a tool case, approaching from the entrance, which made him wonder if there was a problem in the kitchen.

Young, clean-shaven, short, dark hair, big dark eyes, and small ears.

Something furtive about this man, and apparently Lyle wasn't the only person who concluded this, as a man at the next table jumped to his feet and challenged the tradesman.

The next few seconds were a jumble of memories and sensations, hard to piece together for the rest of his life. The tradesman either was tripped by the man at the next table or he stumbled. More than one voice called out in words Lyle could never remember. The tradesman was on the floor a few feet away from him, his face turned away from Lyle. The man at the next table might have been hovering over the tradesman, or touching him, or maybe not. A loud blast, a split second of cacophonous sound, followed by something striking his face.

Blackness. Buzzing, as if he were inside a million-bee hive. As if he were buried and trying to discern what was going on aboveground.

For how long? Minutes, hours, days?

Music . . . familiar . . . da da da da da . . . dadadadada went the piano.

He heard a voice: "Try to open your eyes. Good, what do you see? You don't have to talk if you don't want to."

The man was speaking to him in accented English. Wearing a white coat. Was Lyle at a site? Had he been hurt at an excavation?

The next time he opened his eyes, the white-coated man was shining a pencil-light into his eye. "Can you see me, Lyle? Good. Here are Sam and Beatrice."

Lyle's range of vision, up till then narrowed to the man with the light, expanded to encompass his brother and Beatrice, who were trying to disguise their distress.

"Where am I?"

"Hospital . . . Mainz."

"What do you remember?" the doctor asked Lyle.

"What?"

"Your last memory."

He knew memories were supposed to be linear, but his all seemed to be jumbled, like rice in a jar on someone's shelf.

"The restaurant. A bomb, or something. Someone yelling the place down . . . a woman, I think."

Beatrice reached down and caressed his cheek. Even in his addled state, he sensed her ambivalence, as if something were holding her back.

Sam said, "When he detonated the bomb, it lifted the table, and the tabletop slammed into you."

"Thank God no one was killed," said Lyle.

The look Beatrice gave Sam told him he was wrong.

"How many?"

"Let's talk about how you are feeling," said the doctor.

"How many dead?"

"Six," said Sam.

Lyle closed his eyes, though he quickly opened them again and said, "My arms and legs?"

"Attached and functioning," Sam said, with a reassuring earnestness.

"What's wrong with me?"

Sam looked at the doctor, who said, "Bomb confetti in your legs, most of it out now; a broken rib; concussion that seems to be subsiding; broken nose; bruises on your face. The table protected you. You're lucky."

"That's all?"

"Isn't that enough?" said Beatrice.

"Tell us what you remember?" Sam said.

"The tradesman coming toward me, falling down. A loud noise."

"Did you recognize the man?"

The doctor gripped Sam's shoulder but Lyle's brother wasn't paying any attention to the cue.

"No . . . a stranger."

"Sure?"

"He can't be sure of anything yet," warned the doctor. "And his pulse is racing, that's *gegentherapeutische* for concussions."

"Counter-therapeutic," Beatrice translated for Sam.

Lyle said, "I don't think I know him. Why?"

"The police are trying to decide if this was terrorism or a targeted killing."

Lyle said, "If someone was targeted, why not use a gun or knife, and why in a public place? Was the bomber killed?"

"Yes," Sam answered.

The doctor stepped between Sam and Lyle and said, "He's going to sleep now."

Lyle didn't feel sleepy when the trio left the room, but within minutes he was out cold. This time he dreamed, and in his dream his mother was reading to him: *That was how Beakie felt, as if he had been in deep water for too long. But how was he supposed to get to the surface?*

When he awoke, the room was as dark as deep water, and he was alone, worried that someone would come in while he was attached to this equipment and finish him off. The next time he awoke, Sam and Beatrice were there with the doctor, and light was filtering in through the window.

"Your vital signs are improving," said the doctor.

"Then why do my face and legs hurt so much?"

"Can I give you something for the pain?"

Sam said, "I don't want him falling asleep yet. Who knew you had a reservation at the restaurant?"

"Just the hotel concierge, and the Café, unless they told someone else. I didn't mention it to anyone." As soon as he said this, Lyle remembered that he had told Karine about his reservation, but how could she be connected to the attack, as it was Lyle who had sought her out?

"The Algerian with the bomb worked at the hotel. Why did you choose that restaurant?"

"For the liver, like Mum used to make. Russell recommended it, but he didn't know I was going there."

Sam said, "The man who went after the bomber was a Mainz detective. He's dead."

"He saved my life, didn't he?"

"Probably. Was it a coincidence the bomber worked at the hotel where you were staying?" Sam crossed the room and peered out the window, his profile reminding Lyle of their father. He remembered his father reading to him about ancient Greece, Rome, Persia. His father had sold engineering textbooks in Eastern Europe and he hadn't returned from one such trip when Lyle was eight.

"We're making arrangements to take you home," Beatrice said.

"Just throw my suitcase in the boot and roll me into the back seat."

"If only it were that easy," she said. "You're not well yet, and the police want to talk to you."

"Tell them to talk to Sam. He knows more than me."

"They have, twice," she said.

"I'm glad you're here," he said to Beatrice, emotion welling up inside him.

"Where else would you expect me to be?"

"Your classes . . ."

Beatrice shook her head. "You don't get it, do you?"

"I missed out on the liver," Lyle said to her.

She tried to smile. "I'll learn how to prepare it."

Having rejoined them, Sam said, "Who did you meet when you were in Bosnia, and what did you talk about?"

"Popa and his team. We talked about spearheads."

"Nothing about the artifact or the restaurant?"

"Not a word." Lyle was afraid to look at Beatrice when he said, "I'm going to talk to Sangal and Russell again before I leave Mainz."

Sam erupted. "The hell you are."

Lyle remembered an excavation when he was a doctoral candidate, where Katrivesis had directed his students to pack their things and prepare for departure, but Lyle had held out, telling Katrivesis and anyone who would listen that they were on the verge of a breakthrough. Katrivesis had won out, insofar as the expedition had departed the site, but Lyle had won the opinion battle, and by the time they landed at Heathrow he was the expedition's moral leader. Katrivesis was well aware of this and had made Lyle's life miserable for the next year. Since then, Lyle wasn't going to be wrenched out of any expedition until he was good and ready.

"You talked to Sangal and Russell. What more do you expect to learn?"

"Mainz was the last place Dekeyser was known to have been before he vanished. I almost *vanished* here too. I've been excavating with a spoon—I'm trading it in for an axe and shovel. I've decided, Sam, and I've gotten all my bad luck out of the way."

"Bollocks, that's not how it works," Sam snapped.

"He can't travel for a few days after he's discharged from the hospital, and we'll want to examine him again before he leaves town."

"Thanks for nothing, doc," said Sam.

"That's settled then," Lyle said. "You might be surprised at what they tell me after this."

"Get this through your thick skull," Beatrice interrupted, "We don't care what they tell you, or what they say about the . . . you know what."

That was enough for the doctor, who shooed Beatrice and Sam out of the room and closed the door. A few minutes later, Lyle detached his wires, crawled out of bed, suppressed a groan that came out in a whispered "ooh," and walked to the wall mirror, taking stock of how things were working as he went. Pain, stiffness, weakness, wondering if he'd make it back to the bed without collapsing.

He didn't recognize the man in the mirror: the swollen, beetred face that hadn't been shaved, the section of scalp above an ear that was covered with a bandage the size of an American silver dollar. He looked hideous, like a clown in motley, and felt shaken to the core. He thought of how his namesake had been stabbed with more than an ordinary blade, and how Frodo had responded with resolution, not retreat.

"What are you doing?" a commanding voice said.

A second nurse followed, and each took an arm to lead him back to bed.

"Finding you on the floor won't get you out of here any sooner," the nurse told him.

Just a story, Lyle reminded himself after the nurses had gone, surprised at how deeply it was embedded in his psyche.

Resolution, not retreat.

JANUARY 22, 2017

☺-☺-☺

A Mother's Duty

O N LYLE'S LAST DAY in the hospital, he was eager to leave but, as he still had a concussion test to undergo that afternoon, he wouldn't be discharged until later in the day.

The decision he had made to double down on the search for the manuscript seemed years ago, and irrelevant in the wake of what he had experienced since. No matter what he had said to Sam about his intention to see Sangal and Russell again, wasn't the only rational thing to go home?

Resolution, not retreat. What he had said to himself in the mirror, but this was real life, and the gritty side of it.

These days, events rocketed through and across media. In the few days he'd been cleared to communicate with the outside world, Lyle had turned down numerous interview requests. As for social and business media, he had limited his posts to informing his network that he was on the mend, hoping this would deflect questions he didn't want to answer.

While he had been receiving therapy on a different floor, some-one—Beatrice, no doubt—had left several archaeological journals and his mother's manuscript on the bedside table.

Lyle hadn't read a word of her story since that day in his uncle's office. He ardently desired to hear his mother's voice again in the words of the story. At the same time, he couldn't think of her without remembering those last days—that last night.

What should he do? Give the manuscript to Beatrice and ask her to dispose of it? Would she do it? Try to read it, maybe exorcise those bad memories? Was he strong enough?

It's just a story, he told himself. Not Gloria Stuart. Not even her voice.

He began reading the story, following Beakie the turtle on his decades-long journey after exile from a tribe that thought he had contagious shell sickness.

He was surprised by how the story drew him in, and not just because it had been composed by his mother.

Along the way, Beakie kept hearing about a mighty animal named *zzan Fiel*, who Beakie sought to give him answers to his questions. Was zzan Fiel a myth? A creature turtles would be wise to avoid? A long-dead hero whose legend persisted?

Lyle recognized a Frodo Baggins-like quality in Beakie, and why wouldn't he, considering that his mother had composed the story. Something of his mother too, in how Beakie's sickness had separated him from other shells, and even Lyle's father in the way Beakie had left the tribe and never returned. Had she composed the story to make sense of her own world?

> The sneaker stood over Beakie, who could feel its nose touch the top of his shell.
>
> "What's your name?" the sneaker said.
>
> Beakie turned his head so he could see the sneaker better: an old animal with a long thin snout, and fur that was turning gray. "Beakie," the shell said, trying not to sound as frightened as he felt.
>
> "The letters on your shell," the sneaker said. "Do you belong to humans?"
>
> "Humans did it."
>
> "I'm called Tommie." The sneaker turned and crept toward the rock pile. Beakie noticed that Tommie was lame in one leg.

"When my mother saw I had a bad leg, she left me. I was nearly dead when the humans found me."

Beakie told himself he didn't have to worry about a pond for the white season, because he wouldn't be alive by then, now that he was in the clutches of this sneaker.

"What are you going to do with me?" Beakie said.

Tommie said, "Let me tell you something. I can't eat a thing at night. So don't be afraid. Come to my rock house."

The sneaker limped so badly that Beakie was able to keep up with it. Part of the rock pile had a stone ceiling. He tried to ignore the pile of bones, a pile twice Beakie's size. On the other side of this bone yard was an empty shell that Beakie first thought was just another stone, but now realized had once been a guest of Tommie's.

"Here we are," said the sneaker. "By the way, you don't have to pretend with me."

Lyle felt groggy. His eyes were heavy, his neck stiff. But he couldn't stop reading now.

"What am I pretending?" said Beakie.

"That you're an ordinary shell, when you aren't ordinary at all . . . Beakie. I should say, zzan Fiel. You see, I can read. Remember when I said there were letters on your shell? F-I-E-L, as plain as your face. You told me you escaped from humans, something a shell could never do, not in a million years.

"I want you to do something for me. I'm too old to hunt and I don't want to starve. I want you to bring animals to this den. I'll do the rest. Just bring them here."

"What makes you think a zzan would bring you food. That's not what zzans do."

Tommie's voice was angry when he said, "Now he tells me."

Making a purring sound, the sneaker walked a circle around Beakie. "The humans kept me in a cage, and when they took me out they put needles in me that made me sleep. When I woke up, I had bandages on my head. Do you know what they were doing to me, zzan Fiel, or Beakie, or whoever you are? Making me smarter, that's what. Cutting my head open and making me smarter. They taught me what letters mean, how to read letters that are put together, but my head always hurt."

"Does it still hurt?" Beakie asked Tommie.

"When I'm hungry," said the sneaker, "or angry. But they made me too smart. I watched them lock and unlock the cage, lock and unlock the window. Even ordinary sneakers are good at getting in and out of tight places, and I wasn't ordinary by the time they were finished with me. Not by a mile, old boy. I was sick and tired of being stuck with needles and having my head cut open. One night, after they had gone, I opened the cage and the window and escaped. That wasn't hard, but it was plenty hard when I had to find my own food. As for you, if you are just an ordinary shell, then I will eat you, and get something for all the time I've wasted."

Years after his mother's death, Lyle was experiencing something of her inner life, as if she were speaking to him, telling him things.

What Beakie's birth tribe had thought to be shell sickness were letters inscribed on his shell when Beakie was a yearling: "Fred Ribel," the words having weathered away over the years to **F i e l**.

"zzan Fiel," the little shell said, "tell us the story of the bounder and the flat log."

Beakie was surrounded by young shells, all resting on logs in the middle of the pond.

"Are you listening, zzan Fiel?"

How sleepy he was since he came here. Much of the time he sat on one of the logs, and most days shells came and asked him to tell stories.

Beakie could not have gone on now even if he wanted to. Just paddling around was all he could do anymore.

How beautiful the pond was, and this day, though the sun wasn't as warm, and the white season was approaching. He hadn't thought to prepare for the long sleep that was coming for the other shells, as something else awaited him this season.

"zzan Fiel," little Oleandrix piped up, "Are you going to tell it?"

A spunky little thing. He supposed he would have to tell the story, though a nap would be better. Now, how did it go? Yes, there was that bounder Rascal and happy days and sad days and the flat log that went on and on; that was the story they wanted.

In his memory, he could see Rascal as if it were yesterday.

Now, the whole tribe had gathered on the logs or nearby in the water.

Though he was very sleepy, he cleared his throat and said, "That day the grass was gold and the wind was sweet...Ambrosian—I called him Rascal . . ."

JANUARY 24 – 25, 2017

☺-☺-☺

Mainz

THE SWELLING HAD SUBSIDED; bruises were yellowing; his nose was straight enough; his legs still hurt, though not so he couldn't walk; and his head had stopped throbbing; still a persistent buzzing in one ear, though he'd gotten used to it and didn't notice unless he was in a quiet place or in bed at night.

Before he'd left the hospital, Lyle had been interviewed by the Federal Criminal Police, who gave him the impression they thought the bombing was an act of terrorism, or the brainstorm of a lunatic.

Lyle observed Sam making his way across the breakfast room, and when his brother arrived at the table, Lyle said, "Has Beatrice mentioned returning to Oxford?"

Sam shook his head. "She isn't going anywhere until she's sure you're on the mend. Even though the hotel's booked with a convention of duck lovers, she convinced them to give her the room next to yours. You're going through with these interviews?"

"I tried to walk away."

"After you were attacked . . ."

"There's no evidence I was the target."

"You have your opinion, I have mine."

"You can have an opinion, but you can't choose your facts."

"I'm not here to argue with you, Lyle. You're a stubborn son-ofabitch. I'm your brother, so I don't have a choice, but I don't know how Beatrice puts up with you. Where the hell's the coffee?"

Sam waved a hand at the waiter and pointed to his cup. He looked tired to Lyle, who wondered how much sleep his brother was getting.

"We dug into Desrosier's, Lourdes's, Sangal's, and Russell's affairs. I'm here to tell you what I learned."

"How did you get permission for all this?"

"Maybe I gave myself permission."

"Don't you answer to anyone?"

"Everyone answers to someone. The person I answer to gives me wide latitude, so long as I deliver the goods and don't embarrass him."

The waiter set a pot of coffee on the table and Lyle poured his brother a cup. Sam took several swallows before he said, "That's better . . . Beatrice and Henry are pestering me to keep you out of trouble, so if you insist on trying to find that manuscript, the least I can do is supply information about the principals. But first, something I just learned from the police. Seems the Algerian told the hotel concierge he knew you and asked to be informed if you made a reservation at the Café, a cock-and-bull story about wanting them to serve you a special bottle of wine. Who else have you met in Mainz besides Sangal and Russell?"

"No one, if you mean talking to them for more than a minute."

"No arguments with anyone in the hotel? No off-color comments a neurotic could have overheard and taken the wrong way?"

"Nothing like that."

"The police still think it's random terror, or someone with a fixation, but I'm not buying it."

"It doesn't make sense, Sam. The manuscript is the only thing that could provoke something like this, and I don't have it. I'm not even close to having it."

"Maybe you're closer than you think."

"I'm not running away."

Lyle felt as if his brother could see inside him . . . could see the fear, the competing voices, a far cry from the confidence he was trying to display.

Sam removed a notebook from the inside pocket of his jacket, opened it, and read: "Desrosier's forty-two, born in Normandy, father a teacher, mother a Communist Party organizer. Degree in political science from a small university in eastern France, worked for the French Communist Party until she split from the Party and her mother. When she was young, she was a careful mischief-maker, never caught in any police nets. A librarian in Mainz for almost a decade before moving to Paris. Never married. Any questions?"

"Keep going."

"Richard Lourdes is seventy-three. At the Sorbonne for almost thirty years. Spends lavishly on boyfriends. Not much left over when all the pipers are paid. He's not broke, but close to insolvency.

"Sangal's fifty-three, from a powerful Madras clan, studied in India before coming to Europe, a wife and two children back home, frequents high-priced prostitutes in Frankfurt and Heidelberg. We think his extended family is financing anti-Muslim paramilitary groups, though there's no evidence he's involved.

"Russell's an orphan, brought up at the Mortimer Russell Institute for Advanced Eugenics."

Lyle said, "Russell said he went to a private school that could accommodate his special needs."

"The Institute closed down in 1943. We only learned of the connection because Russell identified the Institute as his primary school on a university application. He's ninety-six, never married, been teaching at the University of Mainz since 1957. We found a 1923 news article about the Institute.

Few are aware of a modern two-story building an hour's drive from Plymouth, on the edge of Dartmoor Forest. The Mortimer Russell

Institute for Advanced Eugenics was built in 1918 and is staffed by a dozen researchers with specialties in neurology, pathology, eugenics, and psychology. Requests for interviews were denied by the director. A communication supplied to *The Times* states: 'The mission of the Mortimer Russell Institute for Advanced Eugenics is to improve the human race, mentally and physically, and to extend productive lives.' Interviewing residents in the vicinity of the Institute, *The Times* has learned that at least one child may be residing there.

"Probably the reason the child took Russell as his last name. The Institute ceased activity during World War II when eugenics got a bad name."

"They treat him like dirt at the university."

"If he's ninety-six and still putting up with it, then he's part of the problem."

Observing Sam pour another cup of coffee, Lyle told his brother about Russell's diet and the jars on his shelf.

"That's not the craziest diet I've come across," Sam said. "As for me, black coffee, steak, eggs, beer, and gin, for as long as I can. If tea and rice are the price of living to a hundred, you can have it."

Lyle said, "You don't think any of them are involved with Dekeyser's disappearance and the manuscript, do you?"

"There's nothing that suggests it."

"So, Desrosier being Dekeyser's cousin and having worked at the University of Mainz are coincidences?"

"We don't even know that Dekeyser and Desrosier knew they were related."

"She was holding something back," Lyle insisted.

"There's a lot of it about. Do you think Sangal wants you to know he pays for sex, or Lourdes wants his secret life known? Did Russell reveal why he hasn't had a promotion in sixty years? I could go further afield, others in Cognitive Studies, Remington, though I don't see any point in it."

Lyle said, "I feel like a voyeur."

"You get used to it in my business. After a while, it's no different than an accountant doing an audit. In fact, auditing how lifestyles compare to legal income is one of our markers, and we didn't see anything that raised alarms when it came to Desrosier, Lourdes, Sangal, or Russell. We have cybertechs who could drill deeper into their communications and connections, but I'm not ready to engage them . . . not yet."

"I'd like you to investigate another person," Lyle said. "Agnes CurLio."

"Who's she?"

"Someone connected to John Hill and Adler Alembert. I found her diary in Hill's archive."

"You still won't call that man by his real name. As I said, stubborn. You must think I'm looking for work."

"Just a quick search."

"Write her name in my notebook . . . here. Timeframe?"

"1932, when she was in England."

"If you feel like dinner, call me. Why couldn't you have gotten in trouble in Paris or Vienna?"

"You always said you lived a dull life."

"My business isn't all truth telling, if you haven't guessed," said Sam, as he left the table.

This comment reminded Lyle of how little he really knew about his brother. Sam had lived with a woman for five years, and Lyle had gone to dinner on one occasion with Sam and Fatemeh, though he couldn't remember why he'd been invited, or by whom—perhaps Sam's birthday. Lyle had only been with them a few minutes before he realized how different they were. Incompatible would have been the word if they hadn't been together for five years. Sam was quintessentially British, or pretended to be, while Fatemeh, ten years younger than Sam, possessed an incandescent personality.

No sooner had Lyle told her about his research than she had accused him of pillaging the historical treasures of her Syrian home and other Middle Eastern states, and she had persisted even after he'd explained that his geography was southeastern Europe.

All the while, a blithe Sam had sat mute with his several gin and tonics, neither correcting Fatemeh nor coming to Lyle's defense.

The evening couldn't have ended soon enough to suit Lyle, and when he learned that Sam and Fatemeh had separated, he was more surprised that they had ever come together, and then stayed together so long.

Shortly after Fatemeh's departure, Sam had embarked on a relationship with a television personality that had flamed out as suddenly as it had kindled, and if his brother had had any relationships after that, Lyle was unaware of them.

After sending his uncle a message that he hadn't found the manuscript but was collecting material for a thriller that would make both of them as famous as John le Carré, Lyle left the hotel and walked to the School for Cognitive Studies.

Gray light penetrated Russell's dirty glass window, and the old man's lamps were illuminated. Russell was writing in a compact notebook, or journal, and by the time he looked up, Lyle was already seated. Snapping the journal closed, Russell deposited it on top of the closest desk stack.

"I'm delighted to see you back on your feet, Dr. Stuart," said Russell, attempting to stand before Lyle waved him off. "Tell me you're feeling better."

"I can't complain. Have all my teeth, both eyes, and most of my wits."

"We live in an ugly world, but then, I've lived long enough to have seen this sort of thing before. Even so, it's appalling. Such misanthropic *Volk* seem to be everywhere these days."

Taking a seat, and feeling like a giant at Russell's small desk, Lyle said, "I thought of a few more questions about Noel Dekeyser, if you'd be so kind."

"I respect a determined man. Actually, I'm glad you came. I found an old article on Paleolithic fetishistic art, and I'd like you to have it." The man looked toward the stacks near the window, shook his head, and began fingering items in the nearest stack.

"Here it is."

"Can I help you, Professor?"

"Done it a million times," Russell said, pulling the binding edge of a magazine that was halfway down the stack. He had almost wriggled it out when the entire pile toppled off the desk and scattered on the floor.

"Goddamit to hell," erupted Russell, his face dark with blood.

Lyle lurched to his feet, doing his best to reassemble the material for the man; afterwards, sitting with the magazine Russell had been after in his lap.

"I hope you enjoy the article. You'll certainly remember how you acquired it, though my outburst was unpardonable. Even after all these years, I sometimes allow my limitations to get the best of me."

"Thank you for thinking of me, Professor. I wasn't completely candid with you the last time we met."

"Nor were you obliged to be."

"So, I'll tell you now we think Dekeyser made off with an ancient manuscript that resided at my uncle's monastery."

"I would never have taken that man for a thief," said a wide-eyed Russell.

"We don't know that for a fact. Problem is, both he and the manuscript have disappeared."

"Isn't this a job for the police?"

Should he say anything about Sam? "The police aren't convinced a serious crime was committed, so my uncle recruited me to assist him. He seems to think I can see through walls."

"Did he say that?" an amused Russell asked.

"Actually, he said I could see around corners."

"Your uncle thinks highly of you. And am I right to say he's an abbot, which speaks to your character as well as your intuition. What can you tell me about this manuscript?"

"A chronicle of a very ancient civilization."

"Where?"

"Here, on this continent." Lyle may have traded his spoon for a shovel, but he knew better than to say a word about Atlantis.

"Have you seen this manuscript?"

"No, but my uncle has, and I've seen the container where it was kept for . . . a long time."

"Please tell me about this container."

Lyle had revealed much more than he'd intended, and not in return for anything tangible about Dekeyser. "A kind of metal, and quite secure for something that old. The thief left it behind. Dr. Russell, can you think of anything at all that might help me find Dekeyser?"

"Not Dekeyser . . . no . . ."

"But?"

"All I have is nonsense, but since this nonsense is connected to you, I'll speak of it. I warn you not to take it seriously, but I feel compelled—that's not too strong a word—to share everything I have with you. I have a client at the University clinic where I volunteer who suggested to me that the Russians were behind the café bombing. It's a crazy notion, and he's inclined to paranoia, but he's Russian himself and his family is well connected."

"Why would the Russians support a terror attack?"

"Who knows? They have motives we can't fathom."

Like protecting the manuscript, if they have it, and if they conclude I'm a threat, Lyle said to himself. As if he were a threat to the Russians, and as if they'd take such extreme measures to eliminate him when there were far easier ways to accomplish it.

"Did this Russian provide any details?"

"Something to do with their consulate in Mainz where my client works. He isn't the most coherent fellow, especially when he's down a rabbit hole. If I went to the police with this, they would pretend to take notes, and dispatch this senile old man as soon as possible."

"Can you give me his name?"

"I'm afraid not—client confidentiality. I've said too much already, but I trust your discretion, and if anyone deserves to hear it, it's you, after what you've suffered. The motives of people who do such things are murky. People killed or wounded in such attacks are collateral damage, or, psychologically speaking, there can be a transference of grievances, real or imagined, onto the victims."

"Is your client insane?"

"That's an elastic term. In some things, he's quite lucid, and he has a responsible position at the consulate. He drinks too much, and that contributes to his phobias and paranoia."

Lyle said, "You've not heard anything from Dekeyser since the day he stopped coming to work?"

"Not a word."

"And he never mentioned the manuscript?"

"Never a word about it. The closest we came was our discussion about artifacts, and I don't recall Noel asking a single question that could be connected to your uncle's manuscript."

On his way out of the office, Lyle stopped in the doorway. "Where did you acquire the skeleton, Professor?"

"It was decades ago. A small museum in Nuremberg that was closing its doors. 'Premeditation of death is premeditation of freedom,' or so said Montaigne. I call this fellow Santini. As you may know, that means great one, or holy one, though for all I know he may have been a scoundrel."

Lyle's walk from Russell's to Sangal's office tired him out, or maybe it was going without the rest he required since the bombing. This time, Sangal was waiting for him, and welcomed Lyle into his office, saying, "You are looking remarkably healthy for your ... ah ..."

"I'm coming along," though he wasn't sure what that meant, as his ears were ringing and a pulsing pain had commenced in his thigh.

"I read that you were protected by a table," said an eager Sangal.

"That's right, though the table did its share of damage."

"You've been speaking with our *Gerontion* again?"

"Who?"

"A pet name for Russell, bestowed by our resident poet, Dr. Moeller. Not disparaging, I assure you," Sangal said, unconvincingly.

Lyle then related what he had told Russell about Dekeyser and the artifact, after which Sangal said, "Dekeyser learned my family had influence in India and asked if they were collectors. That was several weeks before he . . . disappeared. I remember he looked anxious, nervous. You didn't tell me about the artifact the last time we talked. I told him my people are only interested in Hindu artifacts. You see, they have more religious vigor than I do."

"He was anxious?"

"He impressed me as being anxious, though he didn't say anything to suggest a clinical disorder."

"Do you know anyone else with an interest in fine art or artifacts?"

"Do I? Well, there's a woman in Heidelberg who is a motivated collector, but I didn't give her name to Dekeyser."

"Is there anything he told you that might help me locate him? A city he mentioned? A person?"

"Nothing. I tell you, the man was a cipher. What makes you think you can find him, or the thing you're after? You are an archaeologist, not a detective, nor do you have a detective's resources. Don't tell me you haven't considered this."

Sangal had treated him as an annoyance from the moment they met, so on his way to the door Lyle, frustrated, went for the axe.

"What kept Russell from being promoted? He's been here sixty years, and he's still an assistant."

As if Lyle's words were a personal aspersion, Sangal said, "This is *our* University of Mainz, not *your* Oxford, Professor Stuart. Russell is perfectly happy with his status here, whatever you may think."

Returning to his hotel, Lyle felt like crawling into bed. Not yet recovered from the explosion, even those few hours of exertion had worn him out and amplified the symptoms, but no sooner had he untied one shoe than he heard a loud knock.

When Lyle opened the door, the man said, "I must speak to you."

Tall, solid looking, with sharp-edged features and thick, dark hair, wearing an ankle-length greatcoat, the visitor said, "Leonidas Romanov. I work at the Russian consulate."

Lyle's heart started rattling.

"I must tell you something. About the thing you're looking for."

How could this not be the man Russell had told him about? "How did you find me?"

The man closed the door. "The thing you are seeking is in the consulate, but for not much longer. They'll be moving it to Moscow soon. They know you're after it, that's why they tried to kill you."

"I don't believe you," Lyle said. "They could have eliminated me with a lot less bother and publicity. I can't get into the consulate, and it's protected from searches, even if the police believed me."

"I can get you in. I'm deputy director of security. I have my reasons for wanting you to have this thing, but two nights from now it will go to Russia."

Striving to reconcile the man's words and mannerisms with the person Russell had described earlier that day, Lyle said, "Why are you doing this?"

"Does it matter? I have what you want, and I am offering to give it to you. I will need to accompany you, after spreading the story that you are bringing *me* something of value."

"After what I went through at the café, that isn't good enough."

"You are willing to risk losing it?"

"Unless I'm convinced you have it, and there's a good reason for your being here."

The man took a step toward the door, and his hand was on the knob before he said, "My brother is a Russian monk. When I told him what we had at the consulate, and that it had been stolen from a monastery, he insisted I return it. He protected me when I was a boy, and he's never asked a thing of me . . . until now. I promised him I would do this, no matter the cost."

Since Lyle had no idea where the manuscript was being kept, and couldn't recover it even if he'd known it was in the consulate, why would Romanov reveal this to him unless he was sincere? Or insane—a diagnosis Russell had danced around.

"Do you have a card?" Lyle asked the man.

Romanov laughed loudly. "In my business?"

"Then, tell me about the manuscript."

"I've told you enough already. If you don't come, I will inform my brother that I did all I could. This time of year, it's dark by six, when the consulate dines. You will ask for me at the delivery gate, and I will escort you inside."

"What will your people do when they learn the manuscript is gone?"

"I have conceived a story they will be only too eager to believe, because it involves someone they already detest. What happened to your face?"

Why would Romanov ask him this question if the Russians were behind the bombing? "I was run over by a poodle."

His hand still on the knob, Romanov muttered something in Russian, opened the door and, as he was closing it, Lyle called out, "Six p.m."

Sitting on the bed, Lyle tried to make sense of what he'd heard from Russell and from this man. On the surface, everything added up to the artifact being inside the Russian consulate—Dekeyser's disappearance, Russell's story, Romanov's offer. On the other hand, Lyle had barely survived a bomb, and going inside the consulate was tantamount to being on Russian soil. Though he had told the man he would meet him, Lyle hadn't made a final decision. How could he, in his condition and with all that had happened?

He had already decided he wouldn't tell Beatrice or Sam about meeting Romanov, because in his weakened and vulnerable state they'd surely find a way to prevent him. Was there a chance he might accomplish what his uncle had sent him to do, and what both he and Sam had concluded was impossible?

Despite his fatigue, his mind was too active for sleep, so he sat at the desk and began paging through the magazine Russell had given him.

Out fell the journal Russell had been writing in when Lyle arrived at the office, so small and slim it would fit inside a coat pocket. Most of the pages were full of capital and lower case letters, lines, and arrows, no doubt analogs related to Russell's psychology research, the first page dated 1951.

The secret language inscribed on these pages intrigued him. Was this a convention another psychologist would immediately recognize? When he closed the journal, he told himself he'd have to return it to Russell as soon as possible.

Sam called about dinner, but Lyle declined—not because he was tired, but because he was afraid he couldn't keep Romanov's visit secret from his brother.

When he finally went to sleep, he dreamed that Nestor Stuart was sitting on the edge of his childhood bed, reading from *The Aeneid*, the story of the Trojan Horse.

> *O wretched countrymen! What fury reigns?*
> *What more than madness has possessed your brains?*
> *Think you the Greeks from your coasts are gone?*
> *And are Ulysses' arts no better known?*

This hollow fabric either must enclose,
Within its blind recess, our secret foes;
Or an engine raised above the town,
To overlook the walls, and then to batter down.
Something designed by fraud, or force:
Trust not their presents, nor admit the horse.

He was hearing his father's orator voice again, and there the man was, seated next to him—or was it Sam, they looked so much alike.

When he awoke the next morning, the dream was still fresh and fluid. Where had it come from? Perhaps the Russian's name—Leonidas—and his story had sparked it, or Sam's resemblance to their father.

He had a busy day in front of him. Dressing in a hurry, and Russell's journal in hand, Lyle walked out of the room.

JANUARY 25, 2017

☻-☻-☻

Mainz

L YLE EXPECTED BEATRICE to be in the breakfast room when
he arrived, and she didn't disappoint him. In her floor-length
orange, red, and blue *gomesi* and matching headpiece, he couldn't
have missed her.

"You're beautiful."

"I wondered if you'd notice."

"I'm not blind, just distracted."

Beatrice didn't drink coffee or tea. A glass of grapefruit juice
sat in front of her. "How did you sleep?" she inquired

He told her about the dream, his father, and the Trojan Horse.

"In my country, we call it the Gift Horse; any gift that perplexes
should be accepted with caution."

They talked about Lyle's delayed visit to the Lido site, and the
challenges he would have with Gorsey off to Jericho. "I hope I'm up
to it. I know what I have to do, but since the café, emotions, fears,
keep getting in the way. I haven't felt like this since my mother
died."

Beatrice was looking past him when she said, "There was a moment when something deep inside me took over, and there was
nothing I could do about it. Certainly, it felt like that at the time,

181

and afterwards I was shocked at what I was capable of doing." She took a long drink of juice. "Shall we spend the day together?"

Here it was. Lyle said, "Sorry, I'm meeting an archaeologist at the University."

"You didn't mention it yesterday."

"I want to show you something," Lyle said, producing Russell's journal and handing it to her.

"You're an expert at changing the subject. What is this?"

"That's what I want you to tell me."

She put her nose to the leather cover before opening the journal.

"I'll have coffee," Lyle said to the waiter, as Beatrice turned pages.

"Do you recognize the notations?" he asked her.

Beatrice was still paging. "Where did you get this?"

"From Russell's office, by mistake. It was mixed up with something he gave me."

"These aren't psychology conventions I've seen before. When are you returning it?"

He hesitated, but there was no avoiding her. "Today."

"Then, you're seeing Russell. You didn't mention that either."

Beatrice set the journal on the empty chair between them. "Don't forget the doctor. Sam wants to get back to London."

He could tell she was waiting for him to say something. He had to get away before she pried everything out of him. Already, his resolve to keep his plans from her was softening.

"I better go," he said.

"You haven't eaten anything. Here, take this pastry," she said, covering it with a napkin." And one more thing." She handed him an envelope. "Sam asked me to give you this."

He felt guilty about leaving her, but it was as if he were under a compulsion. He put the envelope in his pocket and didn't waste any time in the hotel, making for campus as soon as he'd retrieved his coat. An overnight rain had slimed the pavement, slickening the city grime, and his leg forced him to be especially careful. Lyle was relieved to enter Russell's building and escape the chilly, damp air, though upon crossing the threshold he realized he'd forgotten the journal in his rush to get away from Beatrice.

Their unsettling conversation had reminded him of the night that had almost destroyed their relationship.

Lyle had consumed an entire bottle of wine with dinner, and when he brought Beatrice home, he'd pressed her to let him stay, to the point where she had to push him out the door. After a week of silence, he had sent her flowers and an apology, but it was still another month before she agreed to see him again. During their time apart, Lyle had whipsawed between emotional extremes, disgusted with himself for his behavior and annoyed with Beatrice for resisting him. He sometimes wondered if she harbored doubts about him—and why shouldn't she?—but if she did she never alluded to it, or that night.

Walking down the hall, he recalled what Sam had told him, that Russell had grown up in the eugenics institute, an orphan, a lab rat, someone to help those scientists prevent people like him from being born.

The *Professor extraordinarius* was in his wheelchair behind that little desk, as if he were another stack of material. Looking up from a book, the gnomish man beamed and said, "I'm surprised to see you."

"I'm sorry to come without notice, but I had a visitor last night I think you'd like to hear about. But first, when the stack toppled over yesterday, your journal got wedged in the magazine you gave me, and I didn't notice until late last night. Then, I forgot to bring it with me this morning. I'm sorry. I'll return it as soon as possible."

Glancing toward the stack where he'd laid the journal the day before, Russell displayed a flash of distress. "Psychology notations.

But you mentioned a visitor, and I don't have much time before I have to leave for class."

"Last night, a man who called himself Leonidas Romanov came to my hotel room." Lyle paused to give Russell a chance to respond, though the man was as inscrutable as a sphinx. "He told me the manuscript was in the Russian consulate and that he wants it returned to my uncle's monastery."

"You believe him?"

"Why would he tell such a story?"

"Why indeed?"

"How did he find out I was seeking the manuscript?"

"He's a security officer at the consulate, so he has access to Russian intelligence."

"He wants me to meet him tonight . . . at the consulate."

"I'd be careful about that, Professor Stuart. May I give you some advice? The probability is negligible that Leonidas has the manuscript you're seeking. I told you what I observed in him, and I have some expertise when it comes to matters such as this. Then . . . how can I say this? Directly, I suppose, as we've become friends. You're a renowned archaeologist, but you are no hero, no Ulysses."

Lyle bristled, resentment welling up inside him.

"My advice is to stay away from Romanov and that consulate. Not that I'd expect anything perilous to come of it. Rather, being made to look silly and perhaps dashing your hopes of recovering this artifact. Forget about this fool's errand."

No matter how well intentioned this man was, hearing this wasn't affecting Lyle as Russell might have wished.

"I appreciate your candor," Lyle said.

"But I sense I've said too much. Is the journal in your hotel room?"

Ashamed to admit he'd left it with Beatrice, Lyle answered that it was.

"I'm using the journal in one of my classes, so I'd like to have it back soon. If you'll kindly excuse me, I must prepare for my class."

The last thing Lyle wanted was for Russell to think he didn't take returning the journal seriously, so, before he left the building, he called Beatrice, hoping she had taken it with her. But there was no answer, so he had to leave a message.

He embarked on a hilly walk to the doctor's office, where he was told he was fit enough to go home.

The headaches? Better than before.

Other symptoms? None to speak of.

"You remember my suggestion that you seek counseling? Psychological trauma often lingers after physical wounds heal."

It was still early in the day, but Lyle didn't dare return to the hotel for fear of encountering Sam or Beatrice. Only a call informing him that Beatrice had the journal would prompt him to return and, when she called him back, he planned to ask her to leave it at the front desk so he wouldn't have to face her.

Russell had advised against keeping the appointment, and Sam and Beatrice would prevent it if they found out, but with each passing hour Lyle realized he intended to meet Romanov. Somehow, his pride had entered the equation, to the extent that not going would be cowardice.

He took a cab to the Imperial Cathedral, where he spent the rest of the morning and the afternoon, considering how he'd engage the Russian. He discarded the pastry, as he couldn't eat anything, and left another message for Beatrice about the journal.

On his feet for over an hour, he sat in a pew, and when he put his hand in his pocket he discovered the envelope Beatrice had given him that morning, containing a copy of a *London Times* news article from May 5, 1932.

EARL OF LEICESTER'S GRANDDAUGHTER MURDERED

A body discovered in a flat in Soho has been identified as Miss Agnes CurLio, granddaughter of the Earl of Leicester. Scotland Yard has revealed that Miss CurLio, after death by cardiac arrest, was mutilated. Her body was found by police following receipt of an anonymous telephone call.

Doctors are uncertain as to the cause of the heart attack. Dr. Peter Henry Cooper, chief medical examiner, stated that, if not for the subsequent mutilation, Miss CurLio's death might have been attributed to natural causes. Authorities have not ruled out the use of poison.

According to family members, Miss CurLio had lived abroad for several decades and rarely communicated with them. They were surprised to learn she had returned to Britain.

Neighbors in the building were under the impression that a young actor occupied the flat. They had thought Miss CurLio was a boy employed in the theater district.

One resident stated that the incident has frightened everyone in the neighborhood. "It's a bad business," the man told *The Times*. Scotland Yard has not released any information as to motive or suspects. Police are said to be investigating Miss CurLio's connections to the theater. An anonymous source at Scotland Yard suggested that, considering the brutality of the crime, a madman was likely responsible.

Private funeral services are being arranged by the family. They had no further comments for the press.

On the bottom of the article, Sam had written, *No one arrested. If poison, not identified. A successful murder.*

It rattled Lyle as if he'd known her, as if the article had been published that morning. That was the answer, and shortly after her last diary entry. She had helped Alembert for years before she left him, but he had tracked her down and murdered her. The most likely explanation. But, if Alembert had been such a deadly enemy, obsessed with the manuscript, how had John Hill managed to survive?

As for the consulate, the decision was almost made but, just in case, he stopped at a bar a block from the Cathedral and had a whiskey and soda to settle what remained of his doubts.

A young woman, already drunk, though it was still early, tried to talk him into buying her drinks, at whatever price he asked—she had been direct in both German and English—but he warded her off and plunged out the door. Though this girl was unlike the

Agnes of the diary, she made Lyle think of that long-dead woman, maybe because this woman was desperate too, as Agnes must have been.

Well before six, he found himself across the alley from the consulate delivery gate, walking back and forth in the dark and chill, committed to meeting Romanov, as he'd known he would be ever since he left Russell's office.

A ten-foot fence topped with barbed wire surrounded the consulate, with concrete bollards at the gate to prevent vehicles from crashing through, and with a uniformed guard walking the perimeter inside the fence. The Russian flag extending from the gate reminded Lyle of a site he'd investigated west of Stavropol, not far from the Black Sea, where prehistoric tribes had wintered and marshaled strength. The typical hardships of expeditionary life had been compounded by a Russian official, a Muscovite rather than a local, who had communicated his disdain for Britain. Yuri something or other. He had tried to seduce one of the company's undergraduates. The expedition leader had to confront him about it. In a few minutes, Lyle would be back on Russian soil, in the middle of a German city.

The gate guard didn't give the impression he expected a visitor, though he made the call and instructed Lyle to wait in a small shelter warmed by an electric heater. Sure enough, from the back of the modest two-story consulate, a building old enough to have survived the war, came a coated figure who trotted across the paved yard to the gate.

"Come with me," said Romanov.

It wasn't until they were inside the consulate that Lyle wondered why he hadn't been required to sign in. The place smelled of fish and mildew, giving the feel of a pensioners' flat rather than a diplomatic outpost. Though Lyle heard muted voices, they met no one as Romanov led him down a dark hallway and up a narrow set of stairs.

He wanted to question the Russian, but the man was moving too quickly.

"Here," Romanov said, opening a door.

The time had long since passed for him to balk. He went in.

"Sit."

The room had the appearance of a library and meeting room: a table in the center, a bookcase on one wall, heavy drapes covering both windows, mismatched chairs at the table and badly marred wood floor.

For the first time, Lyle could see the man's face clearly. Romanov all right, but a harder expression, more resolute than the man had displayed the previous night. Suddenly fearful, all Lyle could think to say was, "Russell knows I'm here."

"Sit."

He took a chair, and said in a strained voice, "The manuscript."

Romanov produced a pistol from beneath his coat, with something attached to the barrel that might have been a silencer.

"You will never torment her again."

Expecting the weapon to discharge at any moment, Lyle said, "Who am I tormenting?"

"Caroline, as you know too well."

Desrosier? Despite the chilly room, he was sweating. With the gun pointed at his chest, and the look of fury on Romanov's face, he was struggling to think clearly.

"What did she tell you?"

"The truth. Something I will never hear from you. When she resisted, you slandered her. You threaten her."

"That's a lie." A plea rather than a denial.

If he hoped to change Romanov's mind, he had miscalculated. The Russian clenched his jaws so tight that Lyle could hear grinding teeth. Romanov's hand, and the gun, began to shake.

Desperate to keep the man talking, Lyle said, "Did she tell you this?"

"I swore I would keep you away from her."

Romanov pushed the gun forward, until the barrel was inches from Lyle's chest. He had to force himself to breathe. "Does Russell know?"

A sly look appeared on Romanov's face, and the shaking subsided. "Tell him I intended to kill you? Am I a fool?"

"This is a mistake. I barely know her."

The Russian said, "Enough talk."

"Wait."

"I have waited long enough."

Someone was knocking at the door, but Lyle's world had so collapsed that the door might have been a hundred miles away.

"Do not move. Not one inch." Romanov walked to the door, opened it, and exchanged words with someone on the other side, a back and forth staccato of Russian.

When Romanov returned to the table, he clutched the gun in both hands, as if to make himself more resolute. There were tears in the man's eyes.

Knocking again. This time an older man, bald, with a large scar on his cheek, burst into the room before Romanov could answer. By then, the gun had been concealed, though the newcomer's expression demonstrated he knew something was amiss. He started to speak to Romanov, but glanced at Lyle, and said, "Come with me."

The older man didn't say a word as he led Lyle to the front of the house. The voices were louder now, and the rooms on this side of the consulate were brighter, warmer, and better kept.

"Go," the man said, after he'd opened the front door.

Lyle followed a winding walk to the front gate where the guard let him out, and a man wearing a dark coat and hat approached him. He doubted he'd been in the house ten minutes.

"From the frying pan to the fire, Bilbo."

The man's voice and pet name for Lyle identified him as Sam. Relieved beyond measure, it was all he could do to keep his composure.

"I told them the house was surrounded, that there was no way they could get you past us, alive or dead."

"You have people here?" Lyle asked him.

"This isn't my patch, but I convinced the Germans to post agents on all four corners. These days, I'm better at organization than scaling fences. Now, get a move on."

JANUARY 25, 2017

☉-☉-☉

Mainz

BEATRICE WAS WAITING FOR them in the hotel lobby, alerted by Sam that he'd rescued his brother from the consulate. She grasped Lyle's hand as if she had no intention of ever letting go.

Sam said, "The Russians may not be finished with you. As naked as I am over here, I was lucky to get you out."

"I don't think the Russians are your primary concern," Beatrice observed. "If I'm right, there's an underlying *Gestalt* to all of this. I'll join you in your room in a few minutes, and I'll have dinner delivered. Then, I'll explain."

"And beer," Sam told her. "I'm drier than dry. Upstairs. Now," he said to Lyle.

When they had assembled in the room, Sam said to Beatrice, "Are you packed?"

"Not yet, but I learned to travel light and fast when I was young."

"Good, because I've decided we're leaving tonight."

"Tomorrow. I'm exhausted," said Lyle, prompting a worried look from Beatrice.

"I'd rather have you exhausted and alive than rested and dead. The Russians are unpredictable, and not in a good way. They often act from pride rather than calculation, and we battered their pride tonight. I don't think you warrant the Polonium treatment, but when it comes to murder they have a big toolkit."

"If you say go, we go," Lyle conceded.

"Then, let's eat and get out of here. One of us, not Lyle, will have to drive the Spider. And don't think I'm listening to that mind-numbing music."

Rather, mind healing, insofar as Lyle was concerned. When his mother was undergoing late-stage treatment, he had often sought refuge from the misery in a secondhand bookstore owned by an old man named Adrian Newby. As Lyle explored the books, he was exposed to old Newby's eclectic instrumental jazz. After a month of indifference and confusion, it had taken, and he had been hooked ever since.

"Sam, you admitted you have no authority here, you had no physical evidence I was inside, and the Germans can't enter a diplomatic outpost, so why did the Russians back down?"

"Here's why. When it comes to abductions or killings, three operational stages have to be executed to avoid an international incident or, worse, the loss of operatives by imprisonment or death. Securing the target. Check—they had you. Stationing the target in a safe house until they're ready to dispose of him. Transporting the target to the ultimate destination or disposing of the target, if dead, is the third stage.

"What I did was convince the Russians they couldn't execute the second and third stages without public disclosure or loss of operatives."

"Was it that easy?" asked Beatrice.

"It was *too* easy, and I'll tell you why. The consulate is the last place the FSB would have abducted or killed Lyle . . . too much risk he might have told someone where he was going, or he might have been observed entering, not to mention observation cameras, and not just Russian cameras. An amateur operation, and the FSB are anything but amateurs."

"What's your explanation?" said Lyle.

"A lone wolf, and a clumsy one, but why, unless he's connected to Dekeyser or the manuscript . . . What's wrong Beatrice?"

"I have something to tell you before we leave, and it's going to take a while."

"Then let's hear it," Sam said.

Producing Russell's journal and placing it on the table, Beatrice said, "At breakfast, Lyle left this journal behind. Because Russell and I are psychologists, Lyle asked me if I understood the notations. I didn't then, but I do now, the important parts anyway."

As she spoke, Lyle wondered how he would get the journal back to Russell as he'd promised. Sam broke in with, "This isn't something we need to talk about now."

"This is exactly what we need to talk about, especially with what you said about a lone wolf," Beatrice countered. "Give me five minutes. You've read about Rasputin, a master manipulator, a mesmerizer, whatever you want to call it."

Sam took a zestless swallow of beer. "What does that have to do with the journal?" he asked her.

"It has everything to do with the modern Rasputin who's the author of the journal. The pages are in chronological order, so he's been doing this for years, decades—hear me out, Sam! If I'm right, these notations are an argot known only to Russell . . . up till now, a type of symbolic logic. Lyle left the journal behind when he embarked on his adventure," she said, flashing Lyle a wicked look. "I've always been fascinated by logic trees and symbolic logic, and once I started examining the journal I couldn't put it down. It isn't dense with symbols or mathematical formulas, but it's the kind of thing that's practically impossible to decipher without a key.

"I wasn't going to return Lyle's calls about the journal until I deciphered the code or gave up. I decided early on that the side-by-side capital letters represent names, and when I kept seeing the same capital letters above the arrows I wondered what they could signify.

"Don't interrupt, Sam. You listen to your cryptologists, don't you?

"The more I looked at the letters over the arrows, the more familiar they seemed, but how could that be, as I'd never seen the journal before? I was about to give up when a man and woman started screaming at each other in the hotel lobby. That triggered a memory. Ira—wrath is one of the eight deadly faults that pre-dated Gregory's list of seven deadly sins, and the connection mnemonics I used at the monastery school was *St Agilva*, the name of one of the Ugandan martyrs. In Latin, these faults are *Superbia*—pride, *Tristitia*—despair, *Avaritia*—greed, *Gula*—gluttony, *Ira*—wrath, *Luxuria*—lust, *Vana gloria*—vanity, and *Acedia*—sloth. As to why Russell used the more ancient list of faults—he wasn't interested in sins, except as means of manipulation, and vanity and despondency are powerful motivators.

"These, and only these, letters—*Av* for avaritia and *Ac* for ace-dia—are above the arrows throughout the journal. Russell identifies the weaknesses to which his victims—and that's the proper word to use—are most susceptible, then uses these weaknesses to compel his victims to do what he wants them to do. The lowercase letters to the right of the arrow are abbreviations for his desired outcomes, as I concluded when I examined the diagram, with ND signifying Noel Dekeyser, followed by an arrow to 'art,' signifying artifact, with the 'S' above the arrow indicating the fault to which Dekeyser was most susceptible was pride. Double arrows seem to signify a murder, never by Russell himself . . . by someone he's convinced, compelled, to commit the act, and if I'm right, the killings go back to 1953, starting with:

$$EB \xrightarrow{I} WS$$

"Hold on," Lyle interrupted. "You extracted this from a few letters and symbols in that old man's journal?"

"Once you break the code, everything makes sense."

Sam shook his head. "How could Russell compel people to do things . . . to kill?"

"Because the world sees a feeble old man in a wheelchair, exactly as he desires to be seen, rather than someone who delights in making the world do what he wants it to. Here, look at this notation. Caroline Desrosier is compelled, via *superbia*, to reel Noel Dekeyser in. Down the page, we see Dekeyser compelled to steal the artifact. Didn't Brother Claude tell Lyle that Dekeyser was so resentful when your uncle was chosen to be abbot that he left the Order? Then, here—look—Desrosier is compelled to kill Dekeyser—the double arrow."

"Hold on, Beatrice," interrupted Sam. "When Dekeyser vanished, he was living in Mainz, and Desrosier was in Paris. So, how did she do it?"

"With Russell's help. He guided her, whether she realized it or not, and whatever happened was carefully planned."

What Beatrice was describing was exactly what had happened to Lyle, the way Russell had motivated him to go to the consulate while making him believe Russell was advising against it. This was the second time Lyle had witnessed Beatrice's analytical skills and, if he'd been impressed with her interpretation of Dekeyser's resignation letter, he was even more impressed by this display. He said. "Give me that pen," and wrote:

$$LS \xrightarrow{\text{v}} c\text{ò}h$$

"The way Russell advised me to stay away from the consulate caused me to go there. I can't describe *how* he accomplished it, only the result."

Beatrice said, "People are motivated by other people to do all kinds of things. The difference is Russell used his genius and training to raise this skill to a science. I admit it's a lot to accept, but everything fits, and remember, Russell's genius is making his victims believe what they do is *their* idea. Lyle had gotten too close for comfort, hence the consulate scheme."

Sam said, "He grew up a lab rat, no father or mother. How did that boy become the prodigy you describe?"

"I can't guess," Beatrice said. "He had talent . . . an inner fire, or a diabolical one."

Sam said, "This is a lot to absorb. If Russell is responsible for Dekeyser's death, does that mean he has the manuscript?"

"I'll come back to that. Here's the latest entry. I think this is Lyle's elimination diagram. Do you know anyone with the initials LR?"

$$LR \xrightarrow{\quad I \quad} LS$$

Both Sam and Beatrice were staring at Lyle, who said, "The Russian security officer who visited me last night, Leonidas Romanov."

"A Russian visited you? Here? And you didn't tell me?" Sam said, angrily. "You're damn lucky I decided to keep an eye on you today."

"Your lone wolf, Sam, and I suggest Russell had everything to do with Lyle not telling us. Had Russell introduced Romanov to you?"

"Russell told me Romanov was unbalanced, that the man had told him the Russians were behind the bombing. When Romanov visited me, he said they had the manuscript at the consulate, and explained why he wanted me to have it."

"Russell's genius. Preparing you for the Russian's visit, along with what he told you today that motivated rather than dissuaded you from going to the consulate. You told me Russell sent you a message when you went to the Lido site. Let me see it."

Lyle located the message and handed his phone to Beatrice, who read it and said, "At face value, an innocent message, but knowing what we now know, a devious intervention, intended to bring you back to Mainz: 'You've done your *duty,* you've met your *obligation*,' not good enough for a man who always goes well beyond duty and obligation. As for the liver, frosting on the cake, if liver and frosting can be used in the same sentence. By the way, there are a dozen double arrow diagrams in this journal, meaning Russell was behind at least that many killings, not to mention all the shattered lives."

Lyle had met this treacherous version of Russell before—Tommie the sneaker in his mother's story, also raised by people intent on experimenting on him.

"So that's how it is," Sam said. "Russell intended for Lyle to be murdered tonight by the Russian." Draining the last third of the beer in his glass and wiping his mouth on his shirtsleeve, he said, "I think we'll return Russell's journal before we leave town."

"What a wag you are," Lyle responded.

"Think so? I trust Beatrice, and she said Russell tried to kill you tonight, that he has a dozen murders on his hands. How safe do you think you'll be in Oxford? How long do you think it will take him to send a . . ."

"Trojan Horse, Gift Horse," said Beatrice. "The people he *commissions* are Trojan Horses filled with the malice he packs inside them. Russell stowed his Ego inside Desrosier when she killed Dekeyser, inside the Algerian, and inside Romanov tonight when he tried to kill Lyle. Russell used Desrosier to provoke Romanov, and then Russell suggested, indirectly no doubt, the scheme to isolate Lyle, knowing Romanov would kill him."

Beatrice's observations reminded Lyle of Remington's words. What Russell had written in his journal depicted his *art*, a repudiation of Divinity, the embrace of the Lucifer ego.

"As for the reason Romanov wanted to kill me, he thought I was trying to destroy Caroline Desrosier."

"So, she's in it up to her neck," said Sam.

"Do you think the Russians possess the manuscript?" Lyle asked Beatrice.

"If Russell thought Romanov possessed the manuscript, he'd have it himself by now. Even though he eliminated Dekeyser, I'm not convinced he has it, or knows where it is. Otherwise, he needn't have been concerned about you."

"Russell asked me about it. I didn't tell him everything, but more than I should have done."

Sam said, "I'll need you to come with me, Lyle."

"What are we doing?"

"I'll take care of the doing. You're going to help me find my way."

"I've never been to Russell's home."

"We're going to his office."

"He won't be there."

"I'm counting on that. Take a cold shower . . . here, not your room. Then we'll go. You better stay in my room, Beatrice."

"He's dangerous," she said, "and he'll know by now his scheme failed."

"Maybe, or maybe the Russians have Romanov in a cocoon—they do that with renegades. And even if Russell knows the plan fell apart, he'll expect Lyle to run, not to wheel a Trojan Horse into his lair."

"What are we putting inside it?" Beatrice inquired.

"Lyle, get in the shower or you'll be worthless. Is there anything else you can tell me, Beatrice?"

"Will you be searching for evidence—proof?"

"I have all the evidence I need."

In Sam, Lyle saw a stranger's curtained eyes, rather than the expressive eyes that once mirrored his brother's buoyancy and wit.

Beatrice said, "Compelling, not conclusive. He's entitled to a trial."

"That won't eliminate the threat."

"Is it your prerogative to eliminate him?"

"It's my prerogative to make sure my brother isn't murdered by someone who's already attempted twice."

"What if we're wrong?"

"The evidence is compelling, you said so yourself."

"If there's one chance in a hundred I'm wrong, would you kill him?"

"Judges make mistakes, so do juries. A custodial sentence, even at ninety-six, may not be enough for a man like Russell."

"We don't have all the facts, Sam. I don't want this on your conscience, your soul."

"You don't know me very well. As the Yanks say, this isn't my first rodeo."

"Judge, jury, and executioner? I gave you reasons for bringing Russell to justice, not for vengeance. How is that different than Russell's calculus?"

"Don't psychoanalyze me, Beatrice. Lyle's father didn't come back, because he didn't pull the trigger fast enough."

"What are you talking about?" said Lyle.

"I'm talking about our father. I made sure I learned from his mistakes. You were too young to know that Mum identified with Eowyn. She thought she was getting an Aragorn, but as it turned out she didn't even get a Faramir—she got his brother."

Sam stood and turned his back to them and, for almost a minute, a somber language of looks replaced the spoken word. Though Sam had consumed two bottles of beer, they'd barely touched their food.

"I'm going, and you're coming with me, so shift yourself," said Sam, without turning around.

"Think it over, Sam. That's all I'm asking," Beatrice said.

"Russell could kill Lyle, something you've demonstrated he's quite capable of doing. I'm not taking that chance."

THE CAR WAS SMALL, nondescript, exactly what Sam had ordered.

Driving past the Cathedral, Lyle remembered how their mother would drag Sam to church whenever he was home for the weekend.

"Do you go to church anymore?" said Lyle.

"Not since Mum died, but I went to confession a few times. I'm in a messy business."

"You were just doing your job, weren't you?"

"That's it. Following orders."

Lyle cringed. Then, he realized his brother had intentionally chosen those words.

Sam parked the car in the Cognitive Studies lot.

"When are we going in?" asked Lyle, his ears ringing and his throat dry.

"When I say so. Hopefully, Russell's at home dreaming about how his plan worked to perfection."

Lyle's own dream about the Trojan Horse, and Beatrice's suggestion that the manuscript hadn't been recovered by Russell, had been on Lyle's mind from the time he and Sam had left the hotel. Longer than that, ever since he had made the decision in Heidelberg to commit himself, emotionally and intellectually, to searching for the manuscript. As with the dream, he was convinced he knew something he couldn't articulate, though how could he know anything about a manuscript he'd never seen, or a person—Dekeyser—he'd never met?

"No talking unless there's an emergency. No lights until I say so. When I move, you move. When I stop, you stop," said Sam, sitting in the passenger seat with a plastic tube and a small satchel in his lap.

"Do you think anyone's inside?"

"I wish to hell it would storm . . . there he is. Let's go."

They exited the car and crossed the lot, joining the man at the west entrance to the building. If this person had been any more unkempt, Lyle would have mistaken him for a vagrant.

Handing Sam a card and a key, the man said, "I came as soon as I received your message. He left at nine-thirty. A man wheeled him out the door to a caravan at the curb, where the driver joined them. They lifted him into the rear, chair and all."

"Transportation service?"

"Praetorian Guard: sturdy, busy eyes, no wasted motion. Less than a minute from door to departure, including the thirty yards to the curb."

"He knows his plan failed. On his guard. Anyone inside?" said Sam.

"Circled the building twice. No lights."

The man walked away, and Sam swiped the door with the card, pushing the door open.

"Put these on."

Lyle felt something in his hand. Goggles. Strapping them on, he could see clearly.

"These too, hands and shoes."

The gloves were paper thin, as were the shoes covers."

Handing Lyle the tube, Sam said, "Let's go. Lead me to his office."

The thing Lyle remembered most about Sam from his childhood was his brother's loping big cat walk, easy and menacing, and now, the memory came back in a rush. When he lagged behind, Sam turned and said, "Are you with me or not?"

"To the death, brother."

They took the stairs to the second floor and walked briskly to the end of the corridor, where Sam used the latchkey to unlock the door to Russell's office.

Once inside, Sam locked the door behind them and removed a cylindrical object from the tube Lyle was carrying, an adjustable shade he used to black out the window.

"You can turn on the lights," said Sam, removing his goggles.

As soon as the lights came on, Lyle remembered the first time he'd seen this office, and how he'd scanned the shelves as Russell conversed with the young man.

Sam had removed a gun-like device from the satchel and was attaching a needle thin rod to the barrel, after which he secured a small cylinder to the device. Without a word, he walked to the glass jars on the shelf and placed the end of the rod against the one that contained Russell's tea leaves.

"Wait," Lyle said.

"We don't have time to wait," Sam answered, steadying the driver.

"No, Sam."

"What the hell's wrong with you? This is why we're here. You think this is a game? If we're caught, there'll be hell to pay, and the Germans will disavow all knowledge of the operation. Didn't I tell you I'm naked?"

Gloria Stuart's voice in Lyle's ear: *"Shall we shoot," said Faramir, turning quickly to Frodo.*

"No, Sam."

"I'll take responsibility . . . the blame. I'm used to it," his brother said.

"Put it away. Let's go."

"You goddam idiot."

"If you can put up with Fatemeh for five years, you can hear me out."

He had never seen such a venomous look on his brother's face, as if Lyle were an enemy, or a bug.

For a second, Lyle thought his brother was going to go ahead with what he'd set out to do, but a muttering Sam lowered the tool and began taking it apart.

As for Lyle, he was far from certain that Beatrice was right and Sam wrong. Of one thing he *was* sure, that his own peril was heightened so long as Russell was free to act.

"Alright, let's go," said Sam, as he put on his goggles and stepped toward the light switch.

Lyle's eyes were fixed on the shelves, remembering what his uncle had told him in the repository about John Hill hiding the crate holding the manuscript in plain view, and that Dekeyser had heard the story too. Dekeyser had stolen the manuscript and had brought it to Mainz, as described in Russell's journal. If he'd kept the artifact in his apartment, Russell would surely have found it, and Beatrice believed that Russell didn't have it. The Russians didn't have it either.

What had Lyle seen in the monastery where Dekeyser had lived for years, and here too? "One minute," Lyle said.

"Goddamit. Now what?"

Lyle moved the visitor's chair to the bookshelf, stood on it, and reached toward the highest shelf, taking hold of an ordinary black binder. Stepping down, he read the handwritten label on the spine as he had the first time he visited Russell's office: *Sed libera nos a malo*, words on the placard over his uncle's office door.

Though he only had time to turn a few pages, Lyle knew this was the manuscript. Each page had been inserted inside a transparent sheet protector so holes didn't have to be drilled in the manuscript pages. Russell had rightly appealed to the deadly fault that had motivated Dekeyser—*superbia*, a pride that had provoked the man to write this Latin phrase on the spine of the binder, and then hide it where no one would ever think to look, a needle in a haystack of needles.

"Well?"

"The manuscript," was all Lyle could say, holding it up.

"Put the goggles on . . . now."

Off went the light. The shade came down from the window, and Sam restored it to the tube. After placing the visitor's chair exactly where it had been—something Lyle wouldn't have thought to do—Sam led them out of the office and locked the door.

"Someone's coming . . . the elevator . . . stairs," Sam said as he trotted.

On the first floor, they made for the exit, but before they departed the building, Sam put the goggles, gloves, and shoe covers in the satchel.

"No hurrying when we're in the yard," barked Sam. "If we meet someone or if someone comes after us, I'll handle it. Keep your mouth shut."

Lyle tucked the binder under his arm.

Sam was so hot he didn't say a word all the way to the hotel.

JANUARY 26, 2017

☻-☻-☻

Mainz

HE'S YOUNG AGAIN, *with a nimbleness he never experienced in life, on a beach, building an elaborate sand structure complete with tall towers and ramparts.*

He can feel the warm breeze, smell the sea air, hear piping birds, but the tide is approaching, and he must build a wall to deflect it.

When the tide breeches his wall, he reinforces the ramparts, but to no avail. Inexorably, the noisy sea erodes his creation.

Now, he's an old man. The tide keeps coming, up to his knees.

He glances behind him and sees a shabby little boat on the still-dry sand up the beach. He could get into the boat, but he won't lower himself to the desperate measures of lesser men.

Now, his creation is invisible, what remains of it beneath the water, and the tide is lapping his chin. A sense of dark desperation comes over him, but he can't make himself go to the little boat that's bobbing on the water, even as the vessel drifts nearer.

If he stretched out a hand, he could touch it.

He turns to face the tide. Racing shoreward are massive waves with green bellies and white crowns.

THE MAN IN THE wheelchair woke in a sweat. The first time, he'd tried to laugh off the dream, but it wouldn't go away.

205

He had been thinking about that destructive tide when Lyle Stuart came to his office, had been so preoccupied with the dream that he upset the pile and lost his temper.

This time, he had dozed off while mulling over his bad fortune. Another botched elimination. Desrosier becoming a problem that demanded a solution. Most of all, the precious thing he had been seeking for decades, the thing he had been so close to possessing, had vanished into thin air. The tormenting thought that he would never possess it.

He had never before experienced the sense of failure he had felt since Dekeyser was eliminated, with not even a clue as to what had happened to the manuscript.

A light was flashing on the control panel of his wheelchair, the custom silver chariot he kept in his large penthouse apartment—his security guard signaling an emergency that required his attention. Two-twenty a.m. He touched the control stick, and the chair glided noiselessly into the common area.

He examined the intruder, a bareheaded man in a gray ulster. Not yet fifty. The intruder knew his business, or he could never have gotten into this ultra-secure apartment. So why had he acted so recklessly? Did he have confederates on the street, inside the building?

He addressed the man in German.

The intruder said, "I'm English."

"How did you get into this apartment?"

"I pushed the button and the lift brought me here."

Clapping his hands twice in succession, he said, "*Ferme quatrième étape,*" causing the open shade to descend, so all the glass was covered. If it came to something unpleasant, it wouldn't do to be observed.

"You're Arthur Russell," said the intruder.

"I want to know how you got in."

"What I have to say to you is private."

"You must be mad to think I'd converse privately with you. Niko, where is Heinrich?"

"On his way."

"Does this man have a weapon?"

The wary guard holstered his weapon and conducted a brief search. "No gun or knife. Shall I continue?"

The intruder said, "Would you prefer to speak to me, or to the police?"

The wheelchair crept to within five feet of the man. "Why would the police be interested in me?"

"Nuri Mosbah, Leonidas Romanov, Noel Dekeyser, Caroline Desrosier."

So, this man was a mortal enemy. Something about the intruder reminded him of Lyle Stuart, voice and mannerisms rather than a physical similarity. He was aware that his consulate scheme had failed and had been pondering his next move. Amazingly, this man had connected him with these people, which meant the intruder knew, or suspected, that he had been involved in Dekeyser's death and the attempts on Lyle Stuart's life.

He had struggled with Stuart's elimination, a man with whom he felt an odd affinity. If he hadn't known better, he might have considered it a moral dilemma, though in the end he had done the right thing, if not successfully.

"Niko, return in an hour, and take Heinrich with you."

"Better make it two," said the intruder.

The big guard said, "We will wait in our room, sir."

"Leave the building and return in two hours."

"Yes, sir."

He was already reducing the intruder to symbols, as he had done hundreds of times before. A few words, facial expression, posture, clothing and shoes, eyes, fingers, were often enough to tell him what he wanted to know.

After the door to the elevator had closed, he said, "Would you like a drink? I have a delicious thirty-year-old Scotch."

He didn't miss the signs of internal conflict, though the man did an admirable job of trying to hide it. An alcoholic, as he had suspected.

"I'm with British Intelligence. They know everything I know. So do the Germans."

A combination of truth and invention, but what was true and what was invented?

"I am supposed to believe a man I've never met, who entered my home illegally, who produces no identification or credentials?"

"Nuri Mosbah, Leonidas Romanov, Noel Dekeyser, Caroline Desrosier."

This man was no Santini or Sebastian. Far from it. The intruder's weaknesses weren't that difficult to read: *gula, tristitia*— slavery to drink, discouragement with his lot in life.

"Show me your evidence. But you have none, do you? Mere speculation. Here, a taste of the best Scotch you'll ever have."

Turning the chair more quickly than a ballerina could pirouette, he made for the kitchen, returning with a bottle and two half-filled glasses. If this enemy drank to incapacitation, he would use it to discredit, or destroy, the man.

"You may take the bottle with you when we're finished."

"The British and Germans know what I know . . . everything. If you compromise me, it won't save you."

He could see this man was struggling to resist the Scotch, and the longer the glass and bottle were within arm's reach, the more difficult it would be. "Tell me what they *know* rather than what has been deduced, or suggested, or guessed."

"They know you tried to kill Lyle Stuart twice, using the Algerian and the Russian, they know what's in your journal."

The reason why Heinrich hadn't found the journal in Stuart's hotel room. "Know? The things you mention are subject to interpretation."

"That's not all. We have the manuscript. Dekeyser hid it on your bookshelf. He knew he was suspected of the theft, and he reckoned you were too old and feeble to notice . . . the illusion you created was too good. We broke into your office tonight, after the consulate. A big black binder—rather hard to miss."

Was this possible? Had Dekeyser been capable of such deception? This man's confident words and expression told him it *was* possible, even likely. The manuscript had been on his shelf for months, and now this man had it.

"What do you want?"

The intruder laid a syringe on the arm of the wheelchair.

For years, he too had kept a syringe close at hand, in case he required double-poison measures—drug a drink and finish the victim off with the syringe—though he had never expected he himself would have to take such action. That's what surrogates were for.

"You haven't touched your Scotch."

"Maybe later. When someone tries to kill my brother, he's going to pay a steep price."

By the age of ten, he had realized that most people are capable of only one line of thought at a time, while he had no trouble plumbing a handful at once, including a conversation with someone who believed they were getting his undivided attention. Thus, with every word the intruder spoke, what had transpired in recent weeks made more sense. He had always wondered how an archaeologist had tracked Dekeyser from Folkestone to Paris to Mainz and had learned so much about that renegade monk. The answer was this extrajudicial policeman.

Something was still missing, the skill to decipher the journal. He recalled Heinrich relating that he'd had to delay searching Stuart's hotel room because a woman in African attire had been knocking at Stuart's door. Whoever deciphered the journal had to be here, in Mainz. A trio consisting of the archaeologist, the policeman, and a very talented logician, working as one, the woman probably attached to one of the men—no, not this one; his eminently respectable brother.

All of these deliberations in a matter of seconds. He was battling a three-headed hydra. So, one head at a time.

He suspected that this intruder had been a young turk with dreams of glamor and mystique, but the work had turned out to be poorly paid, and occasionally dirty and dangerous. Now, these agencies were recruiting lawyers and computer hackers, and the old turks were learning their governments didn't have their backs.

"You don't look like an avenging angel. On the contrary, you look like a man who has been put upon and taken advantage of, someone who has earned the finer things in life, the things so many enjoy without having made a fraction of the sacrifices you have . . . I see I am right. You may not have another chance to alter a bleak future, a near future, when you will no longer be useful to your country and will have to scrape by on a meager pension. In the meantime, the parasites sacrifice nothing and take whatever they can. I am right, aren't I?"

He waited for a response. The man's eyes were fixed on the syringe.

"Five hundred thousand Euros, in whatever specie you desire . . . tomorrow, or perhaps today considering the hour, and not a law broken or a trust breeched. A consideration for services rendered in a private matter. Look at this chair and my home. Do you doubt I can make good on this offer?"

"I had you checked out. How did you hide the money?"

"I've been at it for a long time. I've had lots of practice, and I have other names."

He could tell the man wasn't convinced by his offer—not yet. "Have you ever killed a man?"

"I never liked it when I did."

"Then, why compound your misery . . . guilt? You'd better go."

The man said, "I have to see a dead body."

"You're so thorough. Have you arranged for absolution, too?"

The longcase clock was ticking seconds away. They stared at each other, like enemy soldiers hunkered down in trenches a few feet apart.

It dawned on him that he was in mortal peril, something he'd never experienced before. The thought, the sensation, was affecting his thinking. They had his journal. They had the manuscript. What was left for him?

He knew about pain in the way the Inuit know about cold, but he had learned at an early age that the more intellectually active he was, the less aware he was of the pain. He had convinced himself the treasure he sought was the antidote. Was there still a way to obtain it?

"There must be something you desire in life, before you are too old or sick or destitute to enjoy anything. Believe me, I can deliver it. And soon—yes, very soon. I don't think you're a religious man. I don't think you have any illusions about your country standing by you in thick and thin, or silly notions about good and evil. If your brother is safe, will duty keep you from a few years of happiness before the end? Have you ever been to Buenos Aires? I have a lovely house there with its own park and pond. You wouldn't be betraying your country, you aren't a policeman investigating a crime, or extorting anything. It's my money, my property, to do with as I choose. Enough to retire, a new and exciting life in South America . . . with an alluring woman I know who will make you forget all the bad memories."

"You know Romanov failed. You know we have the journal and the manuscript. We know you prompted Desrosier to kill Dekeyser. The deeper we dig, the more we'll learn. You've always relied on invisibility. Now, the spotlight's on you. There's no place to hide."

The spotlight, that platform at the crown of the Big Top, all eyes fixed on him. To the rubes, a pitiful freak. He had been perfectly satisfied to let fools and dreamers pursue ephemeral relationships and petty schemes. All the better for him when he set about making them do what he wanted them to do. Ever since he could remember, this had come naturally, and if he didn't want something, he manipulated subjects for practice, to hone his skills.

The thought that he had failed, that there was no rectifying this failure, had occurred on only one other occasion, in a circus trailer when he realized the only person he ever esteemed had been wrenched away from him.

He had been a young man then, strong and determined enough to use the experience to his advantage. That sense of profound loss was with him again, but this time without the strength to persevere. He was weary with a paralyzing lassitude. *Tristitia.*

Just last week, he'd seen a woman who had reminded him of Madeline. Wasn't it odd that after so many years and a single-minded focus on his craft his old heart had beaten faster when he saw her, like a dog that can't help wagging its tail when it recognizes its master?

He might have rescued her from Santini. Had he wasted *everything?* Could a lifetime's perspective be undone in a matter of hours or minutes? He fought this terrible notion as if it were a parasite bent on destroying him. No cowardly lifeboats for Arthur Alembert.

"You have succeeded in doing what far more intelligent and talented men have never done, backed me into a corner."

"That's why I'm here."

"You've done this before, then."

"In one way or another."

"But you said you never liked it."

"Not until now."

He was confident he could prevent this man from taking his life if he set his mind to it. Depressing the button near his right hand would have him inside the private elevator in his room before this man could take five steps, but even if he avoided death and killed the intruder, how many others of this man's ilk were now aware of his activities?

He could hear the wave.

A panel in the arm of his chair opened, and when his hand emerged, he held a syringe. "I prefer my own Scotch," he said, freeing an arm from the robe and driving the needle into his shoulder.

FIVE MINUTES LATER, the intruder checked Russell's pulse, and put the capped syringe he'd offered the man in his pocket. He had a powerful desire to drink Russell's Scotch to the dregs. Instead, he smoked the unfiltered cigarette he kept for just such an occasion, stowing the butt in a tube on the inside of his belt.

Exhaustion washed over him—lack of sleep, the intensity of the past twelve hours, the dark weariness that accompanied assassinations.

Two stutter steps. He pushed the elevator button and descended.

What had the old man whispered as his eyes closed and his head fell back? "Madness"? "Maddening"?

PART IV

Discoveries

JANUARY 26, 2017

Mainz

"WHAT ARE WE DOING HERE?" said Lyle.

The man behind the wheel of the Spider didn't respond.

"Tell me, Sam."

"It's Beatrice's idea."

"And the two of you decided not to share it with me?"

"That's right."

"You look awful. Did you get any sleep last night?"

"Plenty," Sam snapped.

The tapping on the passenger window meant that Beatrice had parked the other car. A light snow had been falling since Lyle awoke late that morning and had now accumulated to a depth of several inches, with flecks of white in her hair.

"I thought you were in a hurry to get out of Mainz," Lyle said to Sam.

"You're not going to leave Beatrice out in the cold, are you?"

"I just might, considering how the two of you operate," but even as Lyle said this, he opened the car door and stepped out.

"Let's get this over with."

Beatrice took his arm and led him toward the building, as if she were a mother bird coaxing her nestling to take flight. From the curb, he had been able to see the demolished corner of the café, still covered with plywood and plastic sheeting. With every step, an escalating anxiety, accompanied by ringing in his ears. He wanted to protest, but that would display a weakness more objectionable than entering the building.

If Beatrice intended this experience to have an antidotal effect, it was strong medicine, with strong side effects. "Isn't Sam coming?" he asked her.

"Just you and me."

They were met at the door by an older man in jacket and tie who said, "No hurry . . . *prenez votre temps.*"

"Has your business been harmed?" Lyle asked the man, trying to sound as unaffected as he could.

"Are you speaking of paying customers, or the . . . ghouls who photograph the damage and collect souvenirs? We are surviving. It doesn't help that repairs were delayed until the police investigation was complete. May I say I'm delighted to see you on your feet. At first, we thought you were dead . . . like the rest."

"We won't be long," remarked Lyle, eyes trained on the translucent plastic panel and plywood door that separated the intact dining room from the area undergoing repair. "Let's go," he said to Beatrice, who led him to the panel and through the door.

In the midst of the work area was a bare dining table, the same size as the one where he'd been seated that night, and on it had been placed a vase with a red rose, resurrecting memories, sensations, sounds, the split second of terror before the bomb exploded. Feeling as if his bones were burning, and overcome with emotion, he wrenched himself loose from her hand and marched to the place where the blown-out wall had been patched. He was wracked with sobs, but instead of fighting, he offered no resistance.

How close had he been to death? A microsecond, inches? He had seen hundreds of skeletons and mummified corpses, but the syllogism, *all men are mortal, thus I am mortal,* while it had always seemed logically valid, hadn't pertained to him personally.

He looked over his shoulder and saw Beatrice exactly as he had left her, gazing at him with a concerned expression. The table where the detective had sat was right there. How had Russell convinced the Algerian to kill and be killed in the process? Had the man contemplated his mortality, or had he gone on without considering the matter of his own death? Of those other faces at adjacent tables, who had died and who had lived?

The next time Lyle turned around, his eyes so cloudy he could barely see, he beckoned Beatrice to his side and told her everything that had happened, neglecting no detail, no matter how trivial. When he finished, Beatrice said, "May I tell you something I've never told a soul?"

"Only if you want to."

"Something terrible happened to me at a river we had to cross to get to Kampala. It took five years, but I forced myself to go back, and I took a photograph so I'd never forget."

"There's nothing to photograph here. Everything's been blown away or moved. Are you glad you went back?"

"I had to go. It was necessary."

"Did someone die?"

"Paul, Jonathan, and Isaac earlier that day, and I had to kill someone."

He was having a hard time processing what she said. Killed someone . . . Beatrice?

"Did you know Sam left the room last night?" she asked him.

"How long was he gone?"

"Several hours at least."

"Did he say anything when he returned."

"Not a word. He didn't know I was awake. He took off his jacket and shoes, crawled onto the couch, and slept, or pretended to."

"Restless . . . goes with the job."

"I hope that's all it was. Ready to go?"

"I need to watch you and Sam like a hawk. You're more devious than I ever imagined."

"We have to be when it comes to you."

On their way out of the café, the proprietor rejoined them, handing Beatrice something, and when they were outside, she said, "Your precious recipe. The owner has never shared it with another patron, and he swore me to secrecy, but he said you had earned it."

Lyle took one last look at the café. He was alive, while six people in close proximity to his table had died that night, including the man who had saved his life, and the man who had tried to end it. The proprietor had said Lyle deserved the café's prize recipe, but at that moment he felt guilty for having survived while so many around him had perished.

The car window came down and the devious person at the wheel said, "If you're done frivoling, we'll be on our way."

JANUARY 27, 2017

๏-๏-๏

Paris

LYLE AWOKE A LITTLE AFTER three a.m., turned on the room light, and retrieved the black binder that contained the manuscript. Then, he climbed back into bed with the open binder in his lap, oblivious to everything else, as if he'd uncovered an artifact at a site.

His uncle's effusive praise of the manuscript couldn't begin to encompass what he observed. Where in the world had that Oxford linguist found this thing?

Though Lyle knew the difference between remedial, agglutinative, and fusional synthetic written languages, he wasn't a linguist. Still, he was convinced that the people who produced this manuscript belonged to a highly literate culture. Almost every page contained runes in spidery hands, with meticulously illuminated borders of color-rich calligraphic and foliate designs.

Regular breaks in the text—chapters?—occurred every ten to twenty pages, Nothing about the manuscript suggested it was a record of trade, log of bureaucratic activities, law code, or mundane recordings of any sort.

About a dozen detailed maps depicting what appeared to be expansive territories, localized terrain, and walled cities or fortresses, were scattered throughout the manuscript, with the territorial maps evocative of John Hill's cartography. Pondering the missing Mediterranean Sea, Lyle came up with a solution—the *Terra Incognita* explanation for why Africa was poorly depicted into the eighteenth century.

This kingdom's southern boundary didn't extend much to the south of the mountains, the tribes to the south known to be populous and threatening. Thus, known lands were reasonably well mapped, but outside these borders, to the east and south, were vast shadow-lands of little-known peoples and unknown topography, the Mediterranean Sea probably thought to be an arm of the western ocean.

Though Lyle hadn't intended to remove pages from the protective covers, he hadn't been able to resist. The vellum-thin pages had been made of a material, or composite, that was strong and supple, displaying no pigment bleed-through nor any evidence that the text and illuminations had faded, as everything was vibrant. He even put his nose to the paper to see if it smelled like old parchments he'd unearthed at sites. Rather, a faint sweet scent, like early autumn leaves.

In John Hill's story, that great citadel against the mountain had preserved records on many things, including leaves of silver and gold. Had the authors of the manuscript manufactured a kind of parchment from the leaves of that legendary tree—was that the answer?

Lyle had intended to spend no more than an hour with the manuscript, but three hours later he was still at it, and not for a moment had he doubted that John Hill had broken the barrier of time when he deciphered these runes. Without doubt, this was the product of an efflorescent civilization, but even if it was forty thousand years old, how much of that fantasy story was history, and how much was the author's poetic invention? Only a thorough translation of the manuscript could answer that question.

The light coming through the window informed him that he was late for breakfast with Beatrice and Sam. He had been stirred in a way no other artifact had ever stirred him. Otherworldly was the only word he could summon to describe the manuscript.

"Where the hell have you been?" muttered Sam. "With everything that's happened, I expect you to be where you say you'll be, when you say you'll be there. Pass the coffee pot."

Both Sam and Beatrice knew the cardboard box on the table contained the manuscript, and that Lyle wasn't about to let it out of his sight.

Beatrice said, "As brilliant and talented as Russell was, what he desired most in the world was right next to him, and he never recognized it."

A man who resembled the Algerian in the café came toward them, causing Lyle to tremble uncontrollably. Beset by anxiety, and not wanting Beatrice and Sam to notice, he clasped his hands beneath the table.

For years, his life had been like a tightly wound storm over water, but in recent weeks the storm had made landfall, and powerful forces were casting off bands of self-reliance and control.

"What did Henry say when you told him you have the manuscript?" Sam asked his brother.

The longer Lyle waited to answer, the more concern appeared on Sam and Beatrice's faces.

"You haven't told him," Beatrice said.

"There hasn't been time."

"There hasn't been time for a phone call?"

"Do you think I plan to keep it?" Lyle snapped.

"What's on your mind?" Sam said.

"I've examined it. I've touched it. There's nothing else like it. Why should it be hidden away in that box? Think of what we might learn if it's properly studied."

"A question Russell might have asked," said Beatrice.

Lyle jerked to his feet, but his head started swimming, and he dropped back into the chair.

Beatrice said, "The manuscript belongs to your uncle. The man who discovered it gave it to the monastery, not to archaeologists, or science. I don't think that was a frivolous decision."

"I've earned some time with it, haven't I?"

"I don't think your uncle will deny you that time, but you don't have the right to reveal it to the world or turn it over to science. You have to tell your uncle you have it—now, before you've talked yourself into something you'll regret—and ask him if he'll permit you, and only you, to spend more time with the manuscript before it's returned."

"Look what I've gone through to get it."

Sam's face hardened. "Look what *we've* gone through to get it. You're not the only one who's made sacrifices . . . been damaged."

"I know you'll do the right thing, Lyle," Beatrice said, "and you'll feel good about it."

"Feel good about handing off the most precious thing in the world?"

"That's what you believe?" she said.

He forced a smile. "No, I don't. I'll call Uncle Henry after breakfast."

"I want you to see something," said Sam, passing his tablet to Lyle and Beatrice.

A news article in German from the *Allgemeine Zeitung Mainz,* translated into English:

> The oldest and longest serving instructor at the University of Mainz has died. A caretaker discovered Arthur Russell's body in his home. Institutsdirektor Ambar Sangal states, "Professor Arthur Russell, though small in stature, was a giant in the School for Cognitive Studies for sixty years. We shall miss him, and we honor his memory."

"Was it you?" Beatrice asked Sam. Lyle remembered what she had told him about Sam leaving the hotel room the night they'd invaded Russell's office.

"I like French coffee, and no need to hurry if we're not seeing Desrosier until later."

Lyle said, "The article didn't mention suspicious circumstances, or a police investigation."

Sam said, "Russell couldn't have anticipated *black swans*—I mean the collaboration of someone with my resources and training, and someone with Beatrice's analytical skills. If you haven't had the mushroom and goat cheese omelet, you're missing a treat. I woke up early . . . and hungry."

Lyle said, "Hungry for what, news?"

Beatrice was gazing at Sam's tablet when she said, "*This is the way the world ends, not with a bang but a whimper.* Sam, those black swans wouldn't have mattered if Russell hadn't believed he was invulnerable to the deadly faults he used to manipulate others. He believed he was a super-man, above all that. Haven't we seen the effect of Russell's *superbia*? He eliminates Dekeyser before locating the manuscript, certain he knows where it's hidden. He keeps the incriminating journal in plain view, within arm's reach of those who come to his office."

Sam's beckoning hand brought the waiter to their table. "*Trois omelettes, spécialités de la maison, et je veux prendre plus de café.*"

AS LYLE AND SAM entered the small office down the hall from Richard Lourdes, Caroline Desrosier said to Lyle. "Who's this? You didn't tell me anyone else was coming."

Desrosier had adopted an androgynous look, wearing gray slacks and a drab monochrome V-neck sweater over a white tee shirt. As at their previous meeting, no makeup, but hair shorter than Lyle remembered. She hadn't shed all her native beauty, though she seemed to be doing her best to conceal it.

Looking around, Lyle observed nothing of a personal nature. Most of the tombs he'd seen contained more evidence of life than this room. "My brother. He has friends at the *Sûreté* and Interpol."

She looked back and forth from Lyle to Sam. "We're finished," she said, abruptly. "Leave—immediately."

"Don't make that mistake," said Sam. "I suspect you know Russell is dead . . ."

Lyle saw a flash of distress on her features, though not the distress of new knowledge.

". . . and we know more than you think about his enterprises and your close involvement. We're here to learn more and, if you refuse to cooperate, we'll turn everything we have over to the police. With my encouragement, they'll grind you until you're ground so fine you can be sifted. You can cooperate with us and hope for the best or rely on the mercy of the state."

"Why should I trust you?" she said.

"I'll leave that calculation to you. We know enough about Russell to suspect that, where you're concerned, there were mitigating circumstances."

Were there mitigating circumstances? Lyle asked himself. Had this woman been involved in the café bombing and the plot to kill him at the consulate, as seemed likely? Was he sitting next to someone who had tried to kill him? Or had she only been brought into Russell's schemes when he moved her pawn on his chessboard?

"How do I know you're not recording this conversation?"

"Because I give you my word, and you're in no position to strike a bargain."

"Close the door," she insisted.

Caroline Desrosier didn't look like a beaten woman—far from it, just wary. In fact, Lyle felt her magnetism more strongly than he had at their previous meeting, making him wonder if her long association with Russell hadn't made her more protégée than acolyte.

"Arthur and I were acquainted. I met him when I worked in Mainz, and we shared interests in social and political theories."

"Save it. You were associates—collaborators. You reeled Dekeyser in and, when the time came, you killed him," Sam responded.

"That's preposterous," she said.

"You're behaving as if my threat to turn you in is an idle one. Don't make that mistake. This is your only chance, your life preserver."

Except for the night at the consulate and Russell's office, Lyle hadn't witnessed his brother in action, and he could see how perilous it was to be sitting in Caroline Desrosier's chair.

"What do you want to know?" she said.

"You may think my questions are foolish or irrelevant; you'd be wrong. How did Russell learn about the manuscript?"

Desrosier turned a malignant eye on Sam, and apparently saw the way things were, because she said, "Noel told me about the manuscript several years after he'd left the monastery. He'd been infatuated with me since we were young. I informed Arthur, and learned he'd been pursuing this manuscript for years—decades, actually, though along different lines. I convinced Noel to steal it and bring it here."

"Why was Russell interested in the manuscript?"

"A journalistic project."

"That won't do. The truth. What did he find in the Alembert archive that brought him back so many times?"

"Pardon the intrusion." Lourdes had quietly opened the door and beamed a smile that evaporated when he saw their grim expressions.

"Professor Stuart, will you be returning to the archive?"

Why would Lyle be interested in that string of imitation pearls when he'd acquired a Triple-A pearl?

"No, thank you, Dr. Lourdes." Observing Lourdes's interest in Sam, Lyle said, "My brother, Sam Stuart, a commercial traveler on holiday. Sam, Dr. Lourdes, the Adler Alembert Chair of Paleoarchaeology."

A straight-faced Sam stood and the two shook hands, with nary a hint that Sam wasn't a stranger to Lourdes's public *and* private lives.

"Caroline, don't you find Professor Stuart a fascinating man?"

Desrosier looked from Lyle to Sam, and said, "I'm not surprised by his accomplishments. He is relentless."

"Not the word I'd have used, but I suppose one must be to achieve what Professor Stuart has achieved."

The door closed as quietly as it had opened. The other relentless Stuart, Sam, said, "What brought Alembert back so many times?"

"The *paléomythologie* file was rich in information, if one knew where to look, if one could separate the wheat from the chaff."

"And the manuscript?" Sam said.

"Arthur believed there was knowledge in the manuscript to re-make himself."

"Re-make, as in curing his maladies?"

"As in rejuvenation, as in turning back his biological clock, or something along those lines."

"What did you think?"

"I never knew Arthur to be wrong."

Sam's questions kept coming, like machine gun fire. "What were the different lines he'd been pursuing?"

"Arthur told me that in the 1960s he was able to interview a number of Alembert's lieutenants, and he used his talents to compel them to reveal what they knew about that man and his interests. Arthur found out that Alembert had been on the trail of this *thing* when he disappeared in 1932. The *paléomythologie* file was confirmation that Alembert had believed the manuscript to be connected with Atlantis."

"Alembert and Russell believed Atlantis was a real place?"

"That's right."

"And spent decades trying to prove it?"

"Not prove it, acquire knowledge that's been lost for ages."

"That's a hell of a way to waste a life," Sam remarked. "Keep going. I want everything."

"When Arthur learned about the manuscript, the idea of possessing it became precious to him. You could say it became an obsession. I didn't mind, because what made him happy made me happy."

"Did he ask you to move to the Sorbonne?"

"Arthur wanted me to monitor archive visitors, and to investigate the *paleo* file when he had questions."

Though Lyle had met people who had succumbed to cultish indoctrination, Desrosier didn't display any of those characteristics. Rather than receiving a psychological lobotomy, she had been operated on by a surgeon who had enhanced her natural talents, while subordinating her desires and inclinations to his will.

Lyle said, "Did he believe Alembert was the anonymous benefactor of the Institute where he was raised?"

"He *knew* it to be true."

Sam said, "What had Russell done to make him an outcast, to keep him from being promoted?"

"Would it shock you to learn that every member of that faculty, including the *Institutsdirektor,* were in their positions because Arthur desired it, and when he wanted someone removed, they were? That he'd been doing this for decades?"

Lyle and Sam looked at each other before Sam spoke: "You're saying it was his decision to be an assistant for sixty years?"

"That's exactly what I'm saying. He preferred to work behind the scenes to obtain what he wanted. He told me how he did it. First, he invented the narrative he desired. Then, he convinced the person this narrative corresponded to reality. Finally, he convinced them they had worked out this reality for themselves, that it was their own idea."

Exactly what Russell had done with Lyle, pretending to warn him, even as the man was motivating him to meet Romanov at the consulate.

"Arthur had a process that was unfathomable to the person he was interviewing." Staring at Lyle, she said, "I'm sure you heard one of his profiling stories, Arthur's way of assessing the psyche, temperament, biases, of the person he was interviewing.

"He had dozens of profiling stories: the trapeze in the circus, a pet falcon, the cane on the window ledge . . . none of them true," she said. "Or the story about the skeleton. He learned a great deal about people by observing their reactions to Montaigne's quotation."

"Have you ever been inside his house?" Sam asked her.

"Why is that important?"

"Maybe it isn't. I still want an answer."

"He was ashamed to bring me there . . . the clutter, the accommodations to his condition. I didn't care about those things, but I didn't want to upset him."

"So, you never saw the other wheelchair."

"He didn't have another wheelchair. Are you trying to catch me in a lie?"

"You knew about his journal?" Sam said, offhandedly.

It was obvious to Lyle she hadn't known about the journal and, if he saw it, Sam surely noticed.

"He kept a journal for decades, documenting how he manipulated people into doing what he wanted them to do. You were just another entry."

"Liar," Desrosier said, her composure breeched.

Sam removed his own notebook, tore out a page, set it on the table in front of her, and wrote:

$$CD \xrightarrow{S} ND$$

"There are hundreds of entries like this in Russell's journal. A psychologist translated it. Want to know what it means?"

"I have no idea what it means, and I doubt that your psychologist does either."

Sam nudged Lyle, who said, "Caroline Desrosier compelled to kill—the double arrow—Noel Dekeyser, by appealing to *superbia* . . . pride."

She was staring at the piece of paper as if it were a scorpion or a writhing adder. When her sparkling blue eyes came up, they were on fire, like flaming copper salts.

"We were as intimate as any two people could possibly be, and I'm not talking about sex. I know plenty about that."

"That's what he wanted you to think," Sam said.

"Where is this journal?"

Sam produced it, as if from nowhere. After Desrosier had paged through the journal to the year 2016, she paused, and her eyes moved from side to side, up and down, but before she could rip that page from the journal, Sam had snatched it back.

"You know it's his handwriting. You know only he had the talent to do this. You saw your name and Dekeyser's. You were just another entry. Why did Russell decide to kill him?"

"It was the Russian."

"That's not what the journal says."

"The Russian killed him. I'm not admitting to murder."

Lyle said, "Romanov pointed a gun at me, accused me of tormenting you."

"Perhaps I have met him. Perhaps he is a lunatic. I'm not responsible for what other people say and do. Arthur was sure Noel kept the manuscript in his apartment, as close as possible. Noel had suggested as much to Arthur. Afterwards—after Noel vanished—Arthur scoured the apartment but couldn't find it."

"Why did Dekeyser bring the manuscript to Mainz?"

"He was obsessed with having me, with being a rooster. I convinced Noel that Arthur was acting for a wealthy Chinese buyer. The two of them were negotiating a fee in the millions, or so Noel was made to believe. When it came to the manuscript, Noel was all business, knew exactly what he had, what he wanted for it, and how important it was to protect it."

"I know Dekeyser talked to others about art and artifact dealers," Lyle said.

"He told me about that, but I convinced him he could get more from the people Arthur knew. What are you going to do with this information?" she asked Sam.

"I'm not sure. Depends on how reliable it turns out to be. You're safe for the time being."

"Did Arthur die of natural causes?" she inquired.

"That's the public story."

"But you know more, don't you? Did you or your people kill him?" she asked, bitterly.

Sam had opened the journal and was examining it, or pretending to.

"What else do you know about Arthur's death? I deserve to know," she demanded.

Sam didn't look up from the journal when he said, "After he tried to kill Lyle—twice—I let him know we had deciphered his journal, that we'd recovered the manuscript, the only thing he cared about in life, that his every move would be watched from now on, that his behind-the-scenes mischief had come to an end."

So that was it, Lyle told himself. Sam had cornered Russell.

"I see," she said. "You killed him."

Sam said, "Don't do anything stupid. You're in enough trouble as it is. It's not hard to murder someone, but it's tricky killing someone and making them disappear."

"How would I know?" she said.

"You couldn't kill Dekeyser in a public place, especially if you needed to dispose of the body without anyone discovering it. That means, you would have had to kill him in your Paris apartment, a safe house where preparations could be made beforehand. My people found a company that moved a chest to a truck outside the apartment on August 6. You rented a truck on August 5 and returned it on August 7.

"With terrorism involving trucks being such a concern, many companies have installed chips in their vehicles that identify where they've gone and when. Need I go on?"

Her face went white. They had to wait for the woman to compose herself, to remind herself that her only hope in this new Russell-less world was cooperating with these enemies.

"How did he bring people into his orbit?" said Sam.

"Psychometrics, mostly. He advertised—recruited people he was interested in meeting; also, the clinic where he volunteered."

"Don't you wish you'd asked to see the manuscript before you killed Dekeyser?" Lyle asked.

She closed her eyes. "Where did you find it?"

"Go ahead," Sam said to Lyle.

"Dekeyser thought Russell was an old cripple scrapping for a finder's fee. You said Dekeyser was astute when it came to business. He had to have known he was suspected of the theft, and where would anyone search except his apartment, or perhaps a safe deposit box the police could easily trace? Who would ever think to look for the manuscript amidst the chaos of that office? Dekeyser got hold of a master key, and one night he went to Russell's office and placed a binder containing the manuscript high on a shelf, labeling it *Sed libera nos a malo*, the phrase on a placard above his rival's office at the monastery."

"You know all this?"

"I filled in some gaps, and the things you told me about your cousin support it."

Sam said, "Russell's dead, so he can't be harmed for what he convinced you to do, but you can spend years in prison. I want to know about the Café Marseille bombing."

Desrosier placed both hands on top of the table, as if supporting herself, and she took so much time answering that Lyle concluded she'd remain mute on the subject. "It might have happened like this. Arthur might have decided to do something about a troublemaker. He might have learned about that man's passion for liver. He might have stirred up an Algerian he'd come to know in the course of his clinic work, and who was employed at the hotel where the troublemaker was lodging. And after the dust had settled, and the wrong man survived, he might have brought a Russian into the scheme."

Lyle had been skeptical when Beatrice compared Russell to Rasputin, but what he'd experienced and heard in recent days had convinced him the Mad Monk was a novice compared to Arthur Russell.

"What happens next?" Desrosier asked Sam.

"If you're lucky, you never have to think about any of this again. Don't take that to mean we won't be watching you, in case you get a notion to take up Russell's mantle. One move in that direction will be a move too many . . . if you take my meaning."

The forlorn look on Desrosier's face told Lyle that Russell's reach was long, even from the grave.

Telling Sam he'd meet him at the car, Lyle detoured to Richard Lourdes's office, where he had to knock three times before a terse voice shouted, "Come in, then."

"I'm sorry to disturb you, Professor, but we're leaving tomorrow, so *au revoir* and thank you for your kindnesses."

Lyle hadn't finished speaking before he noticed Lourdes's distraught appearance, red-eyed, his body language suggesting dejection.

The older man walked around his desk and embraced Lyle with vigor. "It is I who thank you for seeing me before you depart. I'm afraid I interrupted something important in Mademoiselle Desrosier's office."

"Not so serious as you suppose," Lyle said.

"You haven't located Noel, by any chance."

"He's still missing. A fresh start, I hope."

"As do I."

Lyle noticed the ripped sheet of stationery on the floor, and where was that lovely cloisonné bowl of Lourdes's?

As if the man could read Lyle's mind, Lourdes said, "An accident . . . too damaged to salvage."

Was Lourdes talking about the bowl? "I'm sorry, Professor."

"Yes . . . yes. Was Caroline of assistance?"

"She supplied helpful information . . . about Noel, where he might be, what he might be doing."

"She's a very bright woman. I sometimes wonder why she sought this position and has stayed so long. As for me, I've been here a very long time. Too long, some have suggested."

"I wish you joy, Professor Lourdes."

On the way out, Lyle saw that the trash receptacle contained a pile of colorful shards.

"ARE WE GOING home now?" Beatrice asked Sam, as they finished their dinner at Sam's favorite restaurant in Paris, the Café de la Paix.

"Tomorrow. Brother saved. Artifact recovered. Villain dead."

He pushed his chair back a few inches. "Some memorable meals here, children. One night . . . all by myself . . . the waitress winked at me and delivered half a bottle of a delicious *Mersault* the next table had left behind—that table in the corner. Reading Simenon with a plate of *lamprey à la Bordelaise*."

"I listened to the conversation you recorded with Desrosier," said Beatrice. "You gave her your word."

"I had my fingers crossed . . . like this. And you know the old saying, no honor among thieves. The Russians call it *maskirovka*, the little masquerade, where you create confusion . . . uncertainty. Do you agree that she eliminated Dekeyser?" Sam asked Beatrice.

"The journal says so, and her responses, despite her protestations of innocence, tend to confirm it—the latent content, not the words themselves. Coming from a country brutalized by the Salafists, I studied their psychology by reading transcripts of trials and tribunals, and I learned that many who are initially reticent to admit to atrocities display pride at what they'd done as the trial proceeds. You see this with Desrosier as she went on."

Sam said, "The police let me into Russell's house before we left Mainz, while you and Lyle were sleeping, and I convinced them to hold the announcement of his death for a day."

"Don't you ever sleep?" asked Lyle.

"I can take it or leave it," said Sam. Beatrice gave him a pained look.

"What were you expecting to find?" Lyle inquired.

"Not bodies under the floor; he wasn't the type. How a person lives is a window into their mind. Beatrice could tell you that. Nothing out of place—spotless. Everything electronically controlled. The wheelchair he kept at home was like nothing I'd ever seen, and I've seen a lot of advanced technology. The place must have cost millions. How he lived matched the man Beatrice deciphered from the journal, not the *maskirovka* Lyle and everyone else witnessed in his office."

"We learned something else," said Beatrice. "The chaos in his office was another profiling story, and he used that one on Desrosier, too. Russell made her believe his embarrassment about the house was the reason she hadn't been invited there, making her even more sympathetic and loyal to him, and making her believe he needed her. Russell was more than a genius... a *mere* genius. He became the impresario of his own genius."

"Did you see the body?" Lyle asked Sam.

"The police said suicide. He must have learned about the consulate and the manuscript."

"Do you know what I did while you were recovering?" she said to Lyle. "I read a German translation of *The Lord of the Rings*. I believe in a larger life after death, but there's another kind of eternal life, and Tolkien's story depicts that awful existence in those black riders—hatred and lust for power, while clinging to the miserable existence Alembert and Russell were pursuing, whether they knew it or not.

"Sam, Desrosier probably murdered Dekeyser, and maybe others. Who gave you the authority to let her go?"

Lyle stiffened, anticipating an angry reaction from Sam, but his brother showed no emotion when he said, "In my business, when we aren't given authority, we have to take it."

"For the greater good?"

"Something like that. I made the judgment that with Russell gone, Desrosier's been defanged, and I had to know what she knew. The part about the chip in the truck was invented, but it told me what I wanted to know."

"You have to be careful, Sam."

"I've had a lot of practice."

"That concerns me more, not less."

"You lied to Desrosier about recording the conversation," Lyle said to Sam, "so you could turn her in, even though you said you wouldn't."

"That kind of lie gets around, and I may need to make more deals like that in the future."

"Whether you lie or not is just a calculation?" Beatrice asked Sam.

"When it comes to the firm's business, or Lyle's survival, it is."

"You're better than you make yourself out to be, Sam. I know you are."

"I'm glad someone thinks so."

Beatrice said, "Knowing what we do about Russell, taking such drastic action, killing himself just because a scheme went awry, doesn't fit. We must be missing something."

Sam said, "Even the most careful and resourceful criminals— Capone, Eichmann, Carlos—could be connected to their crimes with enough surveillance and intel. Russell must have decided the game was over."

"He killed himself?" Lyle asked his brother.

"What else?" said Sam.

JANUARY 28, 2017

☻-☻-☻

The Havens

SAM WAS AT THE WHEEL of the Spider, making the roadster do things Lyle couldn't have imagined doing. Beatrice was driving Sam's car, with Lyle in the passenger seat, alternately restless and fatigued. They were on their way to the Eurotunnel and would be back in England by suppertime.

"The way he's driving, I'll need a mechanic when we get back."

"Sam figures that's the way you're supposed to drive a car like that. If he was on a racehorse, he'd make it gallop, whether he knew how to ride or not."

"That's alright if it's your horse."

"You told me you read your mother's story."

"In Mainz, while I was healing."

"Tell me how she died, Lyle."

Anyone else, and he would have been awash in resentment, but as it was Beatrice, he bit his tongue.

"Were you there?"

He turned away from her and fixed his gaze on the gray and brown Normandy landscape. He'd never spoken about that night to anyone, not even Sam or his uncle. But hadn't Beatrice revealed what

238

had happened to her brother, and what she had done on that Ugandan riverbank?

So he told her about how the doctor, knowing his mother was going to die that night, had ordered him to go home. But he hadn't gone. He had hid in the closet of her hospital room until the lights were dimmed for the night, then crept into bed beside her. She was cold as a fish.

A wave of agitation surged through him. "She knew she was dying, and she knew it was me . . . The story she used to tell me, I told it back to *her*. I told her we were on top of a green hill, that when we looked to the west, we could see the Havens, the bay, the sailing ship with white sails, that it was getting dark, but sunlight was still coloring the water, that the path wound down the hill into a darkening valley, but once we crossed the valley we would rise again to the bay, that we were almost there, that I could hear sea birds, the way she used to tell it . . ."

She had hardly moved until the end, when she groaned and struggled to breathe. He'd been afraid, but he couldn't leave, not until he was sure she was gone. "After she died, I climbed out the window and dropped to the ground. Hurt my ankles and vomited in the yard." The doctor had paid for his cab home to the empty house his mother would never again enter.

"You remember everything, don't you?"

"As if it were yesterday . . . an hour ago."

"Do you want to forget?"

"No . . . not a minute of it. Never."

"Where was Sam?"

"Who knows? He was rarely home in those days."

"You did a beautiful thing walking your mother to the Havens."

Had the terrible things Beatrice experienced in Uganda affected her as his mother's death and the bomb had affected him? Had there been anyone to walk her back as she was now doing with him?

"Good God, Sam," erupted Lyle, as his brother took a curve on two wheels.

Beatrice said, "You notice I'm not trying to keep up. When he sees me falling behind, he slows down."

"He's paying me back for defying him."

"He was angry, but Sam cares about you too much to do that. I'm worried about him."

"Sam's the last person you should worry about."

She gave Lyle that *wake-up* look he'd seen before. "You see the older brother you've admired all your life. You don't see Sam's emptiness, that he's adrift, that he desperately needs your friendship."

"Not Sam. He . . ."

"Yes, Sam. He wouldn't admit it in a million years, but he needs you. What else does he have? A job that rubs his nose in ugliness? Can you name one of his friends?"

"I don't see him often enough to know," Lyle protested. In fact, the only close friend he remembered was a witty man named Patrick, who often came to the house with Sam when Lyle was young.

"I suspect he has an addiction, though he hides it well, but no one can hide it forever."

"You're guessing."

"I'm reading signs I've seen all too often, the way you read spearheads and cave art. Not a perfect science, and I hope I'm wrong. I'm telling you Sam needs you. What you do with the information is up to you."

Lyle had never known Sam to need anything, and it was practically impossible to think of him as adrift. While Lyle had been pondering questions about the age and authenticity of the manuscript, he suspected his brother hadn't given these things a second thought, because it hadn't mattered to Sam if the manuscript was authentic. All that mattered to Sam was keeping Lyle out of danger.

"There's a sign for the tunnel," Lyle said. They'd be in Folkestone soon, where he'd met Remington and heard that man expound on Lucifer the liberator. He thought of Russell. How the mighty had fallen . . .

"The mighty?" Beatrice glanced at him.

Had he said that aloud? "Remington, Noel Dekeyser's director at the Folkestone clinic—he had a small replica of the Lucifer of Liège. Do you know it? He called Lucifer the liberator."

The next thing he knew, Beatrice had turned the car off the main road, and soon they were navigating a meandering two-lane road.

It didn't take long for Sam to call them: "Where are you going?"

"A cultural trip," Beatrice answered him.

"I don't have time for culture."

"Then we'll see you in England."

"That's all I get?"

"A cultural trip. Want to hear more?"

"See you in England."

After Sam had signed off, Lyle said, "Where are we going?"

"Mont Saint-Michel. I hope you don't mind. I've always wanted to visit, and even before you mentioned Remington's Lucifer I saw the road sign."

"What about our room in Folkestone?"

"Sam will see to it. We'll find a hotel in Saint-Malo."

"You followed me all over Europe, so how can I complain?"

"When I was a girl, we studied the great monasteries. With all that happened, I'd forgotten how close we were to Mont Saint-Michel . . . until the sign reminded me."

Lyle said, "You haven't asked if I've talked to my uncle about the manuscript."

"I'm sure you have."

Not that Lyle hadn't felt the tug of the thing; he felt it still. Every time he examined an illumination he saw something a casual viewing wouldn't reveal. Ever since he had decided to pursue a scientific career, he had dreamed of contributing something that advanced science by leaps and bounds, and the recognition this would bring him. The manuscript was such a discovery, but to do it justice he would need years, and would have to assemble a team of experts.

He hadn't felt better after speaking to his uncle, and he didn't feel better now. If he accepted his uncle's offer to delay returning the manuscript, could weeks be extended to months, or even years?

He kept coming back to what Beatrice had said to him in Paris. There were no half measures for him. He must restore the manuscript to his uncle as soon as possible, or scheme to retain it forever.

Beatrice said, "You made your uncle happy."

"I'm not sure. He wanted to know about Dekeyser, and when I told him Sam's theory about what happened, he wanted to find the place where she disposed of the body so he could bless it. Unless Desrosier owns up to it, that'll be as hard as finding the manuscript . . . harder. I have plenty of work to do in England, and so do you."

"Your uncle values people over things, even flawed people over spectacular things."

Passing through Caen reminded Lyle that maps and physical terrain are very different things. Up until then, he'd been traveling to a destination on the Normandy coast, but seeing this town reminded him that "Lefebvre's folly" had been located in this region.

It was a longer side trip than he had expected, and he was calculating the probable delay when he saw it rising up like a mountain of stone out of the sea. Except for being surrounded by the sea on all sides, it might have been any castle town: a walled fortress atop the hill, with a stone village and lush vegetation below it.

Exiting the car in a plaza ahead of the causeway, Beatrice said, "An abbey, like your uncle's monastery, but bigger and older."

Though they had arrived late in the afternoon, light from a clear sky reflected off the sea, making it seem earlier in the day. The pinnacle of the monastery, the highest point on the Mont, gleamed as if it was on fire, drawing Lyle's eye. "There's a figure on top of the spire."

"The archangel. This is a departing place, a *periferia*—a border country, like the Havens in the story."

Had she come here to see the monastery, or because of what he had told her about his mother's last hour?

She led him toward the towering monastery, still several hundred yards distant, and an uphill trek. On either side, waves lapped the stones beneath the causeway.

They might have gone twenty yards when Beatrice halted, and turned around. "Wait, Lyle."

Behind them were a woman and man, hand in hand, creeping tentatively in the direction of the abbey.

Lyle followed Beatrice back to the couple. The woman, leaning on a prong-ended cane, was in her eighties, stooped, gray haired, not much over five feet tall, with a horsey face. The stout man, wearing faded blue sweatpants and an oversized pullover, was younger than the woman, had a round Downs face, and was a head shorter than Lyle.

"*Pouvons-nous vous aider?*" Beatrice asked the woman.

"We're English. *Ne parle pas français.*"

"May we help you?"

"Don't bother. We'll be fine."

"How did you get here?"

The woman said, "We rode the bus with a group from Salisbury to Saint-Malo. Jeremy wasn't tops this morning, so we missed the bus. Hired a cab, but no room for my walker, so this cane will have to do. The cab driver said he wasn't allowed to park any closer to the abbey. We'll be fine. Jeremy and me are used to going slow."

"I'm Beatrice, this is Lyle. Why don't we walk with you?"

The old woman looked at Jeremy, and said, "Alright, but we're slow."

"Lyle, you walk with Jeremy, and I'll walk with . . ."

"Catherine Conway," the woman said. "You're an angel."

Beatrice took one of Catherine's arms and the women led the way. Jeremy walked with waddling steps, as much back and forth as forward movement. Lyle had never said more than a few words to those of his kind, and whenever he encountered such a person, he couldn't help wondering what their lives were like, how bleak and constrained they must be.

They had covered the twenty yards that Beatrice and Lyle had backtracked when Jeremy extended a hand, and said, "My name is Jeremy. Who are you?"

"Lyle . . . Stuart."

Jeremy locked his arm in Lyle's, startling him. Up ahead, Catherine was leaning on her cane, and on Beatrice.

"I have a girlfriend. Her name is Loretta. She's pretty. How old are you?"

"Thirty-eight," said Lyle.

"I'm forty-nine. Loretta's forty-two. Where do you live?"

"We live in Oxford . . . teach at the University."

"You're smart. I went to school."

"Did you like it?"

"I'm not smart . . . and I'm slow. I don't like school. My Mum wanted to come here a long time. Saved money. I clean the library."

Struggling for words, Lyle said, "How did you meet Loretta?"

"I have a cat . . . John Wayne. Loretta's in Southampton. I take the bus."

"Is your father back in Salisbury?"

"Daddy died. I know how to write. Mrs. Smith taught me."

"What do you write about?"

Jeremy's expressions alternated between enthusiasm and caution. "Letters."

"To Loretta?"

"Yes, I do. Every day."

As they passed through the town, the way steepened and narrowed, stone buildings crowding the lane on either side. Lyle's leather-soled shoes were unsuited to the smooth stone street, and the bright spire was no longer visible. The effervescent sunlight he'd witnessed on the causeway was absent from the canyon-like lanes of the outer ward. This walled town, the relentless ascent, surrounded by stone walls and buildings, the sense of great age—how could it not remind him of John Hill's city against the mountain?

He could hear his companion's labored breaths, and he noticed that Jeremy's gray hair was thinning, with a bald patch on the crown of his head. Every time Catherine stopped to rest, so did Jeremy, several paces behind his mother.

"Does Loretta write you?"

"Yes. What do you teach, Mr. Stuart?"

"You can call me Lyle . . . archaeology . . . about people who lived a long time ago."

"Like the cemetery where Daddy is. We bring flowers . . . say prayers."

"That's right, but older cemeteries."

"I write Mr. Cuddy letters. He's in jail."

"Why is he in jail?"

"Took things, they say. He's my friend. Mrs. Smith can't walk good. She likes John Wayne. I clean her house."

Lyle caught a whiff of something sweet, and saw that Jeremy was peeling an orange.

"You want some?"

When Lyle declined, Jeremy said, "Know what's in my bag?"

The man's face was screwed up tight, like a ventriloquist's dummy. He removed a box of chocolates from the bag. "For Loretta."

"Does she like sweets?"

"Yes, she does. I do, too. Is Beatrice your girlfriend?"

Lyle hesitated, wondering whether Beatrice could hear them. "Yes."

"She's nice. You going to marry?"

"I don't know."

"I like her. She's black."

"Beatrice was born in Africa, a country called Uganda."

"I want to go there. Lions . . . elephants."

A hairpin turn and a steep flight of steps. With fifty yards to go, Lyle was getting worried about Jeremy and Catherine. Locking arms with the man again, he said, "Does anyone live with Loretta?"

"Her aunt. Nathan used to. He had to go . . . he got rough with Julie."

They took half a dozen steps before Lyle said, "Like hitting?"

"Pushing . . . yelling. Made Loretta cry. I told him not to push girls."

"You did the right thing, Jeremy."

"Can I have your street number . . . for a letter?"

"I'll write it down."

Lyle had taken five-mile walks around Oxford that seemed shorter than this. When they finally reached the abbey entrance, a trio of middle-aged women came down the steps and said, "They're closed for the day."

Beatrice met Lyle's eye as she turned and assisted Catherine in the opposite direction.

"We should have walked faster," Jeremy said.

The old woman was more bent over than when they'd embarked, like a donkey overburdened by its load. Beatrice was propping her up and carrying the cane. Somehow, they managed to get Catherine and Jeremy back to the plaza, where Beatrice said, "Let us drive you to Saint-Malo. We're spending the night there too."

"We'll call the cab," Catherine said. "You've done enough. He'll be here in a jiffy."

"Don't forget your street number," Jeremy said to Lyle.

"Come with us . . . please," Beatrice said.

"Want to see a magic trick?" said Jeremy.

Before Lyle could answer, Jeremy reached into his back pocket and produced linked red and blue handkerchiefs, passing them through his hand twice with no effect, but on the third pass they changed to yellow and green.

"A gift from Cuddy," said Catherine, "before . . . well . . ."

"Jail," whispered Jeremy to Lyle.

Though Beatrice was applauding, Lyle thought she looked weary and sad.

On the road from Mont-Saint Michel to Saint-Malo, they passed fields filled with sheep grazing on the remnants of last year's crop, amidst clusters of ice and snow.

Though Lyle had been a teenager when his mother died, he was mentally and physically vigorous, and he had Sam in a pinch. What would happen to Jeremy if his mother died before he did? How radically would this man's life change?

Lyle was expecting Saint-Malo to be a small village, but it turned out to be an ancient walled city. As he helped Jeremy out of the car, the man said, "I'm sorry I'm slow."

"But you're interesting . . . and a fine man. That's more important. Here's my number. Don't forget to send me a letter."

After Lyle and Beatrice had gotten Catherine and Jeremy to their room, and as they were walking back to the car, Beatrice took Lyle's hand and said, "Catherine's husband died six months ago, and she misses him terribly. They had wanted to make this pilgrimage for thirty years, but things always got in the way. Jeremy is all she has . . . thank you, Lyle."

"If we hadn't come, I wouldn't have met him."

"Are you sorry we're still in France?"

"This adventure began with an angel and ended with one, began with a broken man who was abandoned and ended with a broken man who's loved . . . You didn't see the abbey."

"I saw what I wanted to see."

FEBRUARY 10, 2017

☻-☻-☻

Oxford Archaeology Laboratory

SHE DIDN'T BOTHER TO KNOCK. Why should she, being Andrea Fitzgerald?

Lyle was at his desk, preparing for Lido. There was much to do, not much time to do it, and little assistance, none of it experienced in outfitting an expedition.

"Where have you been?" Andrea asked him.

"The Continent."

"So I heard." Andrea featured large eyes surmounted by elliptical brows, and short silver hair that framed her face like a portrait, or a glamor shot. More than one opponent had failed to recognize the formidable brain behind that beautiful face.

"Where's Gorsey?" he asked her.

"With Marks and the others at the Jericho site. I have commitments in London."

"Are you going back?"

"Of course, when I'm finished here."

"Found anything interesting at the site?"

"An undiscovered city. That's all so far."

And he was excited about a few spearheads. "Circa?"

"2900 BCE, maybe older."

248

"You have the Midas touch."

"I do, don't I?"

"I heard something about a BBC series."

"Not confirmed yet. We're filming the pilot. If it draws an audience, they'll do more episodes. That's how it works."

"Is Marks involved?"

"He isn't interested in that sort of thing."

Nor would Andrea have considered inviting him, or anyone else, to share that spotlight.

"We missed you. We were worried about you," she said.

Naturally, the school had heard about the bombing, though Lyle had downplayed the extent of his injuries, had made it seem he'd been little more than a bystander.

Something was on Andrea's mind, but Lyle knew better than to press her. "I'm going to Lido soon," he said.

"You're up to it?"

"I'm going, no matter what."

"Turn that music down, would you? I heard you were searching for an antiquarian manuscript."

There it was, as nonchalant as could be. He was tempted to deny it. "Who told you that?"

She sat in the visitor's chair, pulled it close to the desk, and said, "I like you, Lyle. I always have, and I don't want you to end up like Lefebvre."

As Lyle had been manipulated by a master, he wasn't going to succumb to an amateur, even an exceedingly talented one. "What do you advise, Andrea?"

"You can start by telling me everything about this manuscript, then I can help you decide what to do with it."

How had she learned about the manuscript? Could it have been Desrosier, in spite of Sam's warning? Desrosier knew where Lyle taught, she could have researched the faculty, or she might have seen Andrea on television, or read about her. And why? Merely to make mischief, a partial payback for the misery Lyle had caused her? That sort of thing suited her down to the ground. A caged weasel's still a weasel, he told himself.

"Desrosier doesn't know what she's talking about," he said, convinced by Andrea's expression he'd guessed correctly.

She said, "I think you found what you were looking for."

He had to give it to her. Resourceful, relentless, unfazed by resistance, no wonder she got what she wanted.

Two days ago, Lyle had returned the manuscript to his uncle— a brisk, uncomfortable visit—and the angst of parting with it persisted. In the preceding days, he had thought about photographing each page. He had committed to returning the manuscript, but nothing had been said about photographs. No half measures, he kept telling himself, but in unguarded moments, he was still pondering how he might have kept it without betraying Beatrice or his uncle. "If I did find it, I've already disposed of it, and why would I dispose of something valuable?"

"What was it, then?"

"The true story of Atlantis."

"I don't know why I bother," she said.

Who could guess what was lurking behind Andrea's earnest eyes? Surely not helping Lyle or protecting his reputation. For sport, after he had rejected her for Beatrice, or an instinctive urge to beat down rivals?

Whenever the subject of the manuscript was introduced, Lyle was sorely tempted to erupt in a torrent of words, until he remembered what Beatrice had said when she first viewed it: "Whereof one cannot speak, thereof one must be silent," and only later had he learned she was quoting Wittgenstein. What could he possibly express in mere words that could begin to describe what he'd experienced in that Paris hotel room?

"Why would the person who informed me about the manuscript lie about it?"

"A woman who has her reasons for wanting to nick me, and the shadows suit her."

"When I return to Jericho, why don't you come too? There's room in my tent for two."

"Marks warned me about vipers."

Rather than meeting him head on; she tried a flank attack. "I've been told Adams is as frigid as the North Pole. She won't keep you warm at night."

Lyle wasn't immune to rancor, but he wasn't as susceptible as he'd been a few months earlier. "Have you ever been close to death, not someone else's—yours?"

"What does that have to do with anything?"

"I was a lot closer to the bomb, and it did a lot more damage, than I admitted. Now, I'm willing to live with weakness, messiness, uncertainty, in myself and in other people. Not malice, though. *Libera nos a malo.*"

"I'm not often wrong, but I was wrong about you. You're nothing but a minnow."

"Are you satisfied being an intellectual minnow?"

Katrivesis was hoping to provoke Lyle. The examiners on Katrivesis's right and left sat stony-faced, waiting for Lyle to respond.

"I'll answer any serious question, Dr. Katrivesis," said Lyle.

"You'll answer every question, Mr. Stuart."

"If I'm an intellectual minnow, does that mean I was spawned by an intellectual minnow?"

The other examiners knew that Lyle was referring to his advisor, who was working as hard to suppress his rage as Lyle was working hard to maintain his composure.

As Andrea rose from the chair, Lyle reached over and increased the volume, letting the music answer her.

Andrea and Desrosier were a toxic cocktail Lyle didn't care to dwell on, so he tried to apply himself to his work, but it was no use as Andrea's powerful presence hung over him like a storm cloud.

His eyes were drawn to the box against his office wall containing Hermann's scholarship. But why bother with it when he had given up the primary source, including the maps?

He gathered up his things, and as he passed Cooper's office, he saw the large map of Atlantis his colleague had tacked to the wall. In bold colors, as if a geographer had prepared the map after visiting the island: cities, including a mega-city; roads and rivers; mountains and forests; even man-made towers and a wharf for hundreds of ships.

"The true story of Atlantis," he had said to Andrea.

He might have disposed of the manuscript, but the manuscript wasn't finished with him.

AUGUST 10, 1960

☻-☻-☻

Oxford

HOW HAD SHE SECURED this interview? He wasn't granting interviews. He didn't want to talk to anyone. He was muddled, distracted, resentful. He'd even abandoned his reading, that last bastion of normalcy. Every day since accepting her request he had been on the verge of rescinding it.

He had never been an impulsive man. Rather, a man of mind— reason and deliberation—but here she was.

The visitor, attired in a green dress and matching pillbox hat, said, "Thank you for seeing me, Professor."

A singular personality, he told himself. Stately, though still young—in her thirties, forties? A woman who could look spectacular if she chose. Certainly, a woman of mind—their correspondence had told him as much, along with identifying her as a toxicologist with something to say about Adler Alembert and that prolific writer the Professor had taken to calling *The Titan*.

They were seated across a low table in a room in his house that was manly in furnishings and appointments, but with feminine touches suggesting a strategic assault on unbridled masculinity. In his drab sweater, slacks, and house shoes, he felt a twinge of embarrassment.

"I can offer you tea or coffee, but the pantry is bare at the moment." The boys were away at school, and he had little inclination to shop for himself these days. "I may have some biscuits and paste."

"Nothing, thank you."

"How can I help you, Dr. Rosman?"

Solemnity writ large on her features, the woman said, "You can help me change the world . . . for the better."

The last thing he'd expected to hear. "*Better* means vastly different things to different people, and I'm less sanguine about changing the world than I once was. These days, I'm content with keeping the man under my hat sane and sound."

"That's Fr. Brown. I met the author in 1936, the year he died. I had read all his books. He agreed to see me . . . yes, I was a young girl then."

The Titan. "Pardon me, Dr. Rosman, but I'm curious what the people in your letter have to do with me."

"The writer I met in 1936 told me about Adler Alembert, and Alembert's . . . *contest* with your friend."

"Why would so circumspect a man reveal those things to you?"

"You know him?"

"I never met him, but I know of him, and I know his work."

"He was aware of Alembert's interest in highly fatal poisons, he feared assassination, and he knew I was studying toxicology."

"Alembert was dead by then."

"Are you sure he's dead?"

He *was* sure, but he wasn't about to explain why.

"That writer and your friend had defied Alembert, and he was convinced he was in danger."

"He told you this?"

"Yes . . . he trusted me. I'm one of you, dismayed at where the world is going. Two vicious, Godless world wars this century, atheism and nihilism everywhere. Something must be done."

The Professor said, "I've learned to be skeptical of human

projects to save the world, no matter how well intentioned. That's not meant to be critical of your noble aspirations, but I doubt if I can be of any assistance."

"I don't mean to impose, especially so soon after . . ."

Every word of condolence like a dagger. Every solitary moment awash in misery. Why not indulge a few distractions, like this woman and her project, an hour's respite here and there, as close to tranquility as he was likely to experience.

Though a sunny day, the curtains were closed, the only light in the room filtered by the green fabric, the pale light bathing one of her arms, staining it green.

"What do you have in mind?" he asked her.

"Bear with me while I tell a story . . . it won't take long. Years ago, I met a man named Erzo, a gypsy peddling on a street in Radley."

"I know the town," said the Professor. "Not far from here."

"Or from Somerville, where I was reading chemistry. When he was unsuccessful at selling me anything, he promised to tell me something spectacular if I'd stand him a few drinks."

Though the Professor had heard that man's name a long time ago, he couldn't place when, or in what context.

"Do you mind if I smoke?" he asked her.

"Not at all," she replied, waiting for him to light his pipe.

The story Rosman had heard from the gypsy matched a piece of the tale the Professor's friend had related years ago in the *Bird & Baby*—the attack on the road after he'd discovered the manuscript, though Erzo had represented the matter to Rosman as a contentious business transaction rather than raw belligerence.

"The container was unlike anything Erzo had ever seen . . . or could imagine. Living silver, he called it. He told me what he knew about Alembert, a man who was missing and presumed dead, and who still terrified him."

Strangers—men and women alike—with whom the Professor had met in recent years were invariably overawed by him; not this woman.

"May I ask why you were standing a Roma drinks in a Radley pub?"

Exhibiting no unease, she said, "Your reputation for cross examination does you justice. I was on school holiday visiting my aunt, and I needed a drink as badly as the gypsy. A bohemian phase I outgrew."

"I don't see how an encounter on the road made that fellow an expert on the thing he observed."

"That wasn't the end of Erzo's story. He was interrogated by Adler Alembert several years later, and he could tell that Alembert desperately desired this thing. At that time, Alembert hired him to follow that big writer and report back on any meetings with your friend.

"Erzo's story inspired me to look the man up, and I was pleasantly surprised at how eager he was to reveal what he knew, that your friend had discovered an ancient—rather, prehistoric—manuscript, had translated much of it, and had somehow managed to keep it from Alembert."

Substantially what the Professor knew to be true, though he was struggling to reconcile the fearful, indiscreet man she described with what he knew about *The Titan*.

"He believed, as I did—and do today—that the existence of an advanced civilization so many millennia before our historical records would weaken the grip of nihilism and help to re-Christianize Europe, that keeping the manuscript secret was a grave error. He was fervently in favor of this chronicle—whatever it is—being revealed to the world. Of course, it has been revealed in a way, hasn't it?"

The Professor knocked the residue from his pipe into an ashtray. "I can't speak to that."

"Or you won't?"

He could feel the intensity of her personality, like a physical force.

"Your friend is a man of high virtue, but he is stubborn and has made up his mind to keep this . . . thing hidden."

"You have spoken to him?"

"Yes."

"You were unsuccessful."

"Yes, but perhaps he would listen to someone he esteems highly, and even if revealing this civilization doesn't re-Christianize Europe, it would drive a dagger into its nihilism."

"You think so? Others have desired this thing, and for their own purposes."

"Exactly, and if we can't convince him to un-hide this thing, someone will eventually get their hands on it and use it for their own ends—vile ends. Even at this moment, there is such a person, and he is formidable . . . another Alembert. I'm not such a person. I don't care about possessing it. By keeping it hidden, your friend is doing a disservice to the beliefs he professes."

"He has told the story."

"He's told *a* story, and not all of it."

"How do you know this?"

Though her aplomb remained intact, he could tell she wasn't used to aggressive questioning. "I know because I've been pursuing this thing for a long time."

"His story wasn't published until years after Alembert and . . . that titanic writer were dead, so how could you know he didn't tell the complete story?"

Her eyes stayed firm, steady. "Ransom would approve of what I'm doing . . . the Lion, too."

What if her timing in coming here so soon after his loss had been intentional? What if she had decided to ply him when he was most vulnerable?

He hadn't moved in the past hour, but he was exhausted, he who had once lectured on his feet for hours on end. Lately, the Professor felt as if all his joints needed grease, especially one shoulder. He started to fill his pipe, and found he didn't have the strength but, by invoking the Lion, she had gone too far. Her words had affected him like an air raid siren in the middle of the night. This woman had heard momentous things from a Roma whose clans revealed little to strangers, had prompted *The Titan* to confide dire things, knew too much about Adler Alembert's secretive organization, and had somehow found her way to him when all the doors were barred. For years, he had engaged in mental jousts with the likes of John, Owen, Hugo, and Dorothy. He might have been beaten down, but those analytical muscles hadn't atrophied—not yet.

He could have equivocated and bought himself more time, but that had never been his way.

"Who are you really?"

"You know who I am."

"I don't believe you."

Her eyes flashed, but she immediately quenched the fire. "Everything I've learned about you suggests you believe as I do about the world . . . and what it needs. I'm offering you an opportunity to help repair this broken world."

He was still holding the empty pipe. "You will not convince me to help you."

"You sit in this dark room as the world erodes, and all the books you write don't change a thing."

She had touched a raw nerve. For some time now, and especially as the carcinoma had advanced, he'd been troubled by the thought that his work was nothing more than chaff. The world continued to lurch in a deadly direction, in spite of all he had tried to do, and even within his own circle of friends and colleagues there was little to celebrate. Now, her suggestion that he'd been building sand castles when he might have been constructing a levy against the flood.

"The manuscript will provoke a cultural crusade, and you can be part of it . . . at a time when your world has come to an end."

His world *had* come to an end. There were moments when he feared he could go no further up, no further in.

"Do you realize this . . . artifact was incredibly ancient when the first pyramid and ziggurat were built?"

As spectacular as this *thing* was—and the Professor believed it was as spectacular and ancient as his friend professed it to be—he also believed what Segalen had proclaimed in his poem: *nothing immobile can escape the hungry teeth of the ages.* Not even the manuscript and its mysterious receptacle. Not forever.

He closed his eyes, and said, "I *have* been part of it . . . I accept his decision."

She stood, a rigid haughtiness in her bearing and displayed on her features.

"Pray let me know when you change your mind."

He stood too, though there was no majesty in him at the moment. "Goodbye, Dr. Rosman."

☻-☻-☻

Oxford

L YLE MIGHT HAVE BEEN preoccupied with Andrea and Lido, but he couldn't have missed the flashing lights at the Waterloo Creek Apartments.

As he walked to his door, he thought he heard his name. He turned around and saw Mary crossing the street, still calling his name in an anguished voice.

Though he rarely spoke to Mary and Burt, he couldn't see either of them without being reminded of the Mary Poppins film, because they were cheerful and optimistic like their film namesakes.

This Mary was anything but cheerful. "It's William," she said. "William Horrigan."

"What's wrong?" Lyle said, eyeing the ambulance.

"He's died."

"What?"

"He's been sick. His immune system was weak."

"Why didn't someone tell me?" William had told him about the cancer, but Lyle had never bothered to find out how he was coming along.

"He said not to bother you, that you're doing important work at the University. William read all your papers. Told me he kidded you about a souvenir. I'm not sure what will become of Lucia—the dog."

Across the street, a stretcher was being pushed inside the ambulance. Crowded around the vehicle was an old woman leaning on Burt, Harold bent over his cane, and many others.

"William thought highly of you."

The ambulance alarm lights went off as the vehicle exited the drive.

APRIL 17, 2017

☻-☻-☻

Oxford

LYLE WAS BACK AT THE Oxford Consolidated Archives, prompted by things he'd learned in recent weeks, and by Cornel Popa's observations during Lyle's just completed trip to the Lido site: "We located the tribe's burial site not long after your first visit. We were surprised to find artifacts in one of the graves, probably a chieftain. Arranged with intent, rather than just thrown in. Weapons on the left, religious artifacts on the right."

"You found iconography this early, and so far from Neolithic centers?"

"It is remarkable, yes? We have more work to do. That set of bones . . . apart from the rest. We think it's a family: father, mother, son. The clues seem to point in that direction, though we may never be certain."

What Popa said reinforced what Lyle had suspected for some time.

The diary was exactly where Lyle had left it. The fact that the diary had been relegated to the *Odds & Ends* box meant it had been deemed of no account.

Agnes CurLio had been forgotten too, deemed of no account. When he'd first examined the diary, he had wondered what had happened to Agnes, and why her diary was in Hill's archive. Now, he knew.

"Grandfather Arthur can't go anywhere without his wheeled chair . . . I only know that my planet must orbit Adler's star . . . They took him away before I could so much as see him . . . I whispered to A. the name I wanted him to have . . . No matter where in the world I go, he will find me and put me in my proper place . . . I left him today, unimaginable a few years ago . . . The channel boat tonight. Almost sure the big man I saw on deck is following me . . . I'm seeing the Oxford teacher today, and I'm leaving this diary behind."

Agnes CurLio had followed Adler Alembert, not the philanthropist honored at the Sorbonne, but a criminal lord and murderer. They had had a child in 1921, whom she thought had died, and whom she had named Arthur, a child who, if it had lived, would have been ninety-six in 2017.

How had Lyle come to these conclusions? By sifting through the evidence, as he did at archaeological sites, and by what he'd experienced since the last time he was here.

Agnes's diary references to Adler/A, South America, their close relationship going back to her youth.

Agnes's entry about the baby—what else could it have been?

Arthur was Agnes's grandfather's name, and Mortimer Russell was the name of the Institute where Arthur Russell was raised.

The Times' evidence of a child Russell's age living at the Institute, corroborated by Desrosier.

The anonymous donor who had funded the Institute must have funded Russell's lengthy residence and treatment, and who could this have been but the boy's father, Alembert?

Arthur Russell's obsession with Adler Alembert's pursuit of the manuscript.

Agnes's arrival in England a few days before the last entry and her murder, her reference to visiting the Oxford teacher, and the diary ending up in Hill's possession.

Had she gone to Hill to warn him because she knew Alembert wanted the manuscript? If Hill had crossed swords with Alembert, how had he managed to survive?

What had happened to Adler Alembert? How much did Arthur know about his father? Had Russell come to lust for the manuscript on his own and for his own purposes, or was the son consciously following in the footsteps of the father?

"You considered that one hair fluttering at my neck; you gazed at it upon my neck, and it captivated you." That was part of Agnes's story too. Lyle had since learned that these were the words of the mystic, Juan de la Cruz. She had left the safety and security of Alembert's empire after encountering this man's writings, so perhaps her world hadn't been as dark as Lyle imagined it to be.

Alembert had disappeared when the boy was eleven. The diary references to Agnes's child made Lyle wonder what Arthur Russell might have been if his mother had raised him, or if he had known someone like Beatrice when he was young. Would the talented Russell have been a very different man, or what he had actually become?

Earlier, Lyle had established a connection between Agnes, Alembert, and Hill. Now, he could add Russell, and himself. Across time and space, they were connected by the manuscript, by something that might have been created by people who lived eons ago.

Beatrice was convinced of what she called a "larger life," but how could one know for certain? Lyle had looked that spectral wolf square in the eye in the ravaged Mainz café, and the experience had terrified him, had dogged him ever since, in spite of his determination to recover the *status quo ante* explosion.

Lyle had balked when Beatrice asked if she could accompany him to Lido for the first week, until she convinced him she was genuinely interested in the site, and not just keeping an eye on him. They had taken a longer route, with a side trip to pay a visit to the sister of the German policeman who had been killed in the bombing—something he couldn't have done without Beatrice.

Lyle had been contemplating asking Beatrice to marry him. He had little doubt what Sam's opinion would be, as his brother thought the world of her. Jeremy had weighed in, too, with Lyle suspecting his new friend's inclinations were better than his own. It came down to this: Lyle wasn't sure he could love her as he suspected she loved him, that he could give it back to her, and this frightened him.

As if he had all the time in the world to make up his mind. Hadn't the bomb and Russell taught him the folly of that kind of thinking?

THEY WERE SUPPOSED TO have dined at their favorite restaurant, but Beatrice had left a message for Lyle to come to her apartment instead—the liver she had promised him in the Mainz hospital?

"I have something to tell you," she said as he was removing his jacket.

"First, I have to tell you something. Sit down for a minute," and when she did, Lyle related everything he'd deduced about Russell from the diary.

When he'd finished, Beatrice said, "His mother was a remarkable woman. What might have been. You hinted at it. A baby needs—deserves—to be loved."

Emotion writ large on her features, along with something Lyle had witnessed in her often enough—resolution.

Keith Jarrett's *Köln Concert*, Lyle's favorite piano jazz, was playing at low volume. The photograph of Beatrice's family at the shrine reminded him of the pen and ink picture the German policeman's sister had given him as he and Beatrice were leaving her apartment: her brother's uncompleted picture of the Café Marseilles with a missing corner, as if the bomb had blown it away.

Looking around the room, he realized there was no food or drink set out.

"I'm having dinner with Sam tomorrow night."

"I'm glad to hear it. It's what he needs."

"I told him Frodo wouldn't have gotten far without Sam . . . You said you had something to tell me."

"I do, but I don't know how, so I might as well just say it."

Jarrett was embarking on a riff that always lifted his spirits, but Lyle felt a sudden chill, exactly as he'd felt when the Algerian approached his table in the café. They were supposed to have dined out tonight, but she had invited him here instead. So, where was the food?

"Maria's husband is missing. They think he's dead. It seems he was working undercover for the police, and the rebels captured him." She stopped speaking to compose herself. "Maria's all alone, with the baby coming soon. I'm going back to Uganda. I'm taking a leave of absence."

Lyle remembered how he'd felt when they were walking back to the car in Saint-Malo, when Beatrice was holding his hand and the world made perfect sense. "When are you coming back?"

"I don't know if I'm ever coming back. If Maria's husband is dead, as they suspect, she'll need help with the child."

His ears were ringing, as they did when he was excited, ever since the bombing. "What will you do there?"

"Take Maria and the baby to Kampala, teach and work in the capital."

"You can't do this, Beatrice."

"Do you think I'd go if I wasn't needed? If I don't live what I say I believe, what do those beliefs mean—what are they worth?"

"I'll find a way to get Maria and the baby to England."

"How do you plan to manage that? Maria's never been out of Uganda. With a new baby, and in a strange place, she'd be lost. At this moment—husband murdered, all alone—she needs as much care as the baby. She doesn't need more turmoil."

"This is miserable," he stammered. "Maybe your God's decided I'm not good enough for you."

He thought that would anger her, and maybe that's what he wanted, but she said, "When we first started seeing each other, I came up with a dozen reasons it wouldn't amount to anything, but you're the best thing that's ever happened to me."

"I love you," he said, realizing he'd never said this to anyone.

"You have to go on with your life, you know."

"How can I?"

"A man who can see around corners will figure it out."

"I can't see around this corner."

She took his hands in hers. "When Dante was going through hell, he kept going. I want to see you smile. That's what I want to remember."

He made a wan attempt, with Beatrice shaking her head. "I have to pack. She needs me."

What he desired most in the world was right next to him, and he never recognized it. That's what she had said about Russell. "When you come back, I want you to marry me," he said.

"You honor me, Lyle, but don't make this more difficult than it already is, and don't commit yourself to something that may be years away."

"Don't you think I know my own mind?"

"Tell Sam I'm sorry I couldn't say goodbye, that I'll write him."

Lyle said, "I'm telling you, I'm not letting you go."

"I hope not. In the meantime, you have your work and I have mine. You're here and I'm there."

LYLE WAS ON THE STREET, turning everything over in his mind, still trying to come to terms with what Beatrice had told him. How could such a thing have happened after all they'd been through?

A car sounded its horn. He realized he'd walked into the street. There must be a way to fix this, he told himself. More than anything, he feared that with the passage of time, one or both of them would lose the feeling they now had, would revert to who they'd been before Lyle Stuart and Beatrice Adams had met, would make of their relationship a fond memory, and not the vital bond he knew it to be here and now. Didn't such things happen all the time, especially in the modern world?

Everything was up to them, he told himself. They, and only they, would determine their futures. At the same time, he knew Beatrice wouldn't agree with him, that she believed in another active agent. As she had said to his back as he walked down the hall, "It's mercy."

MAY 10, 2017

◉-◉-◉

St. Hugh's Charterhouse

LYLE AND ABBOT HENRY had left the Monastery after observing two monks who were sewing the manuscript pages back into the book, using magnifiers and the finest silk thread. They had even learned an elegant stitch in preparation for the work.

"No more than a page a day," Lyle's uncle had informed him. "A few years' work at that rate."

Those stitching monks had been barely aware of them. Heads bowed, only their hands were visible and active.

In a year, three, five, could he and Beatrice sew their lives back together, as his uncle's monks were doing with the manuscript?

Lyle and his uncle were on their second circuit of the monastery park, on a spectacular day that could have been called magical. Lyle had been probing his uncle as to how the magic in John Hill's translation of the manuscript could be reconciled with science.

"I don't suppose there's a word used for as many different things as magic," said Abbot Henry.

Across the park, a young monk was walking toward Lyle's Spider Lusso with a case of the Charterhouse's ale.

"That car looks peppy," said Abbot Henry.

"She's temperamental. This is a good day."

269

His uncle said, "Magic has been used to describe a child's first steps, a card or coin trick, how the universe came to be, the transformation of a caterpillar into a butterfly . . . how many things?"

"Butterflies . . . reminds me of a detour Beatrice and I made to Paris on our way to Mainz and Lido," said Lyle. "Professor Lourdes let me borrow a mounted butterfly from the Alembert archive. I'd never seen anything like this creature—wingspan, color palette—and I wondered if it had been fabricated, but the Oxford entomologists ruled that out."

"Do you still have it? As you know, my interest in nature abides."

"I planned to send it back to Lourdes, but the entomologists convinced him to let them study it. They thought this species had been extinct for at least a hundred thousand years. No comparable species in today's world—none that the bug scientists are aware of anyway."

"So where did it come from?"

"A jungle or forest . . . an isolated microhabitat, or perhaps it perished long ago and was perfectly preserved, like that nodosaur in Alberta."

"Knowing Alembert's obsession, is that what *you* believe?"

"I'm keeping an open mind, Uncle Henry. It's hard enough to accept an advanced civilization forty thousand years ago, without layering it with good and bad wizards, magic, and supernatural creatures. Do you think the magic was literary license?"

Hands buried inside his robe, Abbot Henry said, "That would be taking the easy way out. Remember that, prior to the twentieth century, scientists believed time and space were rigid dimensions, and that no other dimensions existed. Perhaps the modern theory of additional dimensions can bridge the events in the story and the world we know."

"That's a bridge too far for me, Uncle."

"All I'm suggesting is that additional dimensions can be perceived as supernatural. Edmund Abbott described how three-dimensional creatures could confound two-dimensional *flatlanders* inside a locked room by entering the room from *above*, a dimension that seems magical or supernatural to creatures limited to two dimensions. Access to additional dimensions would make someone seem magical to us Earthlings. As for the story your mother read you, those with access to additional dimensions were creatures of another order. Think of them as gods, or angels and devils; our Mr. Hill shared that belief if I understand him correctly. And not just creatures, but devices—rings, wands that facilitated access to additional dimensions. In other words, those devices weren't violating the laws of the universe, they were harnessing forces that aren't accessible to creatures with access to fewer dimensions."

"Do you say this as a scientist, or a monk?"

"Why not both?"

"This talk of additional dimensions, and creatures that move in them, is hard to accept."

"Here . . . listen, is it harder to believe than that the atoms in your body were produced inside stars billions of light years from here?"

"Then, Russell was seeking a door to additional dimensions?"

"It seems so, whether he understood it in that sense or not. He must have discovered something that drew him in, gave him hope."

"Something connected to the manuscript."

"What else could it have been?"

Lyle said, "Desrosier told us Russell was seeking rejuvenation, something that would make him new."

"Weren't those black riders after something similar . . . immortality? Instead, they were consigned to a dimension that suspended mortality, but made them pitiful caricatures of those extra-dimensional beings. That's the 'gift' those chieftains were given, an endless life of slavery—what Russell would have received if he had unlocked that door."

"Beatrice said something along those lines."

"I spoke to her while you were away. Hang on to her, Frodo."

"Do you believe the things in the story happened as they were described?"

"I don't disbelieve they happened. By the way, what did you come here to tell me? It's obvious something is on your mind, something quite different than magic and speculative physics."

"Beatrice has gone back to Africa. Her sister's husband was killed, and her sister's expecting a baby any day now. I asked Beatrice to marry me, but I'm not sure she would have accepted, even if she'd stayed."

"I know you care deeply about each other. Have you ever had a serious relationship with a woman? . . . I didn't think so. What are you willing to give, to change, for Beatrice?"

"I don't expect her to change, so why should I?"

"You're afraid of committing to her, and you're afraid of losing her, but fear isn't a basis for marriage."

"I don't suppose it matters anymore, since she's gone."

"You're accepting that? I want you to ask yourself what you're willing to risk for her."

"What does risk have to do with it?"

"Beatrice is a special woman, but that doesn't mean she's the right woman for you."

"What you mean to say is, I may not deserve her."

"That's right."

It took a lot for Lyle to become incensed at his uncle, but that did it. "Because she's a swan and I'm a duck. Is that it?"

"What I desire is your happiness—and Beatrice's. Can you fault me for that? Let me say it plainly: you will have to woo her. You will have to travel to Uganda to see her when it's inconvenient. You will have to start your day by asking yourself what she needs, and how you can support her. You will have to file off the shackles forged by your father's disappearance and your mother's death."

Without looking at Lyle, Abbot Henry said, "You know how grateful I am for what you did, and you know how I feel about you having more time with the manuscript."

"Better not. If I take you up on your offer, you might never get it back."

"Then I won't say any more about it. There are things we're better off without."

Lyle had asked his uncle if he could view the container again. Ever since that first viewing, he had wondered why so talented an artisan had created a container of such magnificence, an object to dazzle the eye and mind, with a virtually organic closing mechanism and an undetectable closure seam, and then made the thing fractionally off-square.

He was sure it hadn't warped, because the off-squareness was uniform at every corner. Moreover, a warped container couldn't have concealed the seam. The more he thought about it, the more he was convinced that the artist was displaying an intentional admission of imperfection, and doing it by marring his art. The talent—the genius—to create a work of spectacular beauty combined with such humility. What kind of man, woman . . . or being was this?

"This monastery, solitude or song or prayer, is always open to you. You might be surprised at what these Dark Age practices can file off."

"Beatrice asked me to spend time with Sam, and I've been seeing him once a week in London."

Abbot Henry looked at Lyle with an amazed expression. "Persevere in this mission, Frodo. Sam is afraid of me. That's the only way to put it. I've invited our dear Mars to tea often enough, but he always has one excuse or another. Don't get discouraged, no matter how he responds. What do you and Sam talk about?"

"How to stay sane in this world, light-hearted topics like that."

"We must be malleable."

"Desrosier was malleable. See what that got her?"

"You have to start with a strong soul."

"What about those who don't believe in a soul?"

"You're teasing me. Who is Frodo Lyle Stuart if not a soul with a body to help him on his way?"

"Sam drinks, and takes pills."

"Then, we must assist God in saving him."

"That's too big a job for me."

"How many times did Sam save you . . . from Russell, the Russian, yourself?"

"I wish you weren't such a good listener. I'm doing my best, Uncle Henry."

"I'm sure of it. A shame Beatrice had to go. Let's rest here," said Abbot Henry, sitting on a bench that overlooked the monastery pond.

Lyle remained standing. "I've been haunted . . ."

"Go on."

"I'm afraid Sam killed him . . . for me. That Russell's murder is weighing on Sam."

"Russell made his own choices, so has Sam, and so have you. In perfect freedom? I doubt it. You chose to assist your uncle when it wasn't convenient, to struggle with difficult choices involving Beatrice, to support—may I say, uplift—your brother. I'd have done without the manuscript for you to have avoided all the misery."

Looking over the pond, Lyle said, "I'm a better man for it."

"Before you departed, your only concern was being a better archaeologist."

"That's right, though I sometimes wish I could be that man again."

"That *box*?" said his uncle, startling Lyle.

"Do you think the manuscript is safe?"

"When the brothers aren't working, we return it to the repository. We've installed motion sensors in the hallway, and repository door alarms. In spite of these defensive measures, I believe what I once told you, that valuable things are eventually appropriated. What the corrigible devise, the incorrigible defeat."

"I'd like to think all that happened, happened for more than a story, even an excellent story," Lyle said.

"Can I talk you into spending the night with us?"

"Sorry. When my neighbor William died, his poodle had nowhere to go, so I took her in. Sam said he'd keep her when I'm on expedition."

"If Sam is in the throes of something, bring her here. We'll turn her into a free-range poodle. Didn't you have a run-in with a poodle when you were a boy?"

"A fresh start, Uncle, and she's taken to me."

Several large limbs from an ancient oak that extended over the pond had fallen into the water, and on these floating limbs turtles sunned.

"Which one is Beakie?" Lyle asked.

"The one near the fork. See, he's lost part of his shell, but he has clambered up. He perseveres."

"He's content," said Lyle.

"That's not what I see. He's preparing for a journey or a trial. To us, it looks to be an idyllic life, but he has to be on guard. Wild cats and foxes are about. He's not content, not yet."

Time for Lyle's next meeting with Sam. He owed Jeremy another letter. Could he talk Beatrice into letting him visit her?

"Speaking of stories," said Abbot Henry, "if you learn anything that bears on the manuscript, I'd welcome hearing it."

His uncle's words evoked the memory of the ghost now more alive to him than many living, breathing people. It didn't take Lyle long to say, "Let me tell you about a man named Lefebvre . . . and a road."

THE END?

www.ingramcontent.com/pod-product-compliance
Lightning Source LLC
Chambersburg PA
CBHW020611260626
47157CB00003B/955